continued . . .

D0093902

Last Vampire Standing

NANCY HADDOCK

BERKLEY BOOKS, NEW YORK

THE BERKLEY PUBLISHING GROUP
Published by the Penguin Group
Penguin Group (USA) Inc.
375 Hudson Street, New York, New York 10014, USA
Penguin Group (Canada), 90 Eglinton Avenue East, Suite 700, Toronto, Ontario M4P 2Y3, Canada
(a division of Pearson Penguin Canada Inc.)
Penguin Books Ltd., 80 Strand, London WC2R 0RL, England
Penguin Group Ireland, 25 St. Stephen's Green, Dublin 2, Ireland (a division of Penguin Books Ltd.)
Penguin Group (Australia), 250 Camberwell Road, Camberwell, Victoria 3124, Australia
(a division of Pearson Australia Group Pty. Ltd.)
Penguin Books India Pvt. Ltd., 11 Community Centre, Panchsheel Park, New Delhi—110 017, India
Penguin Group (NZ), 67 Apollo Drive, Rosedale, North Shore 0632, New Zealand
(a division of Pearson New Zealand Ltd.)
Penguin Books (South Africa) (Pty.) Ltd., 24 Sturdee Avenue, Rosebank, Johannesburg 2196,
South Africa

Penguin Books Ltd., Registered Offices: 80 Strand, London WC2R 0RL, England

This book is an original publication of The Berkley Publishing Group.

PRINTING HISTORY
Berkley trade paperback edition / May 2009

Library of Congress Cataloging-in-Publication Data

Haddock, Nancy.
    Last vampire standing / Nancy Haddock. —Berkley trade pbk. ed.
        p. cm.
    ISBN 978–0–425–22754–1
1. Vampires—Fiction.   2. Saint Augustine (Fla.)—Fiction.   I. Title.

PS3608.A275L37   2009
813'.6—dc22   2008047391

PRINTED IN THE UNITED STATES OF AMERICA

10 9 8 7 6 5 4 3 2 1

This one is for the Haddock,
Thompson, and Fossett clans.
You not only welcomed me into the family,
you always asked me
how the writing was going.
Thank you for believing!

ACKNOWLEDGMENTS

A kiddie television program of old invited the little studio guests to greet family and friends at the end of the show. I laughed when the children said, "I want to say hi to everyone I know." Now I get it.

In addition to thanking everyone I know, I specifically extend these credits, kudos, and hugs.

For answering my questions: John Galletta, Jr., Esq.; Sgt. Chuck Mulligan, St. Johns County Sheriff's Office; Investigator/PIO Jimmie Flynt, Daytona Beach Police Department; Lt. Lawrence Morgan and Steve Williams, Daytona Beach Fire Department; Mark Wolcott, Volusia County Fire Department; and Tom Donovan, Agricultural Extension Agent, and Tom Tibbitts, Zoning, both of St. Johns County. Any errors are mine.

For the caffeine and laughter, love and support: the partners of Starbucks 8484, my incredible neighbors, my dear chapter-mates, and my treasured friends.

For the feedback, from flattering to insightful: readers!

For being a joy to know and work with: Leis Pederson, my editor; Roberta Brown, my agent; and the entire Berkley Publishing Group family.

Finally, a dancin'-on-the-beach thanks to Lynne, Julie, Jan, Sherry, and Tommy—good friends, great critique buddies, and bright lights in my life!

ONE

~

The villagers marched on Maggie O'Halloran's house, but not at dawn while bearing torches to set us ablaze.

Good thing. August in Florida is plenty hot enough.

Nope, this time they came at happy hour, neighbors and friends bearing potato salad, coleslaw, and grits. Yes, grits. We do live in the South, and this was a housewarming party. A come-one, come-all, fuzzy-feel-good housewarming.

Well, for everyone except Hugh and Selma Lister next door. Oh, they'd been invited, but didn't have the courtesy to send their regrets. Not surprising. The only thing they regretted was that we'd moved in, which they made clear at every opportunity. Right now I heard them talking outside, just over the fragrant jasmine hedge separating our properties.

"Goddamn new people," Hugh growled. "It's almost nine o'clock. How long is this son of a bitchin' party gonna last?"

"Bless his holy name," Selma said, her tone long-suffering.

"Bless whose holy name?" Hugh demanded. "What the hell did *I* say?"

"Never mind," Selma sighed. "Come inside before the you-know-what next door hears you."

That would be me, the you-know-what, the vampire next door.

Vamp senses can be a blessing and a curse, but when I heard the Listers' back door click shut, I grinned. Okay, so maybe Hugh and Selma wouldn't warm to us, but, like it or not, Maggie and I were here to stay.

Yep, praise HGTV, the restoration of the Victorian home where Maggie had unearthed me almost one year ago was finally finished. Since her property spanned two lots, Maggie had sacrificed side yard space to add a two-car garage and an extra parking pad for my sweet Chevy SSR truck. Otherwise she'd simply restored the house to its original glory.

In her "big house," Maggie had furnished each room with classic period pieces. Tasteful and elegant all the way.

In my carriage-house-cum-cottage in the back corner of the property, I'd gone multiple-period mad. British Colonial in my living room. Retro in the kitchen, half bath, and laundry room. Art deco in my master bath, and surf chic in my bedroom, complete with a surfboard ceiling fan.

It sounds like mishmash, but the decor all works. Really. Even the Polynesian-style bar with the carved tikis on my cobblestone front patio. And, though my front patio faces Maggie's back patio, our very different styles don't clash. Maybe because there is a nice, lush expanse of grass to aid the transition from my funk to her fabulous.

*Any*way, to thank the neighbors for putting up with the

construction and to celebrate our move, Maggie and I had decided to throw a luau.

Well, our version of one. I mean, you can't exactly get poi and whole roasting pigs at Publix. Not in St. Augustine, anyway, home of just about the oldest everything.

Including me.

Not that I look much over twenty-five, but then I have the you-know-what, the vampire fountain of youth flowing in my veins.

I'm Francesca Melisenda Alejandra Marinelli, aka Princess Vampire, born right here in St. Augustine in 1780, turned a little underdead in 1800, and buried on this very property in 1803. Maggie unearthed me during the early stages of restoring her Victorian house. Now she's my sponsor and friend.

The Princess Vampire thing? That's what the *St. Augustine Record* reporters and other press people insist on calling me when they write articles. I've made the front page twice, the last time in March when preternatural Special Investigator Deke *(pant)* Saber *(double pant)* and I solved the French Bride murder case. Saber has a few pet names for me, but everyone else calls me Cesca, which rhymes with Fresca, which is what Maggie's now-official fiancé Neil Benson calls me.

Could be worse. Neil could still call me Cesspool, but we made peace a while back—for Maggie's sake at first, and then because we became surfing buddies.

Deke Saber and I are a whole 'nother kind of buddy.

On the other side of the jasmine hedge, the Listers' garage door creaked, and an engine started. Good, they were leaving— for the grocery store, according to my vamp hearing. We'd be on the beach by the time they returned.

I tossed an armful of dinner trash into the giant plastic cans we'd bought at Ace Hardware. Across the floodlit lawn, Saber stood with a group of men, including two detectives we'd met on the French Bride case. They were absorbed in examining the cache of fireworks we'd soon be hauling to Crescent Beach to shoot. What is it with men and things that go boom?

Whatever. Just peeking at Saber made my insides throw their own sparks. And his physique in that black polo shirt? Mama mia! Swimmer's shoulders, tight pecs, titanium abs. The man is a drool fest, so hot he makes my teeth sweat.

My vision swam suddenly, but not from lust. Lust didn't make my skin crawl, either. What the heck?

I pulled my energy back from Saber and paused to center myself. Then I turned in a slow circle, feeling with my vampire senses to find the source of my unease.

There. Twenty paces away, in the corner of the Listers' yard, something hovered on the other side of the jasmine hedge.

Not something. Someone.

Someone who smelled of stale blood.

Ugh, I hate the smell of blood.

Nausea and tension vise-gripped my stomach, and bile threatened to claw up my throat. The Listers, were they in danger? No. I'd just heard them leave. Besides, this blood scent was old. Sour.

So not a complement to the sweet scent of jasmine.

I wrinkled my nose against the stench, willed myself calm, weighed my options. The intruder couldn't be Ike, big kahuna of the Daytona Beach vampires. He was the type to make a grand and spooky entrance. Besides, I had a truce of sorts with Ike. He stays out of my town, and I stay out of his.

I focused and inhaled again. No, the lurker definitely wasn't Ike. He traveled with his entourage, including his second-in-command, Laurel, who radiated putrid hate. This was someone else. Someone whose scent I didn't recognize.

Okay, so, options. I'd been honing my vamp powers—well, speed and strength anyway. I was supposed to come into all sorts of powers when I was no longer a virgin, or so the French Bride killer had insisted. But, hey, the guy was a sociopath, delusional, and, according to Saber, had tapped into some way obscure, completely bogus vampire lore.

When the power faerie failed to smack me with her wand, Saber insisted I practice the powers I did have. He even taught me some slick self-defense moves, which meant I could whip over the hedge and out Mr. Smelly in the flutter of an eyelash.

But wait. Vamp speed spooked humans. We might not have a village uprising, but why risk our delicate relationship with the neighbors? Never mind another outburst if Hugh Lister heard a vamp had been skulking in his backyard. He's the kind of villager who just might take a torch to my house.

I scanned our own yard and took a head count. The cookout crowd had thinned considerably. Not many people to protect from a threat—if it came to that—and they mingled near the front gate, well away from the hedge.

Maggie and Neil circulated among the dozen or so neighbors and friends still chatting in small groups.

Mick and Janie, my coworkers from Old Coast Ghost Tours, waved as they headed off to work the late shift. Those two had danced around each other for months, until a terrifying brush with Ike's fangs bonded them at a deeper level. Now they were openly dating, and they sure made sweet pheromones together.

Millie Hayward and two of her senior friends, Grace and Kay, picked at the Death-by-Chocolate cake on the dessert table. Thinning gray hair aside, these were not your typical old ladies. For one thing, Millie and her cohorts were fanatic fans of the Jacksonville Jaguars football team, and usually wore teal visors with JAG QUEEN embroidered on the bands. For another, their oversized summer purses bore the outlines of the handguns they carried.

Dior and Chanel? Nope. The Jag Queens shopped designers like Smith & Wesson.

When all three ladies bustled my way, the blood odor thinned as if the lurker moved away from the hedge. I had a sense Smelly moved toward the street that fronted Maggie's house but I felt no menace. Still, I quick-stepped farther from the hedge to meet Millie's Shalimar-perfumed hug.

"Cesca, what a great party!"

"I'm so glad you could come."

I included Kay and Grace in my smile, but Millie is my favorite. I couldn't help but love her, even if Saber had briefly suspected her of murdering the French Bride.

"We were just talking and remembered Barb can't make the Jaguar preseason game next Sunday night," Millie said. "You want to come with us and use her ticket?"

"We're wearing T-shirts to spell out J-A-G Q-U-E-E-N-S at the games this year," petite Grace Warner said. "We need you to wear Barb's *E*."

"We tailgate before the game, though," Kay Sims added in a rush, "so plan to leave by four. If you're up by then."

"I'm up, but I'll have to check the ghost tour schedule to see if I'm working," I warned them.

Millie patted my arm. "That's fine, dear. Just let me know as soon as you can."

"Yes." Grace nodded like a gray-haired bobblehead doll. "Because we'll have to find another *E* if you can't go."

"I understand," I assured her.

"Of course, if you have to work," Kay added, eyeing Saber as he strode our way, "perhaps your young man would like the ticket. Does he like football?"

"He wouldn't wear Barb's T-shirt," Millie scoffed, and then cocked her head. "Would he?"

"I'd rather see him paint the *E* on his bare chest," Kay whispered as Saber reached us.

He flashed one of his swoon-inducing smiles. "Hello, ladies. How are you tonight?"

If the Jag Queens had been carrying fans, we'd have had a tropical storm–strength wind going. As it was, batting eyelashes stirred a swirling breeze around me.

"Why, hel-lo, Mr. Saber," Kay flirted. "We were just talking about your—"

"Big *E*," Grace cut in, then blushed.

Saber's brows arched. "My big what?"

"We were discussing," Millie said repressively, "Jag tickets."

"Aaah. Do you ladies need some extras?"

"No, no. Well, we're off for more cake, aren't we, girls?" She grabbed me for another hug and a murmured "Later."

Saber's head cocked as he watched them hustle away. "What was that about?"

"Old ladies don't lose their sense of lust. Did you know that?"

"Sure," he murmured as he slid an arm around me. "I figured *that* out with you."

"I am *not* old," I said firmly, my slow heartbeat stuttering into triple time.

"Of course you're not." Saber's warm lips nibbled a path from my ear to my neck. "Only two hundred and thirty or so."

I angled my head to give him more room to tantalize. "I'm—ooh there, yes—only two hundred and twenty-eight, and you know it."

"I do," he whispered, nipping me now. "It was hell getting all those candles on your birthday cake."

Normally I wouldn't want to trip Saber and beat him to the ground, but I'm sensitive about my age because, well, I'm the older woman. Besides, we did have guests.

"Saber," I breathed.

"Hmmm?"

"Your lips say seduction, but your words are about to get you smacked."

His chest rumbled with a chuckle, and he patted my behind.

"You ready to go set off the fireworks?" His eyes sparkled with double meaning.

"Give me five minutes to clean up a little more."

"You're up all night, Cesca. Can't you clean when we get back?"

I leaned into him and smiled. "Not if you want some private fireworks later."

He gulped. I love it when he does that.

"I'll just go get March and Balch," he said, backing away. "We'll load 'em up and get on the road."

"The detectives are coming with us?"

"Who do you think will keep us out of jail if someone calls the cops?"

"Good point." Shooting fireworks just any old time *was* illegal.

Since Maggie had made the welcome speech, I stepped to the center of the yard to make the good-bye announcement.

"Attention, everyone. Attention please." I waited for quiet, then said, "Maggie and I sincerely thank you for being a part of our housewarming. If you want to grab a last-minute snack, please do. Otherwise, we're ready to hit the beach for fireworks."

Just then, an eerily pained howl that sounded a lot like *"Noooooooowaaaaaait"* rose from the front yard. A dark blur streaked through the gate and across the lawn to throw itself at my feet. When the blur crystallized, a lanky form in navy blue slacks and a stained yellow polo shirt was kissing my toes.

Six weapons clicked to fire-ready. I knew without looking that three of the guns belonged to the Jag Queens, two to the detectives, and one to Saber. His off-duty .40-caliber Glock.

I didn't have time to worry if the Jag Queens would get arrested for packing heat. I didn't have time to worry what the neighbors thought. I didn't have time to worry what the vampire's greasy blond hair was doing to my pedicure.

Yes, a vampire lay prostrate at my feet. Nothing but a vamp moved as fast as he had, and even a tiny whiff confirmed he stank of sour blood.

"Unless you want to get shot," I said steadily, "don't so much as flinch."

"N-not moving," he stammered.

"Good. Now, who the hell *are* you?"

A long moment later, he angled his head to peer at me.

"Would you believe, a part of your destiny?"

TWO

"Forget who he is," Saber shouted. "Step away."

I kept my gaze on the vampire. Part of my destiny? My Aunt Fang, if I'd had one. Still, he'd snagged my attention.

"It's okay, Saber. He's not a threat."

"You can't be sure of that. Please, Cesca, move."

"We've got a clear shot on the right," March said.

"Same on the left flank," Millie chimed in.

I looked up to find Detectives March and Balch and the Jag Queens fanned out ten feet away, frozen in shooting stances. Our remaining guests gawked from the front gate. Saber alone eased toward me.

"Just give me a minute, guys."

I narrowed my eyes at the vamp and tried to read his thoughts. No dice. Fear tumbled in his brain like clothes in my dryer, but that's all I could sense.

"Mister, these folks aren't kidding around," I said firmly. "State your name and business. Fast."

"Are those guns loaded with silver bullets?" he choked out.

"Some of them are. The rest of the bullets will just hurt like hell."

Very slowly, he craned his neck until I saw part of his dirt-smudged face through the fall of stringy hair. Boyish was my first impression of him, but his amber brown eyes carried the weight of age and pain.

"Jo-Jo the Jester."

I blinked. "Huh?"

"My name. It's Jo-Jo."

"Jo-Jo Jester?"

"Jo-Jo *the* Jester. A court jester, at your service, my lady," he said with a slight dip of his head. "May I rise? Looking at you like this is making my eyes cross."

I glanced at Saber, who now stood to my right. The rest of the posse still had Jo-Jo in their gun sights.

"He needs to stand up," I said.

"I heard." Saber scowled and motioned with his gun. "Crawl backward ten feet, then get to your knees."

Jo-Jo the vampire jester—and how many things were wrong with *that* picture?—did exactly as Saber instructed.

Even when he was kneeling, I could guess Jo-Jo to be six feet tall. His polo shirt was more brown than yellow on the front. Were those bug splat spots? A slash wound on his forehead was raw and festering. Small wonder he'd asked if the bullets were silver. From the looks of it, someone had been at him with a silver knife—the only reason a vamp cut wouldn't have healed.

He held his arms slightly out from his lean torso, palms up, as if to show he'd come in peace. Saber's expression said he wasn't buying the innocent act.

"Now what," Saber said, words slow and measured, "do you want with Cesca?"

Jo-Jo snorted. "To me, she is not simply Cesca. She is Francesca, Princess Vampire, Most Royal Highness of the House of King Normand."

My stomach flipped. My breath stopped. Warmth drained from my body faster than blood from a slashed vein.

How did this vampire know my full, formal title? The one Normand had so ceremoniously conferred on me. Every vamp who knew me by that name should have died—really died—over two hundred years ago.

Jo-Jo hadn't been in Normand's court. I remembered the bad old days all too clearly, when Marco Sánchez had kidnapped me, and the so-called King Normand had turned me. I recalled the face of every vampire in that court, had tasted the blood of every wretched human slave.

Absolutely no one—human or vampire—should know my title. So how did Jo-Jo know it?

"Cesca, you okay?" Saber asked.

I snapped to the present, swallowed past the pain, and nodded. We had nervous guests waiting, fireworks to shoot. Maybe a vampire, too, if I didn't get answers fast.

"Jo-Jo," I said, willing my voice steady and my body warm, "Saber asked you a question. What do you want?"

He squared his shoulders. "If the royal princess would but grant my boon, I seek political asylum."

That jerked me back to my normal self.

"Only a country can grant political asylum, so you might as well leave."

"Wait," he said, fear on his filthy face. "How about sanctuary? I will be your slave, live only to serve you, my princess beneficent."

"Slavery has been outlawed for a couple of centuries."

"A servant then?" he pressed, his expression pleading. "I do housework. Even windows, Your Vast Wonderfulness."

I looked down at my size-four green cotton shorts and matching scoop neck spaghetti strap top. I am *not* vast.

"I don't want a servant," I said, not bothering to keep huffiness out of my tone. "This is the US of A. Land of the free—"

"Home of the taxpayer," Jo-Jo interjected.

"Say what?"

Jo-Jo's sharp chin went up. "It's a line from my comedy routine."

Saber shook his head. "With jokes like that, you *do* need protection."

"That's what *I'm* saying," the vampire agreed. "And if you'll put the cannon away, good sir, I'll tell you why."

"A straight answer would be refreshing," I snipped.

"All right, stand up slow and back up another pace or two," Saber demanded as he turned partly to me. "Cesca, be ready to do your thing."

My "thing" is pulling aura, the way I fed while I was trapped underground for two centuries. Of course, I only sipped from a man here, a woman there, but, in the extreme, I can drain enough energy to render a human or vampire helpless.

I didn't have to test my skill on Jo-Jo. He did as asked, and

Saber signaled to the backup crew to holster or purse their weapons. Saber held his at his side.

"So spill," I said. "What do you want from me?"

Jo-Jo sketched an elaborate bow complete with a hand flurry that made me imagine he held a frilly, befeathered hat. I had a quick vision of him in a full jester's costume and frowned. Was he planting that picture, or was I reading his memories? The moon phases didn't fritz out my psychic senses as much as they used to, but still, I couldn't read Jo-Jo's mind, which would've been handy to find out how he'd learned my better-forgotten title.

"My princess, you see before you, sadly misplaced in time, a jester of some former renown. I served the courts of—"

"Jo-Jo," I cut in.

"Yes, Most Royal Mercifulness?"

"Fast-forward. Why do you want protection?"

He deflated faster than a blowfish. His shoulders slumped, and he actually seemed to age.

"The short of it is," he said, meeting my gaze with haunted eyes, "I'm a marked man for leaving the nest in Atlanta."

A twinge of empathy pierced me, but I didn't let it show. I knew full well the Vampire Protection Agency allowed nests of under thirty vamps to exist, but countered, "Nests are supposed to be against the law."

"Yeah, well, tell that to my mast—" His gaze slid to Saber. "I mean to Vlad, the Atlanta head honcho."

"Vlad?" I echoed. "As in Vlad the Impaler?"

"It's not the same guy," Jo-Jo assured me.

"But still. A mother named her kid Vlad on purpose? That's just gross."

"Well, he had an old mother," Jo-Jo said. "No, wait, I mean he's old, so his name was probably hip at one time."

I curbed the urge to roll my eyes. "What does your human sponsor say about you leaving Atlanta?"

"I don't have one, Princess."

"But you have to have one. The Vampire Protection Act specifically requires each vampire to have a sponsor."

"A thousand pardons for contradicting you, Your Nobleness, but after five years, if you've proven yourself to be a completely reformed biter, you no longer need a sponsor."

I gawked at him, then Saber, then searched the yard for Maggie. She stood not far away and, since it was quiet enough to hear a seagull poop, she'd heard every word.

"He's right, Cesca," she said.

My world tilted. Again. Why hadn't Maggie told me this tidbit months ago? That she didn't have to sponsor me for forever. That we didn't have to live partly joined at the hip for the rest of our lives.

That someday she'd want me to go away.

I drew a breath that was supposed to calm me. Instead I got another snootful of Jo-Jo's sour blood scent.

And heard the Listers' car pull into the driveway next door. Yikes. They *so* didn't need to see a vampire standoff.

"Tell you what, Jo-Jo," I said, proud I sounded so reasonable and in control. "We're shooting off fireworks at Crescent Beach. You can come, too, and for heaven's sake, use the public shower while you're there."

Jo-Jo cringed. At the mention of heaven or a shower, I couldn't tell, but he finally nodded.

"What about my request for refuge, Royal Beauteousness?"

"We'll talk about that later."

"Okay," he said, almost puppylike now. "Who's giving me a ride?"

The sound of feet pounding the ground as our guests fled to their cars might've been funny if I hadn't heard Hugh Lister's shout from his front yard.

"Jesus Christ on a stick, these assholes are trampling my goddamn ferns."

"Bless his holy name," Selma said.

Jo-Jo blinked at me. "Bless whose holy name?"

"Never mind. You got all the way here from Atlanta, you can walk to Crescent Beach."

"Thank you, Francesca, Princess Vampire."

Jo-Jo wasn't thanking me an hour later. He flew to the beach instead of walking and looked more bug encrusted for the effort. So, while the guys set up the fireworks, I made Jo-Jo stand fully clothed under the outdoor shower and scrub with a bar of soap I'd bought at Handy Mart. He didn't utter a single protest but only muttered, "I live to serve," like a mantra. Once he was reasonably clean from his hair to his heels, he dried with a spare towel from Saber's SUV.

March and Balch put themselves in charge of lighting the fireworks, which was fine by me. *I* wanted to snuggle with Saber on our blanket under the waterfalls of lights.

What I got was Jo-Jo trying to "attend" me. Between his, "Do you need this, Princess?" and "Let me get that, Princess," my own fuse burned. When I told him to park it and be quiet, the jester wasn't happy. Well, excuse me, but what did he expect after crashing our party? As for giving him sanctuary, I'd set him straight when we got home. Find out how he knew about my title and send him on his way. To where, I didn't care.

The fireworks ended too soon, but since Jo-Jo's clothes were nearly dry, Saber let him ride home with us. My honey was scoring extra points for that kindness tonight, and I'd show him my appreciation as soon as we booted Jo-Jo out the door. Which would be in about ten minutes if my libido had a vote.

Maggie's white Acura and my aqua SSR truck were in the driveway, so Saber parked his black Saturn Vue at the curb. Maggie waited with a scowling Neil under the old live oak tree in the front yard as Saber herded Jo-Jo toward the gate that led to my cottage.

When I approached, Neil turned his ire on me. "You're not letting that vampire stick around. No way in hell."

Maggie laid her hand on his arm. "Neil, Cesca can have any guest she wants in her home."

"Not if that guest will be a threat to you."

"I promise he won't be a threat—right, Jo-Jo?" I said, sensing that he loitered with Saber just beyond the gate.

"Your Most Royalness, I will protect with my life any friend of yours."

"Yeah, yeah," Neil said. "Talk is cheap."

"Silver bullets aren't," Jo-Jo called again.

Neil blinked. "What does that mean?"

I cracked a small smile. "He has delusions of comedy."

"He's a comic?" Maggie asked.

Neil snorted, and Saber echoed it. I ignored them both.

"I promise he's not staying."

Maggie had a peculiar gleam in her eye but only said,

"Thanks for all your help with the party. We'll finish cleaning in the morning before you go to bed."

I waved as Maggie dragged Neil up the sidewalk to the house. I'd clean tonight, surprise Maggie, and then we'd have a talk about that vampire sponsor issue.

I caught up with Saber and Jo-Jo by the tiki bar on my patio. When I opened the cottage door, Jo-Jo whistled.

"Love what you've done with the place."

I loved my living room, too, from the bamboo floors to the rich honey color on the walls, to the espresso-colored wood and leather furnishings. But I wasn't letting Jo-Jo sidetrack me.

"Don't get used to it."

I deactivated the silent alarm system, then made a mental note to reset the code. Jo-Jo probably wouldn't break into my home. Heck, thanks to Saber, my security system rivaled the president's and the pope's combined. However, there was no point in tempting an unknown vampire.

I meant to tell Jo-Jo to sit, but my hostess manners kicked me in the conscience. "Do you want a refreshment, Jo-Jo?"

The vampire slid a look at Saber. "I could use a bottle of warm blood, my princess."

"You haven't eaten tonight?"

"No, my lady. I arrived in town before sunrise and laid low until I found you. I didn't travel with blood."

Okay, so I had to give him credit for not being cranky with hunger. I uncapped a Starbloods bottle and popped it in the microwave, then uncapped a beer for Saber and grabbed a glass of ice chips for myself. I do love my new fridge with crushed ice in the door. Napkins and beverages on the teak tray—another splurge for my new home—and I was ready to deal with Jo-Jo.

Until I handed him his drink, and he scowled at the label.

"Not to complain, Your Tastefulness, but do you have any-thing to drink that's less, um, girly?"

"Like what? Fang Bang? Monster Mash?"

Saber snorted. "I imagine O Positive would do."

"I don't stock a variety of vampire drinks," I reminded Saber, then looked at Jo-Jo. "It's this or nothing."

"Of course, Your Graciousness. Caramel macchiato is fine."

He sat stiffly in the coffee-colored, cloud-soft leather chair opposite from where Saber and I sank into my matching couch. The old vampire, who didn't appear any older than I did, also looked better now that he had cleaned up. His shaggy shoulder-length hair was sandy blond instead of just plain dirty, and even the wound on his forehead didn't seem so raw. However, I was not—with a billboard-sized *N*—getting involved in his problems.

And caramel macchiato is *not* girly.

I didn't hold my nose while Jo-Jo drank, but I didn't watch him, either. By the time he'd finished, recapped the bottle, and set it on the dark wood coffee table, I was ready to crawl down his throat to drag the truth out of him. On the other hand, Saber got people to reveal all kinds of things just by chatting. Did I have that much patience?

Jo-Jo cleared his throat. "Will Your Magnificence give me leave to speak?"

"As long as you knock off the royal name-calling," I snapped. So much for patience.

He gave a short nod, and his gaze settled on Saber. "I saw your name in the paper with that of Her Highness. I know you used to hunt us, and I know you're a special investigator now. May I speak freely?"

"I won't arrest you for past crimes, if that's what you mean," Saber assured him.

"Thank you."

"Okay, so take it from the top," I said with a flip of my hand. "You're Jo-Jo, a jester."

"*The* Jester," he said without an ounce of modesty. "I performed in the courts of medieval Europe, my princess. Kings vied for my services and loyalty. Why, I—"

"Jo-Jo," I interrupted.

"You want me to fast-forward again, my lady?"

"Yes. I assume you were turned in the Middle Ages and couldn't work anymore."

"I might have if I'd been able to juggle."

"I thought juggling was part of the whole jester shtick," Saber said.

"It was, but you see, I wasn't used to having vampire speed. I lost control of the knives and, uh, took out a few members of an august audience."

"Such as an entire royal family?" Saber asked.

Jo-Jo shrugged. "Only one crown prince and a visiting head of state, but then the bloodlust hit me and, well—"

"You vamoosed out of town," I finished. "What then?"

"I found refuge with a master vampire and relearned to juggle so I could earn my keep entertaining for his court."

"How did you get to the States?" I prodded, intrigued in spite of the whole kicking-him-out thing to come.

"I immigrated with a small band of vampires in 1871. I moved out West for a while, then to New York City. The others moved to the South."

If he was telling the truth—and he did seem sincere—then I'd already been buried for decades when he came to this country. So how did he know my title? I itched to ask, but Saber cut in.

"How long have you been in Atlanta?"

"Since about 1930. Before that I worked in vaudeville."

Saber arched a brow. "Onstage?"

"I may not have been a headliner," the vampire said with exaggerated dignity, "but I had a gift for making people laugh. Even if we couldn't do the matinees."

"We?"

"I had a partner for my routines. Jemina. I met her in New York City. We moved to Atlanta together."

"Is she still living?" I asked.

His brown eyes blurred, and a wave of sadness hit me.

"Yes, but she says I'm too far behind the times. I'm not funny anymore, and she doesn't want me." He touched the wound on his head. "Her new boyfriend gave me this."

"With a silver knife?" Saber fired. "He's not a vampire?"

"Oh, he is, but he seems immune or something. Anyway, I knew there was no use in staying, so I used Google Earth to navigate to St. Augustine, and here I am."

"Which brings us back to the real question," I said. "Why are you here?"

"To ask for your help."

"Help doing what?"

He clasped his hands together so tightly, his knuckles whitened even more than a vampire's should. "To build a new career. I want to be a stand-up comic."

Saber and I exchanged a glance of disbelief.

"Oh, I don't expect you to teach me to be funny again," Jo-Jo hurried on. "The thing is, even if I had a good routine, Master Vlad runs his nest like a fiefdom. We have jobs—I'm a technician on a computer help line—but our jobs are low-profile. He'd never let me work in a comedy club. Even if a higher salary increased the amount of tribute I could pay him."

"Tribute?" I echoed. "Like taxes or like protection money?"

"I think of it as room and board."

I frowned. "Can't you just move out? Leave the nest but still live in Atlanta?"

"Not and stay alive." Jo-Jo shuddered. "The master would make an example of me. He may track me down and execute me just for leaving. That's why I asked for your protection."

I should've said that I didn't want any part of this. That bucking the head vamp in Atlanta was *so* not going in my day planner. But, darn it, this is supposed to be a free country. Even for vampires. We're a flipping protected species, for heaven's sake.

Almost nothing makes me fighting mad, but injustice will do the trick. This Atlanta creep was cruisin' for a bruisin' if he thought he could kill vampires just for leaving his highly illegal—if ignored—nest.

"Cesca," Saber said, jarring me out of my thoughts. "Let's excuse Jo-Jo and talk privately for a few minutes."

"Why?"

"Because I know that look you have. Do us a favor, Jo-Jo. Take a walk."

"To where?"

"Around the block."

Jo-Jo glanced at me, then bolted for the door. At least he didn't slam it.

"Now just what look do I have?"

"Your avenging angel look."

"It's unfair, Saber."

"I know, but do you want to pick this battle?"

I turned to him, took his hands in mine. "Do you? Vlad sounds like the kind of guy you used to hunt."

"Yeah, he does, but I can't guarantee I'll be here if the jerk does come after Jo-Jo. Or you."

"And I might not be able to take on Vlad, because I don't have enough superpowers?"

"You've barely explored your superpowers, but you can defend yourself to a point. And we have the Vampire Protection Agency for backup."

"Backup how?"

He squeezed my hand. "I'll check out Jo-Jo's story and get the scoop on Vlad. I'll also ask the Atlanta VPA agent about this immunity to silver. That bugs me."

"Immunity sounds flat-out impossible. As long as you're talking with the VPA people, will you ask them to watch for any vampires who might be on the move out of their usual territory?"

"In case this Vlad guy sends a hit man after Jo-Jo?"

I nodded. "Of course, that's only going to work if all the Atlanta vampires are wearing their GPS implants."

"Honey, they have to be. The rogue vamps are dead or on the extermination list."

"Oh, right." I thought a minute. "Let's say we help Jo-Jo. Where is he going to stay?"

My front door opened with a whoosh, and Jo-Jo stuck his head in. "I got a motel room when I flew in this morning. I'll stay there."

I bit back a grin at his eagerness, and waved him to the chair. "Is your room sunproof?"

"I slept in the bathtub with both the bathroom and room door locked, and the Do Not Disturb sign out."

"Not the most secure," Saber said, "but it'll do. How are you set for money?"

"I have enough to last awhile."

"Enough for new clothes and a haircut?" I pressed.

Jo-Jo raised a protective hand to his head. "Clothes, yes. The haircut I'll have to think about."

"All right, just one more thing I need to ask." I took a steadying breath, glanced at Saber's dear face, then at Jo-Jo's expectant one. "How do you know my formal royal title?"

"I read the articles about you and Saber. About the way you solved the French Bride murder case."

"My full title wasn't in the papers."

"It wasn't? Then where did I hear—" He scrunched his face in a thoughtful frown, then snapped his fingers. "I know. I overheard Vlad. He was on his usual rant about being controlled by the government."

"He should take a number on that one," I said.

"Yeah, well, he threw a tantrum every time there was a news story about you working with Saber. He hates it that you're, like, a vampire Nancy Drew."

"But I don't know Vlad, and he couldn't know my title."

"He didn't. Not until a sneaky, backstabbing vamp told him."

"This vamp have a name?" Saber asked.

"Marco."

THREE

Marco?

My lungs seized. My heartbeat stopped.

Panic squeezed my vision to a pinpoint.

It couldn't be the same Marco. The one who, with his vampire henchmen, had followed me to the beach at the dark of the moon on July 21, 1800.

As a human, he'd been incensed when I refused his offer of marriage. As a vampire, he kidnapped me and offered me to Normand to turn. As a conniving Judas, he'd incited the townspeople to burn us out.

The villagers had come at dawn to the stone-and-timber house King Normand ruled, but they hadn't killed me, because they couldn't find me. The night before, Normand had sealed me in his own coffin in the half basement under the house. This was my punishment for making daylight escapes from his little kingdom, and he'd watched while his human slaves bound the coffin in silver chains. I'd known from a vision that the townspeople were attacking, but I hadn't warned Normand. I'd wanted to die.

Instead, I'd lain in the coffin listening to the pleas and screams of those dying aboveground. I was certain the villagers had turned on Marco, too. That he had died with everyone else. He must have, or he would've come back—if not for me, then for Normand's treasure. Wouldn't he?

When Maggie had unearthed me and the newspapers ran a story about her "bizarre" discovery, I lived in quiet terror for months that Marco would learn I was out of the box and come back. To keep daymares at bay and to protect Maggie, I'd checked the historical society records for any trace of Marco. Predictably, the city fathers had failed to record mention of local vampires.

Searching the church records was a bust, too, so I turned to Dave Corey, my handler at the Vampire Protection Agency. Some vampire hunters had taken fangs to prove kills, rather like taking scalps. There was a set in the VPA records attributed to a Marco of Spanish or Mexican descent, but that's all Dave had.

I stewed in silence for a long seven months about Marco coming back when I got a clue—and a boyfriend who did more digging through his own official channels. Saber found scores of Marcos registered with the VPA, none of whom seemed remotely connected to me. More vamps named Marco had been slain before the VPA was established. Conclusion? The Marco I had known was either stoking fires in hell or had moved on. Way on. Looking over my shoulder was only holding me back.

Still, how curious that the Marco in Atlanta would know my full title. It may be nothing, but probing Jo-Jo for more answers was smarter than sticking my head in a sand dune.

I dragged air into my lungs, and my heart restarted in painful thuds. Vision returned with a rush that left me dizzy.

I eyed Jo-Jo, who looked paler than normal. Had I frightened him? He'd sure scared the bejeebers out of me.

"What is Marco's last name?"

"Uh, I don't know, Princess. We're not big on keeping our human surnames, if we ever had them."

"Does he have a nickname?" Saber asked.

"We call him Marco the Mouth because he's—pardon me, Your Highness—a kiss-ass and a snitch."

Which fit the Marco I'd known, but I kept my breathing even. Lots of vampires were double-dealing, backstabbing, power-tripping pains in the fang.

"Have you ever heard anyone call this Marco by the name Sánchez or Vega? Or Sánchez y Vega?"

"No, never. In fact, Saber here looks more Latino, and Marco sure doesn't sound Spanish or Mexican."

A ray of hope sparkled. "What *does* Marco look like?"

"Pretty much white bread, like me. His skin is a shade darker than mine. Blond, blue eyes, maybe five foot eleven."

Though the height was off a few inches, it was near enough with shoe lifts, and he could've dyed his hair. But Marco's eyes had been black brown, and he wouldn't be caught—well, dead—wearing contacts. He'd been sensitive about so much as dirt specks in his eyes, even as a vampire.

The specter from the past vanished, and I sagged into Saber.

"It's all right, Cesca. It's not the same vampire."

"Princess," Jo-Jo cried, falling to his knees and thunking into the coffee table on the way down. "I could die a thousand deaths that I upset you. What can I do to make amends?"

"You can teach Cesca how to fly," Saber said.

I elbowed Saber even as Jo-Jo uttered a choked, "The Most Royal Highness doesn't fly?"

"No, and I don't want to learn."

"Sure you do," Saber insisted. "You bitch about gas prices all the time."

"Everybody complains about the price of gas."

"Yep, but you can do something about it. Learn to fly." He grinned. "Unless you're afraid of flying."

"Flying would be fun. It's the falling that sounds like a downer."

"Jo-Jo wouldn't let you fall."

"Oh, no, Princess," Jo-Jo said, still on his knees. "You will never come to harm with me."

"See?" Saber jabbed.

I scowled.

Jo-Jo frowned at each of us in turn, then brightened. "The princess and her consort obviously have much to discuss. How about if I just leave you two alone now?"

"Good idea, Jo-Jo."

"I'll go back to the motel then," Jo-Jo said, backing away in a half bow. "See if they have Comedy Central on cable and research jokes on my laptop."

"Hold it," I said, one hand up. "Your laptop computer?"

Jo-Jo looked puzzled. "Yes, Highness."

"You didn't bring clothing or blood along, but you flew here with your computer?"

"Well, sure, it's top-of-the-line. I have to keep my night job until I break into show biz again."

"But what if you'd dropped it?"

Jo-Jo shrugged. "It's insured. Is nine too early to come by tomorrow night? You know, to run through my routine for you?"

I shook my head, bewildered by the gadget-mad male mind. "Ten would be better. I work the eight o'clock tour tomorrow."

"The ghost tour?" he asked in hushed tones. "Wow, do you think I could come?"

Eeeks, no, I thought, but said, "It won't be sunset yet, and I think that tour is full tomorrow."

"Oh, then, another time. Good night, my Princess. Good night, royal consort."

"Wait, Jo-Jo."

"Yes, my lady?"

"How do you think your Marco knew my full title?"

"He's not my Marco, but your title is easy to figure out if you just follow the rules of royal titles. Di was called Princess Diana, but her proper title was Diana, Princess of Wales. You don't have a country to claim, but as the acknowledged daughter of Normand, Vampire King, you become Francesca, Princess of the House of Normand. Of course, that's in British terms. In French, your title could vary."

Yeah, like my gas mileage. "Oooo-kay, then."

"Should I explain that again?"

"No, I've got the gist. But one more thing."

"Yes, Highness?"

"Be extra quiet coming and going, okay? I don't want Maggie disturbed, and you definitely don't want to annoy Neil."

"I'll be quiet as the dead, Princess."

He closed the front door with exaggerated care, and I leaned into Saber with a long sigh.

"Feeling better?" he murmured in my hair.

"About Jo-Jo's Marco, yes, but I need to talk with Maggie about the sponsorship issue."

"Just remember, whatever she did, it's because she cares."

"So do you, but you haven't lied to me."

"Well, not any more than you just lied to Jo-Jo about the ghost tour."

"You've got me there."

"I have you here."

He pulled me into his lap and inched my thin blouse strap off one shoulder. "You know, that five-year clause *is* in Vampire Protection Act provisions. You didn't read them, did you?"

His groin hardened against my hip, and my breath hitched. "No, just the brochure. I was too excited to get on with my new afterlife."

"How about your love life? Want me to amp that up to-night?"

"Mmmmm, is this what consorts are for?"

"Honey, why do you think I doubled my vitamins?"

He kissed me, softly at first, then urgently. I caught fire with explosions of pleasure like the fireworks at the beach.

"Bed . . . room," I panted in his mouth.

"Why . . . move?" he panted back.

I cupped his erection and whispered what I wanted.

I don't know which of us hit my California king bed first, but waiting for him to strip me was excruciating. When it was my turn, I kissed and rubbed and teased each inch of skin I exposed. And then he slipped into my body, and I matched his rhythm until we climaxed as one.

I love it when our pheromones mingle at midnight.

Later, when Saber's breathing evened in sleep, I smiled at the waxing moonlight streaming through the window and enjoyed his warm body until my mental to-do list nagged me out of bed.

I closed the drapes to keep out the light come daytime. Not that sunlight fries me. It doesn't, and my naturally olive skin provides some protection, too. But UV overexposure will make me break out in lesions similar to what lupus patients experience.

I wear super sunblock when I'm outside in the daytime, of course, but I don't wear it to bed. So for my bedroom I made blackout drapery panels that, when closed, look like surfboards stacked against the wall. I'd also sprung to have wonder windows installed that are both UV reflective and impact resistant.

Yes, Saber had wanted bulletproof windows to protect me from the vigilante vampire hunters, but the expense was astronomical, and they didn't come with UV protection. Instead, I had a perimeter alarm that was triggered by weight. If the siren sounded, I hit the floor and crawled to the secret escape hatch in the walk-in closet.

I also built an alcove in the living area to house a computer cabinet. It served as my study and office space, and, dressed in my penguin-on-the-beach sleep shirt, that's where I headed to run a computer search for Marco.

Sure, I knew Marco Sánchez was dead. Jo-Jo's Marco was a whole 'nother creep, a whole 'nother set of fangs. On the other hand, the vamp knew my formal title. Peace of mind is priceless.

I reset the security code and alarm system while the computer booted, then zipped to the Vampire Protection Agency website and their version of America's Most Wanted. The pages listed the names of vampires who'd been declared Rampants, along with their aliases, descriptions, and notations of "at large" or "terminated." This list dated back to 1997, when vampires were first designated a protected species, but Saber had accessed older archives for me, and I'd memorized his codes. Okay, it was a little sneaky, but for a good cause.

A click on this button, a password and verification code in that box, and I was in. I typed M-A-R-C-O, waited only seconds, and had ten hits. There, just as I remembered when Saber showed me. The next to last entry on the page read: Marco, surname uncertain, approximately two centuries old, of Spanish descent, black hair, dark brown eyes, five feet eight inches. He'd been killed three years before the VPA was launched.

If the villagers hadn't killed Marco, and if someone else hadn't squashed him like a stinkbug before vampire hunters kept good records, then this was the proof I needed. No new daymares for me. Ding-dong, Marco was dead. My lingering doubts lifted.

I cruised the VPA site awhile longer, found the five-year rule, and read the history of the Vampire Protection Act and Agency. May as well read up now before I talked with Maggie.

I learned that a crime reporter had stumbled on the scene of a slayer disposing of a vamp body in the early 1990s. With conspiracy theories and Pulitzer visions merrily dancing, he'd broken the sensational story. *Vampires Among Us. Film at eleven.*

Disbelief, confusion, and terror summed up the initial human reaction to the news that vampires walked the earth. Governments of the world couldn't pooh-pooh the story, because a select conclave of vamps flew out of the closet to prove they were real. Course, that's when the scientists injected themselves into the picture.

With the help of some not-so-scrupulous slayers, vamps

were captured for scientific study. One biologist with terminal cancer insisted on being turned so results could be verified. His cancer disappeared, and his DNA proved altered. Conclusion: vampires were Homo sapiens with DNA and other markers just different enough to be classified as a unique species.

Enter the ACLU to argue for vamp citizenship rights. Enter the government to tax its new citizens. Enter commerce to create new products. Shock and fear passed, free enterprise and regulations reigned.

Made me want to sing "from sea to shining sea."

On the downside, the Covenant had formed. The anti-vamp version of the KKK left their sheets at home but cornered vamps using crosses and silver, crossbows and stakes. Some vampires were killed outright. Others defended themselves, only to be branded as dangerous and legally executed.

Come to think of it, I hadn't seen my Covenant stalker, Victor Gorman, in, gosh, close to a month. He must be on vacation because, in spite of a restraining order against him, he consistently tailed my tour groups. He'd never pulled a weapon on me, so I dealt with the harassment by adopting a policy to polite him to death.

I closed the VPA site and spent the next few hours catching up on my Psychology of Color homework. Yep, I had passed my GED test, held my high school equivalency now, and was officially enrolled in the art institute online. Could I find work as an interior designer someday? Why not? Designers consulted with clients in the late afternoons and evenings. I was up by then.

I tiptoed back to my bedroom and kissed Saber awake at six thirty. Since we did ever so much more than kiss, it was an hour later before we were out of the shower and dressed.

While Saber poured himself orange juice—Florida orange juice, of course—I filled a bowl with his favorite cereal, Frosted Mini-Wheats. He settled at my turquoise and chrome retro table, splashed soy milk in the bowl, and dug in. I plucked a dry wheat square, heavy on the frosting, from the box.

"What's on your agenda today?" I asked, feeling very Sunday-morning domestic.

He grinned. "I'm serving a search warrant on Ike's club in Daytona Beach."

"You're searching Hot Blooded on a Sunday? In the day-time?"

"Element of surprise strategy, my dear. We blow by Ike and deal with the human day manager."

"Well, spill already. What's Ike done this time?"

"Let's just say summer tourists have reported memory losses and missing jewelry."

"He's enthralling and robbing people?"

"Or drugging them."

"But no bite marks?"

"None that the complainants are admitting to. An emerald ring and a classic Swatch watch turned up at a pawnshop, and the owner recognized one of Ike's human employees as the person who brought the items in."

"Does he have a record?"

"It's a she. Donita Ward. No record, but supposedly she's Ike's new squeeze."

"Whoa. Isn't Laurel still Ike's second-in-command?"

"Yes, and before you ask, Donita is a slender, short-haired brunette, but that's all I can tell from the grainy videos."

"Bet Laurel's seething mad about the girlfriend."

"You know it, and Laurel's even scarier than Ike is."

He leaned back to glance out the kitchen window that faced the back of Maggie's house. "If you want to catch Maggie, she just came outside."

"That's okay." I studied my nails. "I'll go see her later."

His brows shot up. "Since when do you procrastinate? Go. You have an hour before you crash, and you'll sleep better if you've talked to Maggie."

He leaned over his cereal bowl to kiss me. "Believe me, you'll need your rest for what I have in mind later."

"How much later? I work a ghost tour tonight, and then Jo-Jo will be here."

"Does the term 'afternoon delight' ring a bell?"

A bell, no. A gong, yes.

I dashed outside but stopped short. The yard was spotless. Trash was bagged and set at the corner of the house, and the tables and chairs we'd rented were folded and leaning against the front fence. No litter on the ground, and the teak furniture was tastefully arranged on Maggie's cobbled patio. Cobbled just like my patio, except hers is three times bigger and covered by an arbor. And, yes, we'd gotten a bulk deal on the cobblestones.

Maggie stood in the yard, hands on her hips, her engagement ring flashing in the sun.

"Did you clean up last night?"

"Not me. Jo-Jo must've done it."

"Helpful and quiet, too. Not bad. Come on, Cesca," she added with her usual briskness. "We need to talk about the five-year sponsorship rule."

We sat under the wooden arbor in the still morning heat,

me in a teak chair with a striped cushion, Maggie on the matching love seat.

"How come you never told me about the five-year thing, Maggie?"

"Bottom line? Because I didn't want to lose you as soon as I found you. I figured I'd let things fall into place in their own time."

"Did Neil know about the rule?"

Maggie smiled. "He does now."

"And? How does he feel about it? Would he care if we kept living near each other past the five-year mark?"

"Hard to say at this point. He is *not* happy this Jo-Jo guy showed up."

"I'm not wild about it either, but apparently he can live wherever he wants to."

Maggie tipped her head. "And you don't want that to be here. Why not?"

I leaned back and watched the play of sunlight through the wood slats of the arbor.

"I don't know how to be around other vampires. I hated the ones I had to live with in the old days, and the thought of being buds with Jo-Jo isn't giving me a warm glow."

"Plus you're used to being the only vampire in town. The only fish in the pond gets all the attention."

"I don't want the attention. Not from the newspaper and not from Jo-Jo. He sees me as the head fish. He looks up to me."

"And he's depending on you to help him?"

"Yes, and it scares me. I don't want to be his comedy coach, his princess pal, or anything else."

"It is a lot of responsibility," Maggie allowed as she shifted

LAST VAMPIRE STANDING 37

positions. "Looking out for someone else, guiding someone else, encouraging someone else."

I met her dancing Irish green eyes. "I get it. You took me in, and now it's payback."

"They do say payback is a bitch."

"And no good deed goes unpunished." I sighed. "The thing is, I don't know how to help Jo-Jo. I don't have the means to protect him, even if I were batty enough to let him move in with me. I sure can't wave a wand and make him funny."

"You *can* be his friend."

"Neil will go ballistic if Jo-Jo hangs around here."

"I'll take care of Neil." She paused. "Look, Cesca, we're going through a lot of changes with the move and my engagement."

"And now Jo-Jo shows up."

"Helping him is a personal decision, and staying in your cottage will be, too. If you live there forever, I'll love it. If you ever want to move, I'll support you."

I took her hand for a quick squeeze. "Thanks. You have any advice for handling this whole Jo-Jo the would-be comic thing?"

"Try not to stomp on his dream."

I snorted. "He's doing that all by himself."

"He does come out of left field, but give him time."

"Do you think being an interior designer is too big a dream for me?"

"No. Neither was being a ghost tour guide, and I have a feeling Jo-Jo is every bit as determined to succeed as you are. Who knows? He could do amateur night at the comedy club and be a huge hit."

I shuddered. "From what I've seen, even amateur night is a long way off."

Saber came back to my cottage at four. His raid on Hot Blooded hadn't been productive, and duty still called that night, but we indulged in a delightful afternoon tryst that stretched into hours. My mellow mood held even when Saber left again to stake out Ike's club. He promised he'd be back, though he didn't mention when.

If Saber's absence was convenient, it wasn't an obvious dodge to being there for Jo-Jo's practice run. Neil was another kettle of mullet. He *said* he was cleaning his house in Davis Shores, just across the Bridge of Lions. Sure, he was preparing to put his home on the market, but Neil cleaning when he could be with Maggie? *Riiight.*

Maggie and I might've invented somewhere else to be, if we'd planned ahead. But Jo-Jo showed up right after I'd changed from my Minorcan ghost tour guide costume into shorts and put my thick, unruly hair in its customary ponytail.

Jo-Jo was rather endearingly excited to try out his new material on us, and he'd cleaned up pretty well. His hair was loose but washed, and he wore blue jeans, a white T-shirt, and black flip-flops. Guess he'd hit Wal-Mart sometime last night.

Maggie left the floodlights off, so we took seats under the glow of rope lighting strung on the arbor. Settled on the comfy teak chairs for the private floor show, we hoped for the best.

Jo-Jo gave us comedy carnage. I was certain his jokes alone had put the first nails in vaudeville's coffin.

He started with, "How many vampires does it take to

change a lightbulb? None. We don't change no stinking light-bulbs."

Maggie stayed silent, I worked not to grimace, and some-where a kitten meowed like it was in pain. I could relate.

Next Jo-Jo tried, "Take my ghoul friend, please."

Maggie cleared her throat. I winced. The feline meowed again—louder, longer, closer—and I felt the brush of magick in its cry. What the heck?

I glanced around, while Jo-Jo tried a belligerent, "Hey, you. Yeah, you, white bread. Are you undead or are you always that pale?" He paused and shook his head. "No good, right?"

"Frankly, no," Maggie admitted.

Jo-Jo waved her off. "No problem. I got a million of them. A priest, a rabbi, and a gnome go into a vampire bar—"

"Rrryyyow!"

No stranded kitty made *that* sound. It was a brain-jarring panther cry, and it came from Maggie's roof.

I looked up to see Cat, the magical shape-shifter who had helped capture the French Bride killer. She sprang from her crouch at the junction of the roof and arbor, sailed gracefully through the air, and landed with a thud a slim paw's swipe from Jo-Jo.

"Rrrryyyow," Cat screamed again.

Jo-Jo screamed, too, some variation on *"Aaaiiieeee,"* as he half-jumped, half-flew to the top of the arbor.

It was the funniest Jo-Jo had been all night, but I didn't have time to enjoy a laugh, because Hugh Lister banged through his back porch screen door and barged straight through the jasmine hedge, shouting.

"Goddamn it, can't you people be quiet one— Jesus H. Christ in Dockers, what the hell is *that* thing?"

FOUR

"What thing is that, Mr. Lister?" Maggie asked calmly.

We'd both shot to our feet the second we heard the screen door slam, hoping to shield Cat from view. Had it worked? Had she downsized yet?

I glanced over my shoulder as Hugh snarled, "That thing."

"*Rrryyow.*" Cat emerged from between my legs, still making a racket, but she'd shape-shifted to look like a hefty house cat with a silver-colored chain around her neck. A chain that was scads too large. Was that a charm hanging from the chain?

"You mean the cat?" I asked. "Is she yours?"

"Hell and damnation, no, that animal isn't mine. I hate cats, and I could've sworn that one was bigger a minute ago."

Maggie blinked oh-so-innocently. "Bigger than what?"

"Bigger than it is now. It looks stupid in that necklace."

Cat parked on her haunches, stared at Hugh, and let out an eerie wail that made him take a step back.

"They make awful noises when they're in heat, don't they?" Maggie said.

Cat snorted, and Jo-Jo moaned theatrically from the slatted arbor roof.

Hugh whirled and stared at Jo-Jo neatly caught in the outer halo of rope lighting. "Why is a man crouched on your arbor, Ms. O'Halloran?"

"Allergies," I said quickly. "Really bad allergies to—"

"Cat hair," Maggie supplied.

"Cat claws," Jo-Jo corrected.

Hugh shook his head at Jo-Jo, then eyed Maggie and me. "You're running a nut farm over here, and I won't stand for it. I'll rally the whole neighborhood if I have to, but you people will not be rowdy at all hours of the day and night." He stomped back through the jasmine hedge and shouted, "Selma, I need a goddamn drink."

"Bless his holy name, the bourbon's in the bar."

Bless whose holy name? I heard in my head.

The breath of relief I'd started to take lodged in my throat. Maggie hadn't spoken, and neither had Jo-Jo. Uh-oh.

I looked down to where Cat rubbed against my bare leg.

"Please tell me you didn't say that."

But I did, Cat replied.

My pulse thu-thudded in my ears. This couldn't be happening. I'd taken one too many smacks in the head from my surfboard, that's all. The vampire "curse" on my psychic senses might be wearing off, but there was only one person I'd heard this well telepathically. That was in my past. Plus, well, Cat wasn't even a person.

Was she?

No, I am not part human, and I am not called Cat. I am called Pandora.

I blinked. Ai-yi-yi, she *was* talking to me, and in a superior, snippy tone, just like a typical cat.

I sputtered something like *"Ohmygarrrgghh,"* and staggered to a patio chair.

Maggie rushed to me. "Cesca, what's wrong?"

I couldn't find my voice, so I pointed at Pandora as she glided to sit a few feet away, out of Hugh Lister's line of sight. Then, like time-lapse nature photography on high speed, she grew back to panther size and licked a platter-sized paw. The chain around her neck disappeared into her thick ruff of golden fur.

"Princess, if the panther is threatening you, you and Miss Maggie should slip into the house. I mean, you know I'd protect you with my life from most things, but—"

"Pandora isn't a thing, Jo-Jo," I croaked, still staring at the panther. "She's a shape-shifter. A sentient being."

Thank you for the support. Tell the odd vampire to get down before he breaks the arbor.

"Jo-Jo, get down from the arbor before you break it."

"Nuh-unh. Panthers bite."

I glanced up. "So do you."

"Not anymore."

"Come down here and meet Pandora."

"Pandora?" Maggie echoed.

"With all due respect, Your Royalness, I'm not meeting a wild panther, sentient or not. He interrupted my act."

Pandora raised her head to stare at Jo-Jo and chuffed low in her throat.

Jo-Jo sniffed. "Everybody's a critic."

"Pandora is a she, Jo-Jo, and for heaven's sake, get down," I commanded.

Maggie knelt beside me. "Cesca, what's the problem? We've seen the cat—Pandora—before. She helped Saber save us from that killer."

"Yes, but she didn't talk then. Or she didn't talk to me."

Maggie cut her gaze to Pandora. "She's talking?"

"Like that horse on TV, Mr. Ed?" Jo-Jo asked, shinnying down an arbor post.

"No, not like the horse. This is telepathy."

Pandora sighed. *I realize you are surprised, but you must listen. I have a message to deliver.*

I gave Pandora a long and probably stupid look. "A message from whom?"

"Is she talking to the panther?" Jo-Jo whispered to Maggie as he drew cautiously nearer.

Pandora narrowed her eyes on Jo-Jo and jerked her head toward my cottage. *We will talk in private.*

Jo-Jo about climbed into Maggie's arms as Pandora rose and trotted across the yard into the shadows. Good thing my porch light was off. I didn't need Hugh Lister spotting her.

I looked at Maggie. "Pandora has a message for me."

"Fine. Go find out what it is so we can get back to work with Jo-Jo."

Oh, yeah, Jo-Jo's act. What with the neighbor who hates us almost catching us with a shape-shifting panther who now talks to me, I'd almost forgotten my priorities. Silly me.

I plopped on one of the tiki barstools facing Pandora. My mother drilled manners into me, but she never covered a formal visit from a shape-shifter. Should I start the conversation?

"Uh, thank you for coming," I said. Constantly striving to be a gracious hostess, that's me. "What do you want to tell me?"

The message is from Triton.

My heartbeat faltered. Triton was my first crush, the long-lost friend with whom I'd shared a strong and mutual telepathy. He was the only other soul I'd shared that gift with until now.

Pandora swiped a paw at my foot, forcing me to focus.

"How do you know Triton?"

Pandora simply blinked. Nothing stonewalls like a cat.

I sighed. "What is the message?"

Triton will meet with you soon, but he sends a warning and a talisman.

Aha! Triton *was* nearby, probably in town, just as I'd suspected. After one hundred and fifty-six years of telepathic silence, he'd appeared a few months ago just long enough for me to get a glimpse of him standing on a sand dune. He'd left a golden dolphin charm in the sand, one like he'd worn during our childhood. Then he'd vanished. I'd mentally searched for and found a shadow of him, but he blocked me.

Yes, he is blocking your telepathy, Princess Vampire, for both of your sakes. There is great evil rising. You must beware of betrayal, of treachery.

I shivered. "Betrayal from whom?"

Triton did not say. You are to be on your guard.

"That's all? Does Triton need help?"

He needs only for you to be safe.

Okay, I could do that, but questions whirled. "Um, are you Triton's panther?"

Pandora looked affronted, and I rephrased the question.

"What I mean is, who takes care of you? Do you live with someone?"

Pandora tilted her regal head as if considering whether to answer. *Old Wizard is my closest companion.*

"I see." And I did as I received a vague mental picture of a bearded man from Pandora. "Where is Old Wizard? Does he know you're here?"

While the Council of Ancients meets, I am charged to watch over you.

I didn't know what or who the Council of Ancients was, but hearing the phrase gave me goose bumps the size of hives. What did my body know that my brain didn't? How was Triton involved with this wizard and Pandora? Would Pandora tell me if I offered to pet sit while the wizard was gone?

Pandora read my thoughts and shook her head. *I live wild. I will patrol and keep watch from a distance, but you must be alert to danger.*

"You won't answer questions about Triton?"

I cannot. It is for him to tell you.

"The way things are going, it'll be another century before he does that," I groused. "All right, Pandora, I'll be careful, and um, thank you for your help."

You are polite for a vampire. Pandora rose, padded the few steps to my barstool, and thrust her head into my lap. *You must remove the chain now.*

I hesitated. My nose didn't itch—my usual reaction to silver—but then a necklace or ring here and there didn't always set off the reaction. Now the one tourist who'd been draped with enough Native American rings and necklaces and bangles to be a walking jewelry store had worn just the amount to make my allergy go bonkers.

Pandora must've read my thoughts again. She nudged me with her nose. *The talisman is pewter and the chain is steel. Neither will burn you, but there is no clasp on the chain. You must slip it over my head.*

"Okay, but no biting if this hurts."

It will not hurt.

And it didn't because, as I sank my fingers into Pandora's richly furred neck, she shrank herself just enough for me to lift the chain off before she returned to full size.

Weird to watch, freakier to be touching her while she changed sizes.

"Cesca, don't move."

I flinched at the sound of Saber's voice. Well, what did he expect when he startled me? Pandora merely backed up, sat, and stared at him.

So did I, but not so much with the usual lust as with concern. He pointed the business end of his matte-black semi-automatic at Pandora.

"It's okay, Saber," I said, smiling my assurance. "Pandora is giving me a message."

"Pandora?" Saber shifted his weight. "Is this the same cat that had our French Bride killer by the neck a few months ago?"

"Yes."

"And why was his head in your lap?"

"Pandora's a female, and she was giving me this." I held up the chain with the charm dangling from it.

"So you're good here?"

"I'm fine, Saber. Better than fine. I can communicate with Pandora telepathically."

Saber relaxed but didn't holster his weapon. He held the Glock at his side, and I couldn't blame him. He and other slayers had hunted werecreatures until they were extinct. Last time we'd seen Pandora, I'd explained that she was a magical shifter, not a were. Weres, real lycanthropes, had an earthier smell and an energy signature that lacked a spark of magick.

I met Pandora's amber-eyed gaze as she rose.

I will be on guard. Remember to do the same.

With that, Pandora loped across the yard past Saber and sailed over the fence gate. I hopped off the barstool and went to Saber as he holstered his gun.

"How did the stakeout go at Hot Blooded?"

"Slow," he said, sliding an arm around my waist. He dropped a kiss on my nose, then on my waiting mouth. "Did I hear right? That the cat—"

"Pandora."

"—brought you a message you heard telepathically?"

"You did. Isn't that cool?"

"It's different. What was the message?"

"To beware of betrayal and treachery."

"That's succinct. Are the chain and charm part of the message?"

"It's supposed to be a talisman."

Saber caught the two-inch pewter charm in his palm and squinted at it. I didn't have to squint.

"A mermaid sitting on a treasure map?" Saber said. "That's supposed to ward off evil?"

"Maybe it looks lame, but Pandora said Triton sent it with the message."

"Triton, as in your old boyfriend? He's back in town?"

"I don't know where he is," I admitted. "Triton is blocking our connection."

I balled up the charm and chain in my palm to stick them in my shorts pocket, and startled when a strong, white noise buzz vibrated from the pewter. Interesting, and something I'd have to explore later. Like when Saber was asleep.

Right now, I needed to deal with a boyfriend who, in spite of his cop look, I could swear was a little jealous.

"You still want to find Triton," Saber said flatly.

"Well, yeah. I want to smack him upside the head. Repeatedly. With a sledgehammer."

Saber cracked a smile. "I remember when you wanted to smack me every other minute."

"And now I want to kiss you just as often. But only you."

He took the hint and brushed his mouth over mine. The kiss was too short but satisfying.

"So, a mermaid and a treasure map. Do they have special significance to you or Triton?"

"To me, mermaids mean the ocean, and treasure maps mean pirates. I don't know what they could mean to Triton."

"Pandora didn't give you a hint?"

"Nope. She only mentioned a great evil, betrayal, and treachery, and said she'd be watching out for me."

He shifted to gaze across the yard where Maggie and Jo-Jo sat in deep and earnest conversation. "I suppose she didn't say who you should beware."

I sighed. "No, but she would've told me if Jo-Jo was the threat. Besides, he's only dangerous to an innocent joke."

"He's that bad?"

"He's worse. Come on, I can't leave Maggie stranded any longer."

Arms around each other, we reached the patio just as Maggie looked ready to implode.

"No, no, no. Don Rickles could do insult comedy. From you, it would scare people stupid." She spotted Saber and me and twisted to face us. "Tell him I'm right, and take over, Cesca. I have to go to bed."

"No problem, Maggie, thanks for helping."

She started off, then paused. "What did Pandora say?"

With Jo-Jo there, instinct kept me mum about Triton. "Nothing critical. I'll tell you tomorrow."

Maggie nodded and went into the house. I plopped into the love seat with Saber and eyed Jo-Jo.

"Maggie's right, you know. You don't want to copy another comic, especially someone famous. You need to be yourself. Have your own style."

"But myself isn't funny anymore," he grumped, slumping in his chair, "and my style was built on my vaudeville act."

"Can you adapt that act to stand-up?"

"The bits won't work without Jemina or another partner," he said, a sudden gleam in his eyes.

I held up a hand. "No. I'll do what I can to help you find an angle for your comedy act, but I'm not performing with you."

"Then I'm doomed," he intoned.

"You will be if you don't stop moping. Being negative won't

get you anywhere, so let's look at what's possible. What kind of comedy do you want to do?"

"The kind I'll get paid for."

I grinned. "Good start. We know you can juggle. You could use that in your act."

"But not with knives," Saber warned.

Jo-Jo winced. "Agreed, but is juggling hip enough for a twenty-first century crowd?"

"You won't know until you try." I tapped my chin. "You need to relate to both humans and vampires."

Jo-Jo gave me a double take. "You think vampires would come to see my act?"

"I don't see why not, but your audiences need to see themselves and their lives in your jokes. In normal stuff like working, family issues, paying taxes, aging."

"Vampires don't have old age issues, honey," Saber said.

"What if we did? What if we had to have—" I thought of the Jag Queens and grinned. "—false teeth. What would we do?"

Jo-Jo looked blank, but Saber grinned.

"Vampire denture cream," he drawled. "Available in mint, cinnamon, and O positive."

"Perfect," I said, squeezing his hand.

"Can I use that?" Jo-Jo asked eagerly.

Saber shrugged. "Sure."

"Okay, let me try one." Jo-Jo frowned in concentration. "Taxes. Vampires live long enough to pay more taxes than a small country, but it's not enough to clear the national debt."

"Rough, but you're getting the idea."

Jo-Jo looked cautiously hopeful. "Do you think this will give me enough material for a whole act?"

"I'm no expert," Saber warned, "but you could throw in one more thing."

"What?" Jo-Jo and I asked in unison.

"Poke fun at vampire lore."

I grinned at my honey. "You mean myths like being repelled by garlic and not having reflections in mirrors?"

"People will think that's funny?"

"Depending on how you tell it, sure," I said. "Plus you could defuse some of the fear people have about us by letting them laugh with you."

"If Vlad hears I'm making fun of vampires, he'll kill me."

"Not while Saber and I stand behind you. Besides, I thought you wanted to take charge of your afterlife."

Jo-Jo straightened. "I do."

"Then stop worrying about Vlad," I said.

"Yeah," Saber drawled, "and start worrying about how you're going to teach Cesca to fly."

FIVE

I stiffened. "Saber, Jo-Jo does *not* need to worry about teaching me to fly."

"I don't know. From what Maggie said, Abe's Traffic School worried about teaching you to drive."

Jo-Jo looked appalled. "Don't tell me Her Highness is a bad driver."

"I'm a great driver," I snapped. "I don't tailgate or lane weave or cut people off."

"But you do have a lead foot, and you can't parallel park to save your life."

"Afterlife," I snipped, "and parallel parking is overrated."

"All I know is that the driving test examiner was afraid you'd bite him if he didn't pass you."

"I would never!" I sputtered, hoping I didn't blush. I hadn't exactly soothed that nervous examiner's fears.

Darn it all, I'd hoped Saber would forget about the flying lessons. He'd pushed me to claim my vampireness since we met, and overhearing the French Bride killer rant about a passel of powers day-walkers were supposed to possess only made Saber shove harder. He said he wanted me to be all I could be. Heck, if that's what *I* wanted, I'd join the Marines. They were looking for a few good vamps.

Flying? I wasn't going up without a fight.

"Jo-Jo has enough to do, Saber," I argued. "He needs to focus on working up an act. Besides, you told me not all vampires day-walk. Maybe flying isn't one of my talents."

"Day-walking isn't a universal vamp trait, but flying is. You need to learn this skill."

Jo-Jo picked up the banner. "Your consort is right, Highness. Knowing how to fly will strengthen your power base."

"I don't have a power base, Jo-Jo, and stop calling me Highness."

"Yes, Your Graciousness."

I gritted my teeth. "Gentlemen, now is not the time for flying lessons."

"Why not? Jo-Jo can work with you right here."

"In the backyard? Hugh Lister would have a stroke."

"Maggie taught you to drive in empty parking lots. That's an option."

"Sure. Like playing Peter Pan in a parking lot won't attract undue attention."

"You are not wiggling out of this, Cesca."

"Um, we can start with simple levitation," Jo-Jo offered.

Saber and I snapped our heads in his direction.

"Simple?" I gulped. "Levitation is simple?"

"Of course. Any year-old vamp has mastered—uh, I mean, it's basic enough."

"See, Cesca?" Saber said. "Driving a car is probably more complicated."

Translation? If I couldn't fly, I was the lamest vampire on the planet. Which didn't bother me, really. I'd rather cling to being as normal, as human, as possible. But, with Saber all but daring me, this was a challenge I had to meet. A fear I had to conquer. A vampire party trick I had to master or never hear the end of it.

I heaved a defeated sigh. "Up, up, and away."

Jo-Jo popped out of his seat with more energy than he'd shown since he leaped atop the arbor. Saber flashed a diabolical grin, pulled me up, and paced after Jo-Jo to the shadows beside my cottage.

"Okay, Princess," Jo-Jo said, rubbing his hands together. "Let's start with an overview. Now watch what I do."

I crossed my arms as he took three steps and just, well, lifted into the air until he hovered about two feet off the ground. It was as impressive as the one time I'd seen Ike fly, though Ike and his vamps had taken more steps to get off the ground. Guess Jo-Jo was older and had more air miles.

When he sank down to the grass, he turned to me.

"Now you try."

"No."

Saber hip-bumped me. "Go on, Cesca."

I planted my hands on my hips. "Saber, I walk all the time without that happening. I saw the mechanics, but that doesn't tell me how to actually go up."

"Princess, what don't you understand?"

"How do you get your lift, Jo-Jo? Are you thinking 'come fly with me'? 'Walk this way'? Are you thinking happy little thoughts?"

"Uh, I believe I just expect to fly, and I do, but let me go over the steps again."

Jo-Jo walked back to us, brows furrowed in concentration. He turned, took a breath, and started off. When he reached the fourth step, the one that should've hit only air, he stumbled. Muttering something colorful, he started off again, and then stumbled again.

Houston, we have a problem. Failure to launch.

Jo-Jo faced us with chagrin. "Maybe we should try a different approach."

"Maybe we should do this later."

"Now, Cesca, you don't want Jo-Jo to feel like he failed as your teacher, do you?"

I glanced at Jo-Jo's embarrassed expression. "No."

"Plus," Saber said, leaning close and whispering, "it would be hot to levitate during sex."

My knees went a little weak, and I had to clear my throat, but I was suddenly motivated. Highly motivated.

"Bring it on, Jo-Jo."

My flight instructor nodded. "Okay, Highness, have you ever flown by accident, without meaning to? Or come close to flying?"

I shook my head, but Saber contradicted me.

"Yes, you have. You flew into my line of fire when that killer captured you in March."

"That was jumping, Saber, not flying."

"You hovered."

"I did?"

"You did." He pitched his voice low and sexy again. "Now jump for Jo-Jo so we can all call it a night."

For the record, white vampires might jump like NBA stars, but this white vamp can't fly.

We worked for twenty minutes, and I did have some success. I never figured out exactly how, but I finally managed a leaping hover about six inches off the ground that lasted for all of three seconds. Still, it was a toss-up whether Jo-Jo would be funny before I could fly.

Good thing we took a break when we did. Though Jo-Jo tried not to let me see his frustration, he'd slapped his forehead during the lesson so often that the wound Marco had inflicted with the silver knife was now red, raw, and seeping.

Saber sat Jo-Jo on a barstool on my patio and peered at the cut by the porch light.

"What have you been putting on this, Jo-Jo?"

"Antibiotic ointment." He winced when Saber carefully probed the wound.

"Cesca, where is that special salve I had made up for you?"

"That smelly stuff I haven't had to use yet? It's in the first aid kit."

"Would you mind sharing some with Jo-Jo?"

I smiled and trotted into the house. Anything to get out of flight school for the night.

When I'd been shot during the French Bride case—on two occasions, no less—Saber had insisted that I keep some anti-silver salve on hand. I'd argued that none of the bullets had been silver, but he gave me two one-ounce jars anyway. One I kept in the car, the other in the house. I didn't know where he came by the salve or what was in it, but I hoped Jo-Jo had a weaker gag reflex than I did.

I grabbed some gauze pads and white medical adhesive tape for good measure and dropped everything in one of the plastic bags from Publix I saved to line trash cans.

When I handed the bag to Jo-Jo, he frowned and peeked inside. "Highness, why does a vampire have a first aid kit?"

"Because she has human friends."

"Ah, that would explain it." He stood and gave me a little bow. "Thank you for the medicine. I'll see you tomorrow night."

"What for?"

"More help with his act," Saber answered, almost too quickly.

I let it pass because Jo-Jo left, and Saber murmured his pet name for me against my ear.

"Princesca, ready to come fly with me?"

We didn't levitate in bed that night, but we did soar to the moon and stars a few precious times. In the afterglow, with our legs still tangled and our breathing returning to normal, I snuggled my head into the curve of his shoulder.

"It just gets better and better with you," Saber murmured, his hand lazily caressing my hip.

I kissed his chest. "Glad to hear I'm holding your attention."

"You hold more than my attention." He paused and turned to face me in the light of the candles scattered throughout my bedroom. "What would you think of me moving to St. Augustine?"

I pulled back enough to see him without my eyes crossing.

"You could be based here instead of in Daytona Beach?"

"I can now. Since the Vampire Protection Agency is federal, they're reorganizing. All former slayers who want to stay on the job as special investigators will be federal employees instead of working solely for each state."

I took that in for a minute. "Is there a chance you'd be transferred out of Florida?"

"Some, but it's not likely. The powers that be know we're familiar with the vamps in our areas. Moving us around could create more problems than leaving us alone."

"Wow, a federal reorganization designed to be more efficient instead of less? I thought that was unconstitutional."

"Ha-ha, funny girl. If I buy my own place in St. Augustine, would you feel like I'm crowding you?"

"You couldn't crowd me, Saber. St. Augustine isn't *that* small a town."

"It might be with Triton and me both here."

I frowned and propped up on my elbow. "You're not jealous of Triton, right? You know there's nothing between us other than an old friendship. Emphasis on the old."

"I'm not jealous. Not exactly. But I don't understand why he came back, left you that dolphin charm you said he used to wear, then vanished only to send you another charm and a warning."

"He's turned into a drama king?"

"Cesca."

I shrugged. "I don't know what's going on with Triton. Why he came back or why all the cloak-and-dagger stuff. I do trust that he's not playing an elaborate game, but, whether he's here in town or not, you're the only man I want to be with."

"Even if we don't know where we're going in our relationship?"

"Even then." I scooted into his arms and kissed his chin. "And I think your moving here is the best idea ever, Saber."

He gave me a scowl and growled, "What happened to calling me Deke in the bedroom, woman?"

"Well," I drawled, stroking a hand slowly down his chest, "moving is business, not pillow talk."

"Princesca, we're in bed, we're naked, and the South is rising again. If that's not pillow talk, what is?"

I moved over him and whispered against his lips. "This is, Deke, darling."

The moon and stars were even more spectacular on our next trip, and I didn't feel the least bit slighted when Saber— Deke—sank into sleep when the eagle landed. I was too blissful, spooned in the curve of his body, dozing and drifting in dreams of us sharing beds in both of our homes.

My sexually sated daze didn't last long. I needed to get to my homework and run a few loads of laundry. Since the washer and dryer are super quiet, and since the laundry room is off the kitchen next to the half bath, the noise wouldn't bother Saber.

I pulled on my flamingo sleep shirt and blew out the candles as I moved through the room, folding Saber's discarded clothes and gathering my own. The necklace and charm jingled in the pocket of my shorts, and Saber made a noise in his sleep as he turned over.

I gazed at his face in the moonlight, the angles softened in sleep. Suddenly, my chest tightened with a crashing wave of tenderness, stealing my breath.

I loved this man.

When the best I'd hoped for were some dates and, okay, semicasual sex just so I wouldn't spend my afterlife as a virgin, I'd found love.

Sure, Saber pushed and prodded me to do things I didn't want to do, like fly. He'd challenged my idea of a safe, secure, normal afterlife since we'd met, but he'd helped heal me in places I hadn't acknowledged I hurt. No, we didn't know where our relationship was going long-term, but it didn't matter. He loved me, and I loved him.

Nothing, not even Triton, would get in the way of me being with Saber for however long we might have.

I slipped out of the bedroom with new determination. Not about the laundry, though I started the first load right away. Nope. This was about getting through to Triton. He might block me from his thoughts, but there was a chance he might hear mine.

If nothing else, a good ole telepathic rant would make me feel better.

With the washer whooshing softly in the background, I settled on the sofa, the rich leather a warm caress on my partly bare legs. I laid the mermaid charm within reach, then went through the centering routine I'd learned from reading books on how to tap psychic energy. The reading was at Saber's insistence, but, hey, I was woman enough to admit the focusing techniques worked.

I was soon ready, and scooped the chain and charm into my left palm. The white noise buzz began as soon as I closed my hand around it, but the longer I held the charm, the more the radio-type static morphed into the sound of the ocean. I imagined diving beneath the waves, then pictured Triton until I saw him clearly. A few more deep breaths, and I knocked on his mind door. It opened a sliver, and I stuck my ethereal foot in. My little voice cautioned me against using Triton's name, but, otherwise, I let 'er rip.

Of all the nerve! You show up after eons of silence—and just when I finally met a great guy, I might add—then vanish and appear again? I don't think so, bub. I don't know what's going on, but getting that obscure message was annoying as hell.

I sensed Triton raising a brow.

Yes, I said hell. I'm that ticked. And, okay, it was good to hear from you, but this popping in and out is not acceptable. I want to know where you are, why you're back, and what this big evil is that has you in hiding.

Very, very softly, I heard, *Not safe.*

Well, when will it be? Because I have a nice afterlife filled with friends and activities, and I don't want anyone screwing it up.

Nothing.

You hear me? I will not be yanked around, not by you and not by anyone else.

Again, nothing, but Triton's mind door ever so slowly closed on my ethereal foot.

Ouch.

I came back to myself, blinked at the room, and opened my fingers to find I'd squeezed the charm hard enough to make an impression in my hand. Damn.

Well, all right. I'd given Triton my bit of what for. I hadn't expected *any* response from him, so I suppose it was a victory that he'd answered me at all, however briefly.

What could be such a big darn deal that we couldn't do a mind hookup? Was someone telepathically eavesdropping? Hunting Triton? It would have to be him, because I was a breeze to find. My crazy Covenant stalker did it, which is why Saber insisted on all the security.

Sitting here wondering what kind of danger I was in and where it was coming from wasn't getting my homework done. Much as I loathed our current assignment on period furniture, I went to my desk and dropped the chain and charm in a tiki-motif mug by the monitor. While the system booted, I added fabric softener to the wash load and grabbed a Fig Newton to chew on. Beat chewing on questions about Triton.

I waded into my *History of Furnishings* textbook wondering why anyone had thought heavy styles like baroque looked good. To me, they just looked hulking. And, once you got that furniture into a room, no way did you want to move it out again.

Of course, the wealthy had servants to drag furniture around. I wondered how many had suffered hernias. Then again, people weren't so mobile in earlier times. Family homes were passed down through generations and still were, for that matter.

I set my chin on my fist and thought about my own family. I'd been raised with furniture just as chunky as some of the pieces in the book, though not as elaborately carved and costly. The tables and chairs, chests and bedsteads in my family home were sturdy, serviceable. They had to be to stand up to the beating that first my brothers, then my nieces and nephews gave them. Had my family missed the things they couldn't take when they'd finally fled St. Augustine?

I looked at the full-page photo of an oak trestle table darkened to black brown with age. The surface looked pitted, scarred, beloved. I hesitated, then touched the photo with one fingertip and was jerked back in time.

The children huddled under the table, shooed there by the women. They didn't cry, but their eyes were huge and frightened as they peeked at me between their mothers' skirts. I'd cared for these babies, coddled and laughed with them, but no more. I was a vampire now, and if they knew not what that meant, they'd been told stories enough to fear me.

I raised my gaze, and my heart bled to see the face of my mother contorted in horror. Her pallor was severe, so much so that I feared she would collapse. Instead, she gripped a cleaver in her arthritic, trembling hand. Two sisters-in-law, they who had chided me for not choosing a husband, wielded long knives and regarded me with loathing. My youngest sister-in-law, the one I best loved, clasped the newest baby to her breast. I ached to touch that fuzzy head, to croon a lullaby.

To be a family again.

"Please, don't be afraid," I said over and over. "I'm here to warn you."

They didn't heed me. They couldn't. Their terrified screams begging me to spare them and the children drowned my anguished voice, and I wept as I slipped out the garden door. They thought me a monster, with no soul, no love, no loyalty in my heart. They were wrong.

Later, I asked Triton to get them out of town so that King Normand could no longer threaten them, but I relinquished my family that day. I was alone with no one to love and no one to live for. I would survive or find a way to forever die.

The memory faded, and I wondered for the first time if I had relatives somewhere. Descendants of my nieces and nephews who would be happy to learn about their ancestors and perhaps to know me. If so, they hadn't shown up yet, which was telling in itself.

I shook off the past and closed the textbook, then about screeched out of my skin when a hand landed on my shoulder. I spun in the old-fashioned swivel desk chair to face Saber.

"Easy, babe, it's me."

"Geez, make some noise next time," I said, my heartbeat still in overdrive, my eyelashes wet with the remnants of tears.

"I did make noise, honey," he said gently. "Are you okay? Is your vampire hearing on the fritz?"

"My hearing is fine. I was hyperfocused." I surreptitiously wiped my cheeks dry. Then I noticed that, except for his shoes, he was dressed. I glanced at my dolphin desk clock. "Where are you going at three in the morning?"

"Daytona."

"But you were just there, like, eighteen hours ago. What happened?"

He rubbed his hand over his whiskered cheek. "The cops found a guy in an alley a block from Ike's club."

"Dead?" I asked, rising to hug him.

He shook his head and held me. "The guy is alive for now, but he's in shock and sporting some vicious fang marks. Not clean or neat."

"You need to go talk to the victim?"

"More than that. The guy is claiming he was robbed, but he can't give a coherent description of who lifted his wallet and ring or of who bit him. We're serving another search warrant on Ike. The Daytona cops are waking a judge now, and we're planning to hit them right about the time they close at four."

I stepped out of his arms. "If you're raiding Hot Blooded while Ike and his nest are awake, I'm coming with you."

"Cesca, I'll have a squad of city cops there."

I shook my head and headed for the bedroom. "Not good enough. Somebody there bit a man, and I might be able to tell who it was. Plus, I can do my energy-draining trick if the natives get obnoxious."

"No way. I can't have a civilian at a possible crime scene. Besides, weren't you going surfing with Neil this morning?"

I paused at the bedroom door. Actually, I'd forgotten about the date with Neil, and this was far more important.

"Surfing can wait, and you can deputize me or something so I won't be a civilian."

He frowned but didn't have a comeback, so I pressed my case.

"I'll follow you in my car and leave as soon as I know everyone will be safe. I'm going to tail you anyway, so you might as well give in."

By the time he had his sneakers laced up, I was dressed in blue jeans and a tank top, and ready to kick fang.

SIX

We sped south on A1A, Saber with his light and siren bubble stabbing the night, me streaking behind in my SSR. I'd never been to Daytona but had heard the drive took an hour or more at normal speed and in normal traffic. I'd bet both fangs we'd be there in thirty-five minutes.

Enough time for my bravado to wane, but not my resolve.

Not that I *wanted* to confront the Daytona Beach vamps. Been there, survived that. Ike's rich voice oozes over a body like a controlled oil spill, but he's a quiet flavor of scary next to Laurel. Vampzilla is bossy, bitchy, and wears human bones in her cornrowed hair. The other two vamps I'd met in March were Ike's muscle. Tower and Zena are very tall, very built, and very loyal to Ike.

Ike had left me alone since our meeting five months ago. Would he take my turning up on his turf with Saber and the Daytona cops as a declaration of war?

If so, I'd just have to talk him down out of the boughs. A vamp had chomped on a human, and that simply wasn't kosher.

Of course, there was the off chance—way off—that the biting had been consensual. In March, I'd also met four blood bunnies that hung out with Ike, and I'd later asked Saber about their bite marks. He'd explained that biting could be consented to during sex. Not an encouraged practice, but the VPA overlooked love bites just as it ignored small nests. Sometimes, bureaucracy bites.

Consensual or not, a vampire should never leave a bitee to wander around under a partial thrall. The effect was like turning a drunk loose. Without the upchucking.

Saber killed his light and siren and turned into a parking lot behind a two-story cinder-block building painted Caribbean blue. Not the color choice I pictured for a place called Hot Blooded, but I imagined City Hall controlled the colors of buildings. St. Augustine's city government did the same.

The parking lot teemed with official vehicles and uniformed men and women from the Daytona Beach police force. I joined Saber, and we headed for a tall, rangy black man wearing a Daytona Beach cop uniform and a scowl.

"Captain Jackson," Saber said, "this is Cesca Marinelli."

"I know who she is," Jackson snarled. "What the hell is she doing here?"

That's me. Making instant friends wherever I go.

"I've deputized her on the good chance she can ID the biter, and we can get out of here fast."

"How is she gonna do that?"

I smiled, being perfectly pleasant. "I have a sharp sense of smell for blood, Captain Jackson."

"Just stay out of my way." He turned the full weight of his gaze on Saber. "Are you clear that this is our operation? You're here as a consultant for now."

"You mean until you throw your hands up and dump the mess in my lap?"

"That was Hake's style. It's not mine."

"Then your way will be a nice change," Saber said.

Jackson blinked, then nodded and handed Saber a photo of a man with ragged, bloody bite marks on one side of his neck.

"Since you know the head vamp, you can assist me in questioning him while my teams conduct the search."

Saber murmured his agreement.

"We round up all the vamps and any humans still in there and put them at opposite sides of the room. I've assigned people with silver ammo to guard the vamps."

"Good plan."

Mollified that Saber wasn't here to upstage him, Jackson seemed to stand down.

"Fine. So you question Ike, and she"—he pointed to my quiet, respectful self—"can do her bloodhound thing."

"Arf," I muttered too softly for Jackson to hear.

Saber did hear and shot me a zip-it look.

At Jackson's signal, one group of officers fanned out to cover the back door while others took up positions with rifles aimed at windows. Another five men marched along the sidewalk to the front entrance, with Jackson leading. Saber and I followed.

Tower was on doorman duty. Skin and eyes the color of dark chocolate, he nearly filled the double doorway in height and breadth but wore a flat expression.

Jackson flashed his badge under Tower's nose. "Daytona Beach police. We have a search warrant."

"Ike is expecting you."

Well, of course he was. It's not like he could've missed the circus in his parking lot. I kept quiet and slinked behind Jackson and Saber into a cavernous room dominated by an empty dance floor. Two massive flat panel TVs hung suspended over an elevated DJ booth, and both were tuned to ESPN.

ESPN in a vampire club?

A bar of rich, dark wood sprawled into the shadows on my left, and tiny colored lights winked around the perimeter of the room, maybe twenty feet high. No disco ball here, but the blinking lights gave a strobe effect.

One that made Ike's dark looks more foreboding, even from across the dance floor. He uncoiled from his seat at a cocktail table, and I noticed he wore black dress slacks and a silky black shirt.

Huh? No leather?

I took a quick peek at the other seven vampires seated at the table in a haphazard semicircle. The Scandinavian-featured Zena wore jeans and a tropical-print button-up blouse that looked great with her pale blonde hair and white skin. An older-looking female wore a modest sundress, and a younger one sported a red and white cheerleader outfit.

Rah, rah, Fang U?

Tower and three males I didn't know wore jeans and shirts; one was built like a linebacker sporting a Florida Gators T-shirt. What was up with the normal clothes? Had they all come fashion forward, or was this costume night?

And *what* was that smell in the air? It wasn't blood. I

didn't catch the slightest whiff of blood in the room, and I was a shark when it came to that odor. This essence was more a light citrus scent. Oranges? Had Ike installed an air freshening system, or did I smell the fruit the bartender used for drinks?

Captain Jackson finished sizing up the vampires but didn't seemed fazed by the anger emanating from Ike or by having to cross the expanse of dance floor to reach him. Nope, Jackson strode forth, slapping the warrant against his palm, until he stopped close enough to Ike to crowd him.

"Daytona Beach police."

"I know who you are, Officer." Ike held his ground.

"Captain," Jackson corrected.

"As you see, I have gathered everyone for questioning."

Jackson's gaze swept over the assortment of vampires. "There's no one else in the building?"

Ike waved a hand. "The humans are there, in the booth on the far side of the bar."

"Is your light-fingered girlfriend over there?"

"Allegedly light-fingered." Ike paused, looked like he was waging an inner war. Or eating dog poop. "Captain."

I squinted at the booth, my vamp vision kicking in. Sure enough, four women sat at a barely lit booth, three of them blood bunnies I'd met in March. Last time I'd seen that trio, they'd been dressed like they'd mugged a herd of cows for the leather. Tonight they wore shorts, Capris, and jeans with casual blouses. Maybe this *was* costume night.

The last woman in the deepest shadow, was that Donita Ward? All I could see in the dimness was a slim figure with short brown curls scribbling on a clipboard.

Maybe my vamp vision wasn't twenty-twenty, but Donita didn't look like a hardened criminal. Even her energy signature felt soft. Calm. If that was Donita.

Jackson dispersed cops to question the women. Another group headed upstairs, and a third went down the hall where a sign read Restrooms. Saber sauntered over to stand with Jackson, but I stayed put. I made myself a shadow so I could observe and puzzle over that elusive scent.

"Now perhaps you will explain, Captain," Ike said with a sharp edge of impatience. "Why am I being targeted for a search twice in less than twenty-four hours? What is the complaint?"

Jackson handed Ike the warrant. "We have a male victim with bite marks who also claims he was robbed here."

Ike lifted a brow. "The victim is alive?"

"That surprises you?"

"What surprises me," Ike said as he scanned the warrant, "is that a mortal has the nerve to complain about being bitten when the bite had to occur during sex."

Cheerleader Vamp gave Ike an odd look. "But Ike—"

"Silence, Susan."

The female twitched her shoulders at the rebuke but still looked puzzled.

"These bites weren't clean or neat." Saber held up the victim's photo for Ike to see. "If this was a consensual bite, the vamp involved either didn't put him in a deep thrall or didn't keep him there."

"You recognize him? Know who bit him?" Jackson demanded.

"I do not recognize him, but then I am upstairs in the office, not in the club. May I?" He indicated the other vamps with a sweep of his hand.

"Sure, show them." As the photo was passed around, only Tower and the guy in the Gators T-shirt showed a clear reaction.

"He was here tonight," Tower said and nodded at Gator guy. "Coach served him at the bar."

Coach nodded. "He stayed about an hour. Had two beers and paid cash."

"He say anything?" Saber probed.

"Naw, man, he was the surly kind. Just watched the crowd for a while and left. Ya ask me, I think he was Covenant."

I sucked in a little breath. If the victim was one of the vamp-hating Covenant members, any vampire might have gone after him for that alone. And yet, I didn't have the sense Ike or his buddies were lying.

Ike folded the warrant and looked at Jackson. "There you have it, Captain. This man was here but he left whole. None of my people harmed him."

Saber ran a hand through his hair. "You didn't happen to install outside security cameras like I suggested, did you?"

"I have hardly had time to replace the computer hard drive," Ike responded, heavy on the sarcasm. "The only cameras we have record activities in this room."

"You'd save yourself a heap of hassle if you'd wire the outside, too. Where's Laurel tonight?"

Ike's mouth tightened. "As of our wakening, she is being punished."

"For what?" Saber asked sharply.

"Normally this would be our business and ours alone, but I

will tell you. Laurel gave Donita the stolen property to pawn. After my day manager informed me of your search, I forced the truth from Laurel."

"Why didn't Donita tell us Laurel gave her the stuff when we were here earlier?" Saber asked.

Ike gave a negligent shrug. "Because she knows I can deal with Laurel as you cannot."

I gulped, remembering the discipline Normand dished out in the old days.

Jackson snorted. "What'd you do, Ike? Slap her hand? If Donita didn't lift those things, then Laurel did."

Ike's mouth stretched into a most unpleasant smile. "Laurel has not adequately explained where she . . . acquired the jewelry, but I am persuading her. I have banned her from the club for now and given her the task of cleaning our residence. Thoroughly, nightly, and in shackles."

"Laurel can break shackles, Ike."

"Not these, Saber. Laurel is not free to leave and will not be until I allow it." He paused. "When I am satisfied she is telling the truth about where she came by those items, naturally I will inform you."

"We'll still need your surveillance feeds," Jackson said instead.

"I understand. Take the hard drive, and leave another receipt." This time Ike sounded resigned. "I suppose you want to examine the lost-and-found box again as well?"

Jackson nodded, and Ike signaled to Zena. She and one of the cops headed to the bar.

As they passed near me, Ike made full eye contact, and I fought the instinct to flinch.

"Francesca, Princess Vampire," Ike purred. "Welcome to my humble establishment."

The blonde in the cheerleader outfit gave me a double take, squealed, and bolted from her chair.

"Oh my little G-god, you're the Princess Vampire!" she said, bouncing toward me. "Can I call you Francesca? I'm Suzy with a 'y.' Am I supposed to curtsy?"

I peeked at Saber's amused smirk and deduced that Suzy wouldn't perk me to death.

"Uh, no. No curtsying."

Her nod sent her ponytail dancing around her neck. " 'K. Can I have your autograph? There are napkins and pens at the bar."

"I don't think—" I got out before Ike interrupted.

"Susan, escort the princess here to meet your nestmates."

"But Ikey—"

"Susan, come."

Suzy pouted a little but grabbed my hand and practically galloped me to the table where Ike now sat at his leisure.

"Saber, may I ask the humans to join us now?"

Saber raised a brow at Jackson, who hesitated, then called his cops away from the booth.

While the human women came toward us from one direction, Zena and her cop escort closed in from the other.

"Thank you, Zena," Ike said when she placed a file-sized cardboard box on the table. "Princess, you remember Zena and Tower, of course."

My manners kicked into high gear, and I offered a smile. "Of course. Nice to see you again."

Saber, the smart-ass, made a choking sound beside me. Tower and Zena remained impassive.

"And may I also present," Ike went on, "Susan and Coach, Ray, and Miranda and her husband, Charles."

Ray looked enough like Antonio Banderas to make my heart thud the fandango. Then he smiled, the sparkle reaching his chocolate brown eyes, and my tongue swam in a pool of drool.

Oh, my. A vampire whose eyes sparkled with humor instead of glittering with hunger? Talk about babe bait. For the club, of course. Not for me. I had Saber. I wrenched my gaze from Ray to study the older couple who looked like they'd been in their mid-forties before they were turned.

"Miranda, how long have you and Charles been married?"

The woman smiled back. "Oh, my goodness, Princess," she said in a British accent, "it must be close to a hundred years."

"One hundred and two," Charles said in an equally clipped tone and took Miranda's hand.

"Miranda and Charles normally act as my household staff," Ike put in. "I brought them here to get them out of Laurel's way. And Ray is my longtime friend and attorney."

A *vampire attorney?* That was as bad as a vampire comic, and my eyes watered with the effort not to laugh.

Ray startled me by chuckling. "Yes, a vampire attorney is somewhat redundant, is it not?"

I returned his grin. "No comment."

"Ah, and here is Donita. Donita, this is Francesca, Princess Vampire of St. Augustine."

Seeing Donita Ward in brighter light vaporized the last of

my expectations. Medium height and slender, her hazel eyes were clear, her gaze direct, her expression open. She wasn't a sweet young thing, either. Maybe thirty-four, she was dressed in a beachy version of business casual.

She stuck out a hand for me to shake. "Francesca, good to meet you."

"Uh, you, too." I motioned to the clipboard in her left hand. "You must be very organized."

She laughed. "I hope so, since it's my job. I'm a business consultant focusing on organization and image."

"And working solely for me," Ike said, his hand on her shoulder.

Donita smiled up at him, not like she was infatuated out of her mind, but something comfortable passed between her and Ike.

Ike going domestic? Nah, couldn't be.

"Captain," Donita said. "Would you like to go through the lost and found now?"

In silence, Jackson lifted the cardboard lid and pulled out one thing after the other. A lipstick, two brown plastic hair clips, a Dallas Cowboys cap with a bent bill, and a dingy white sweater. I swear he growled in disappointment.

"I assume what you seek is not there?" Ike said.

"No," Jackson snapped.

"Not to tell you your job, but has it occurred to you that bite marks are not always the work of a vampire? As Saber and the Princess know, the French Bride's bite was made using a fanged prosthesis."

"We'll check that out," Saber said, "but we'll also be contacting the VPA to compare the casts of your fangs with the entry wound."

"By all means. We have nothing to fear."

"Do they, Marinelli?" Jackson shot at me. "Do you smell blood on them?"

I knew he'd be disappointed. Unless the security cameras showed something, the search had been a bust. But I wouldn't lie, so I shook my head.

"No one here has bitten anyone tonight, Captain. Not even each other."

"You're sure?"

"Absolutely positive."

"All right." He signed a receipt for the computer tower his officers had brought down from Ike's office and left.

"Thanks for your cooperation," Saber said when the cops were gone.

"It kills you to say that, does it not?" Ike returned.

Saber hesitated. "No. I've learned to give credit where it's due. You seem to be making changes, Ike."

"As does the princess." Ike pinned me with those inky eyes and a sudden flare of suspicion. "I hear you have taken a vampire under your wing. Is this so?"

I gaped. "How did you find out about Jo-Jo?"

Ike waved a hand. "Laurel told me, though I didn't know his name until now."

"Uh-huh, and how did Laurel know about him?"

"If Laurel's been spying on Cesca—" Saber began.

"It was not on my orders. But I believe Laurel heard the news from that lispy chatterbox, Cici."

Had I not been watching the blood bunnies—Claire, Tessa, and Barb—from the corner of my eye, I'd have missed the startled look they exchanged.

"Ladies," I asked them, "where is Cici tonight?"

Claire tossed her long black hair over her shoulder. "We don't know. She moved to St. Augustine to go to school and work at"—Claire leaned forward to stage whisper—"Wal-Mart."

"Well, good for her," I said, doing an inner happy dance that Cici had dropped out of the bunny club. "But if Cici's been in St. Augustine, when could Laurel have talked to her?"

Tessa shrugged. "Cici stopped by on Saturday night to hang awhile. I guess Laurel talked to her then."

A quick psychic flash, and I knew that wasn't true. Not even Tower and Zena bought it, and they didn't seem to have two thoughts to rub together. So, who was lying? Laurel or Ike? And why?

"You have strayed from the point, Princess," Ike said testily, pulling my attention back to him. "You told me in March that you would not set up a competing nest. Have you gone back on your word?"

"I said I haven't. I'm not the nesting type."

"Why, then, is this vampire in town?"

"He's working on a comedy act," Saber supplied.

Vamps and blood bunnies exchanged puzzled glances, but Donita leaned forward.

"Is he any good?"

I opened my mouth to tell the truth but reconsidered. "He's getting there. In fact, you might want to book him for a gig here at Hot Blooded."

"But this is not a comedy club," Ike objected, making *comedy* sound both foreign and dirty.

"We'll bill it as a special performance," Donita said. "Trust me, the curiosity factor alone will pack the house."

Ike still looked appalled, but Donita whipped out a business card, sparing a glance at her simple, utilitarian watch as she did. "Francesca, talk to your guy and call me when he has an opening."

"Donita," Ike said with an edge of warning.

It didn't faze her. She patted his arm.

"Ike, it's cool. Now, we have about two hours before dawn to get this place closed down."

Saber and I took the hint and left at four forty-five, me wedging Donita's card into my jeans pocket.

A breeze hit us outside, brisker than it had been an hour ago. Saber slung an arm around my shoulders as we walked to our cars.

"What do you think of Donita?"

"She's sure not what I thought she'd be, but she's telling the truth about that jewelry."

"I'm convinced, too. Wish she'd have come clean earlier though. I would have liked putting the silver screws to Laurel."

"What I'd like to know is how Laurel found out about Jo-Jo. There's no way Cici told her."

"You're right. Jo-Jo didn't crash the cookout until after nine o'clock, so the timing is impossible unless Cici saw Jo-Jo at Wal-Mart."

"He did have new duds by Sunday night."

"I still think Ike's had Laurel keeping tabs on you."

"There's a spectacularly creepy thought. Saber, why is Ike so paranoid about this nest competition business? Why doesn't the VPA shut nests down entirely?"

"Nests bind vampires together. Gives them a sense of community and safety."

"Huh. Like a club?"

"More or less. You might be in one now if you hadn't been buried and out of circulation."

I snorted. "Not likely."

"Why not?"

"Been there, despised that. I wouldn't feel safe in a nest if my afterlife depended on it."

He grinned and opened my car door. "Go keep your surfing date with Neil, and imagine flying is as easy as surfing."

SEVEN

All right, so maybe surfing might feel a little like flying. Neil and I sure flew through the bitchin' waves that an offshore storm was kicking up on Monday morning.

Falling was still another matter. Taking a tumble into waves, I could handle. Concrete? Not so much.

I'd last seen Neil on Saturday night after the fireworks. The ones we shot off at the beach *and* the ones caused by Jo-Jo's appearance. Neil must've still been ticked, because he'd been terse with me during the hour we'd surfed. I didn't expect him to stick around after we'd stowed our boards, but he did.

He leaned against the fender of my SSR, frowning as I dried off with a palm tree beach towel.

"Tell me you sent that creepy vampire packing."

I used the towel to squeeze water out of my ponytail and prepared to fudge.

"Neil, I can't ship Jo-Jo back to Atlanta against his will."

"I get that, but you're not letting him hang around the house, are you? You're keeping him away from Mags, right?"

"It's Maggie I need to keep away from Jo-Jo."

He scowled. "What does that mean?"

"She insisted that we both help him with his comedy routine last night. Not for long," I added when Neil's fists clenched. "Maggie went to bed before midnight."

"Are you telling me that she's sponsoring another vamp?"

"No, *I* am. Sort of. And before you erupt, I doubt Jo-Jo will stay around long. He'll work this comic thing out of his system, then he'll move on."

"You want to put that in writing?"

"It's a no-brainer," I bluffed.

"Fresca, it's no secret it took me a while to warm up to you, but that's in the past. I'm focused on my future with Maggie, and I don't want her involved in vampire business."

I tossed my towel onto the passenger seat. "Hell, Neil, *I* don't want to be involved in vampire business. Haven't I done my best to steer clear of other vamps, period?"

"Yeah, but trouble has a way of finding you."

"Only that once, and the killer was a human," I shot back. "Neil, listen. Anyone can see you're wild about Maggie."

His eyes softened, and his gaze shifted to the ocean. "I waited half my life to find her."

"I love her, too. The sooner you two get married and keep each other busy at night, the happier we'll all be."

He looked back at me. "You mean that?"

"Duh."

He straightened and yanked on my ponytail. "Just so we agree on boundaries."

"We do, but I need a favor from you," I said as he started toward his Jeep parked next to my Chevy.

"What favor?"

"Talk to Maggie about this whole Victorian wedding theme, and get her to scale back a little."

"Excuse me? She has her heart set on doing it up big."

I draped my arms on the hood of my truck. "Have you been to many weddings, Neil?"

"I'm staring at forty years old. Of course I've attended a lot of weddings."

"Then think ugly bridesmaid dress and add a bustle."

He cocked his head in thought. "That bad?"

"Could be."

He shuddered. "I'll see what I can do."

Neil's protectiveness of Maggie didn't bother me. When the French Bride killer had kidnapped Maggie in order to entrap me, I was ready to snatch his head off. Or die trying. Which is saying a lot considering I'm pretty much a pacifist and a chicken to boot. I knew firsthand that being in danger is no fun, and neither is taking a bullet.

Which is how my first two ghost tour costumes had been ruined. Oh, I'd managed to save the skirt of the Minorcan costume, but the blouse was shot. In the back, to be precise. My Regency gown was a total loss, but I'd teamed up with Shirley Thomas, a superseamstress who made costumes for Flagler College productions.

With Shirley's help, we'd made a new Minorcan blouse to go with the salvaged skirt, two Regency gowns—one in emerald, the other in sapphire—and a female pirate outfit just for fun. I also hired Shirley to work on a Victorian bridal gown to surprise Maggie. I loathed bustles, but had to admit Shirley's design would be stunning on Maggie.

I must've dreamed about clothes because when I awoke at four o'clock Monday afternoon, I recalled that three of my costumes were at the cleaners. The Minorcan outfit I'd worn last night hung in my closet, but had been awfully hot to wear in August, especially before nightfall. And, though the wind from the storm moving up the coast was strong, the air was still muggy, and the skirt would blow between my legs and trip me. The pirate outfit would be a much better choice for tonight.

I tossed off my Starbloods, then showered and dressed in shorts and a bra-top camisole. My wild hair I pulled into its standard ponytail. With plenty of time to run to the cleaners and dress for my tour at eight, I decided to knock out some housework first. I set the microwave timer for an hour, and with the Beach Boys blasting on the CD player, I dusted, ran the vacuum, and put the laundry away.

Yes, there was a fortune buried with me in King Normand's smelly old coffin, but I was no spendthrift. I'd bought my custom-interior SSR used, and Wal-Mart was my mecca.

Which reminded me. Though Saber and I were sure Cici, the former blood bunny, didn't know squat about Jo-Jo, we needed to talk with her. I scribbled a note on the magnetic pad shaped like a hula girl, the one that I kept on the fridge so Saber and I could leave each other messages. It was a way to bridge the gap between our different schedules.

When the timer dinged, I headed out to pick up my costumes. The health food store was nearby, so I stopped to pick up the case of Starbloods I'd ordered, too. I thought about buying a he-man brand to have on hand for Jo-Jo but figured he had his own stock by now. Call me unadventurous, but caramel macchiato was all I'd drink.

Except for sweet tea, heavy on the ice, of course.

I arrived back home to find a message from Saber on voice mail. He'd completed his official reports on the search of Hot Blooded and then called a Realtor to start his St. Augustine house hunt. *Yippee.* He went on to assure me he'd be at the cottage in time to hear Jo-Jo's act.

Saber had better show, since he'd set up the session. If I had to sit through another round of bad jokes, I just might spontaneously learn to fly. To someplace exotic. Like Texas.

When I first started guiding ghost tours in March, they weren't what you'd call normal. Not with my Covenant stalker in one group, a murder victim in another, and Ike and company in the third.

My tours had improved over the last few months, but the occasional nutcase still showed up. I spotted tonight's oddball among the fifteen normal tourists as soon as I walked through the old city gates and made my way to the waterwheel at the Mill Top Tavern, where my tours started. What was my first clue the guy was a nut?

Besides being dressed in camouflage cutoffs paired with a matching sleeveless vest and a dingy green T-shirt, the Ichabod Crane look-alike wore five huge crosses around his neck.

My second clue? He was laden with at least eight cameras

and other gizmos, the straps crisscrossed Rambo-style over his thin chest.

The third clue came when the guy stuck a gadget in my face and smacked me in the nose.

"Argh," I sputtered and stumbled back.

Since I wore my pirate costume, the crowd laughed.

"Stand still while I get a baseline," the guy commanded, moving in on me again.

Being polite to tourists is one thing, but I refuse to be ordered around by them. I took two deliberate steps away and planted one hand on the hilt of my rubber sword in its plastic scabbard.

"Matey, it is *not* a good idea to stick things in a pirate's face."

The young man blinked big brown eyes. "My name's Kevin Miller, and this is an electromagnetic field meter"—his gaze dropped to the gadget—"that's going nuts. Besides, you're not a pirate. You're the vampire."

"Exactly. A vampire might bite."

"You won't. You don't bite people." He grinned at his fellow tourists like he'd won a prize. "I did my research."

"Yes, but did you leave your manners at home?"

He shifted from one foot to another at my schoolmarm tone and fingered one of the crosses with his free hand. He looked down at the one he held, then back at me.

"My crosses aren't lighting up."

"Unless you put batteries in them, why would they?"

"Because you're a vampire."

I smiled at him and the crowd. "Not much of one, according to my friends. Now, is everyone ready to visit the ghosts of St. Augustine?"

Amid murmurs of assent, I dodged Kevin to collect tickets and headed for the tour substation. The substation is a square cabinet with padlocked doors. Two-by-fours screwed to the sides of the cabinet support a sign that reads Old Coast Ghost Tours.

I stashed the tickets in a manila envelope in the cabinet alongside our ghost tour pamphlets and snagged a battery-operated lantern with plastic panes. I didn't need the lantern, and it didn't give off much light anyway, but carrying a lantern was part of the tour guide ambiance.

"Welcome to the Old Coast Ghost Walk. Gather around, now. Don't be shy.

"I'm Cesca Marinelli, born in St. Augustine in 1780. My parents were among those immigrants from Minorca, Italy, and Greece, who came here as indentured servants to work in the New Smyrna Colony. My mother was Minorcan Spanish, my father an Italian mariner.

"We're standing at the north end of what is called the Minorcan Quarter, or the Spanish Quarter, or simply the Quarter. This is largely where the immigrants settled, and many downtown properties are still owned by Minorcan descendants.

"We'll start our tour by going through the city gates to the Huguenot Cemetery and wind our way through the historic district. If you have any questions along the way, just raise your hand."

Three hands waved, one of them Kevin's. I called on a young woman in lime green shorts and a white blouse.

"Will we see the place where you caught the French Bride murderer?"

"I didn't catch him alone, but yes, we'll see Fay's House toward the end of the tour."

"Are we going into haunted buildings tonight?" a man at the back called out.

"We'll be going into the oldest drugstore."

Kevin shouldered his way closer. "I need time to take readings and photographs."

"I appreciate that you want to document the ghosts, but these tours run on a schedule."

Kevin shook his head. "I'm not here just to document ghosts. I'm here to document your abilities as a ghost magnet."

Ghost magnet?

Okay, so maybe spirits *did* relate to the underdead part of me, but my fellow tour guide Mick Burney is the only one who'd ever called me a ghost magnet. Had Mick gotten this guy to pull a gag, or was Kevin serious?

From his expression, I was going with serious. Sheesh.

"You can take any measurements you want, but I can't wait for you. Now," I said, sweeping the group with a bright smile, "come along, and let's meet the ghosts of St. Augustine."

I saw the usual ghostly suspects in their usual haunts. Elizabeth the gatekeeper's daughter waved to us as we passed through the city gates. Judge John B. Stickney also waved. The judge was a prominent citizen who had died of typhoid while on a business trip to Washington, D.C. Buried in the Huguenot

Cemetery but later exhumed, the story is that he searches the cemetery for the gold teeth that grave robbers stole.

Erastus Nye and John Hull made themselves known at the Huguenot, as did a lady wearing a snood. A cat ghost brushed against at least four tourists' bare legs.

At the Catholic Tolomato Cemetery, we saw the Man in Black—a black robe—who is said to be a Franciscan missionary murdered on the grounds of the then Seloy Indian village. The Bridal Ghost made a brief appearance, too, but the tourists were even more absorbed with the orbs of light that zipped around the cemetery for a good five minutes.

That is, when Kevin left his fellow tourists alone long enough to be amazed instead of annoyed.

His cases of equipment thumped and bumped the other tourists until they stayed as far from him as they could get and still hear my ghost stories. He EMF metered me and anyone else who found a cold spot, flashed the camera darn near continuously, and made such a big pain of himself that I half hoped the biting ghost who hangs around the oldest drugstore would nibble him. But, no. The biter ghost must've taken a camera case to the kisser and backed off.

An hour and a half later, we had covered about one square mile of town and were back at the waterwheel. There waited Victor Gorman, my Covenant stalker.

Dark hair, black ops outfit, scar running down his right jaw. Eerie light blue eyes. Same old Gorman. His breath reeked of jalapeños, garlic, and cheap cigar, just as it had the first time he'd confronted me. Guess he figures onions would be overkill.

"Hello, Mr. Gorman," I greeted him pleasantly. "Have you been on vacation?"

Gorman blinked, not expecting my warm welcome. Okay, lukewarm. I smiled sweetly back.

His eerily light blue eyes narrowed, crinkling his weathered skin. "What are you up to, vampire?"

His voice was as gravelly as ever, and his personality just as grating. I stuck to my kill-him-with-kindness policy.

"I'm just wrapping up my tour," I answered him, then turned to my audience to do the closing spiel.

"Ladies and gentlemen, thank you for joining me on the Old Coast Ghost Walk this evening. We appreciate your patronage, and, if you want to turn in an evaluation form, you can get a discount on a future tour."

"But," Gorman yelled, "don't count on takin' it with the vampire."

"Why not?" one of the tourists asked.

"'Cause you never know when she might get herself kilt."

"Stupid man. She's wearing a pirate getup, not a kilt," I heard an older lady say as she and her husband toddled off.

I grinned at the couple, letting Gorman's comment pass. After all, this is what we did. Gorman threatened, and I ignored him. I didn't underestimate him, though; I had a feeling he would try my patience tonight.

"You're Gorman?" Kevin asked, clomping closer. "Ms. Marinelli's stalker? The one who was shot when you distracted the French Bride killer?"

Gorman straightened, preening as Kevin snapped yet another photo. "I'm the guy."

"Did you see any ghosts?"

"Huh?"

I didn't understand what ghosts had to do with the shooting either, but zippity hot damn do-dah, I saw my chance to dump Gorman on Kevin and make a clean getaway.

"It's a great story," I gushed. "Mr. Gorman challenged the killer right there in the street. You should let him tell you the whole thing firsthand. Oh, sorry, where are my manners? Mr. Gorman, this is Kevin Miller."

While the men shook hands and awkwardly talked, I put my lantern away, relocked the cabinet, and edged toward the bay front to slink away.

"Hold it, vampire, I wanna talk to you."

Rats. Foiled.

I pasted polite on my face and turned. "I can't imagine what we have to discuss."

"Just this." Gorman stalked closer, Kevin on his heels, until the two of them flanked me. "I hear rumors there's other vampires in town, and I wanna know two things. What'd you have to do with it, and what you gonna do about it?"

"Nothing, nothing, and where did you hear this rumor? I don't think your source is reliable," I shot back, hoping to confuse him.

It worked. Gorman's face screwed up in thought. He was not the sharpest stake in the Covenant woodpile.

"Oh, look at the time. Must run," I said, stepping back to skirt around Kevin.

But Kevin grabbed my wrist, clonking me with a camera case.

"Wait, Ms. Marinelli. Are more vampires really coming here to St. Augustine?"

"You heard the rumor, too?" A mean grin spread over Gorman's puffy lips, and he grabbed my other arm to trap me between him and Kevin. "Tell me who the scum are, vampire. Where do I find 'em?"

My heart raced, but I didn't panic. "There's nothing to tell," I said calmly, "so, both of you, let me go."

"Indeed, you blackguards," a voice roared behind me. "Unhand Her Highness this instant, or face my wrath!"

In a rush of air, a hand brushed my side, and there stood Jo-Jo, brandishing my rubber sword.

Ay-yi-yi.

EIGHT

Gorman and Kevin released their holds on me out of pure shock, and well they should have, because Jo-Jo was a sight to bemuse. In black leather pants, a white poet's shirt, and his hair tied back to show the healing wound on his forehead, he looked like a Shakespearean biker dude.

His eyes, though, blazed with dead serious intent. In spite of that outfit, I realized that Jo-Jo could be as potentially dangerous as anyone else, human or vampire.

"Who the hell are *you*?" Gorman demanded.

"I am Jo-Jo the Jester, champion of the fair Francesca, Most Royal Highness of the House of King Normand."

"You're one of the freakin' new vampires in town?"

Jo-Jo waved the sword. "Step away from the princess before I run you through."

"Uh, Jo-Jo," I said, having eased from Gorman and Kevin on my own. "That's a rubber sword."

He blinked, twirled the sword in a blur of speed, and tapped the tip on the bricked surface of the plaza.

"Zounds! Never mind, my princess. I shall fight with my bare hands if necessary."

Gorman's perpetual scowl contorted. The corners of his mouth twisted upward, and he wheezed a sound I realized was laughter. Really creepy laughter.

"Damn, this'll get those pansies in the Covenant seein' things my way again."

"Pansies?" I said. "What are you talking about?"

Gorman gave me shifty eyes. "I kept warnin' 'em about you. Told 'em it was a matter a time before they'd regret decidin' to leave you alone."

I blinked. "Do you mean that all this time the rest of your Covenant buddies haven't been out to get me?"

"No, but they hafta listen to me now, else be overrun by a bunch of evil pervert bloodsuckers."

"But, Mr. Gorman, you can't just kill vampires," Kevin objected, squaring his strap-laden shoulders. "It's against the law, and, besides, I'm not finished studying Ms. Marinelli."

"Whaddya mean, studyin' her?"

"I'm getting my doctorate in paranormal phenomena." Kevin fished in a pants pocket, pulled out some slightly battered business cards, then shoved one at Gorman and one at me. "I have a theory that vampires are predisposed to attract ghosts."

Gorman snorted. "So what?"

"I'm here for a few weeks to take Ms. Marinelli's tours and compile data. And if this guy"—he hooked his thumb at Jo-Jo—"is a real vampire, maybe he'll let me study him, too."

"Kevin, why don't you go to a city with a large vamp population to study?" I had to ask.

The young man flushed. "I tried, but none of the groups would cooperate."

"Hell, son, what'd you expect from a bunch of monsters?"

"We are not all monsters," Jo-Jo informed Gorman haughtily, "any more than all humans are criminals."

"Yeah, right," Gorman sneered. "We'll just see how long it takes you to attack when we're watchin' your every move and back you in a corner."

Gorman walked off with such a spring in his step, I expected him to click his heels. And that awful horror movie laugh? He was scarier as a happy man than he was an angry one.

"Well, the witch hunt is on again," I said to no one in particular.

"That is one twisted dude," Kevin chimed in.

"What do you think of my outfit, Highness? Is it too over-the-top for my act?"

"What act? Do you do ghost tours, too?" Kevin asked, fumbling for the camera hanging beneath all those crosses.

Crosses that were now faintly glowing. Yikes. I needed to shake Kevin before he noticed. He might not freak, but I wasn't taking the chance.

"He doesn't give ghost tours, and it's time for us to go."

"Okay. Just a few more shots."

Jo-Jo posed, slashing my rubber sword in the gusting wind as the camera clicked. I counted to five, grabbed his arm, and led him off toward the city gates.

"See you tomorrow, Ms. Marinelli," Kevin called after us.

"Not if I call in sick," I muttered.

"Uh, Highness, vampires don't get sick."

I shot Jo-Jo a sour look. "I get sick whenever I darn well feel like it, and stop swishing my sword."

Jo-Jo wisely handed me my prop and kept his mouth shut.

Saber waited at the tiki bar on my patio and gave me only a welcoming peck on the cheek since Jo-Jo was there. The men settled in the living room while I changed out of my pirate costume, but I put my vampire hearing to good use and eavesdropped on them.

Saber probed for more information about the vampire who was immune to silver, the one who had wounded Jo-Jo. Jo-Jo, though, seemed to have already told us what little he knew. Marco hadn't been in Atlanta more than a year, and Jo-Jo avoided him. The confrontation over his longtime sweetheart Jemina had come only after Jo-Jo had caught her with Marco.

"You can't tell us anything else about this guy?" I asked as I joined them, comfy in my baggy blue shorts and a T-shirt. "He doesn't have one single scar anywhere on his body?"

"Princess, we may all live together under Vlad's rule and roof, but I had no reason to see Marco without clothing," Jo-Jo said, then pursed his lips in thought. "The skin on his arms is whiter in some places than others."

"Like sun damage or a skin condition?" Saber asked.

"I suppose, but the scarring or whatever it is would've occurred before he was turned."

"Yeah, but it gives me another detail to check with the VPA.

Now, how long have you known about Marco's immunity to silver?"

"Personal knowledge? Only since he cut me." Jo-Jo looked disgusted. "He ran his finger along the blade to gather my blood, then offered a taste to Jemina."

"Did she, uh—"

"No, Highness. She spared me that humiliation, but Marco sucked his finger clean."

"Gag," I said, fighting my own reflex.

"That's when I decided to flee. I didn't pack so as not to alert Vlad's spies. I left two days later, because everyone's busy on Friday nights."

Of course they were. The long workweek over, they kicked back on Friday nights. Happy hour with blood on tap, then hook up later for a little bite. Yuck.

"So the only things missing from Vlad's nest are you and your laptop?" Saber asked.

Jo-Jo looked sheepish. "Well, there are a few other things, but nothing that didn't belong to me."

Saber narrowed his eyes. "Like what, and if this will bring trouble down on Cesca, you're a goner."

"As in dead or just gone away?"

Saber gave Jo-Jo his cop face.

"Okay, okay. I brought the cash I had on hand, and my bank account books. I still have the Christmas Club account I opened in 1952," he said proudly, but he hadn't spilled everything yet.

Saber made a growling sound as I opened my psychic eye to take at peek at what Jo-Jo was dancing around.

"A key?" I said, a picture of it suddenly clear. A small version of a brass skeleton key but flat rather than rounded. "You brought an old key with you?"

Jo-Jo's eyes rounded in amazement. "Yes, Highness, but how did you know?"

"Never mind that," Saber said. "What does the key unlock?"

"J-just my safe-deposit box in New York City, honest," Jo-Jo stammered, clearly shaken that I'd read him.

Since I hadn't been able to read him until now, I was surprised, too, but that was beside the point.

"Why are you being so cagey about a safe-deposit box?" I demanded.

"Well, I've had the box since 1927, and some of the things in it could belong to Jemina. Like a piece of jewelry."

"Is she or anyone else likely to come hunting you for the key?" Saber asked.

Jo-Jo frowned. "I don't think so. She mentioned the box to me about a week before I caught her with Marco, but not like it was important. It's been so long, I'm not even sure what's still in there."

Saber and I exchanged a glance.

"You getting anything else from him, Cesca?"

"There's an opal ring and a jet necklace in the box, and he knows it. Jemina swiped them both a long time ago, and Jo-Jo's kept them for her. Other than guilt that he's holding out on her now, that's it. The coins, a few rings and some papers are his. Oh, and he knows what's there, because he made an under-the-radar trip to New York last winter to check on the contents."

Jo-Jo paled a little more than even a vamp should. Saber gave a single nod.

"I'll contact the agent in Atlanta and put out a general call for information on immunity to silver. If there's any scoop on this, one of my contacts should know."

Jo-Jo sank back into the club chair with a shaky sigh and a wary eye. "Princess, how did you—"

"See the key and the other things in your thoughts?"

"Yes, and without me knowing you were in my head the first time? I didn't even feel you when I knew you were reading me."

I shrugged. "I don't know. I don't mind-probe that often."

"Did you probe those guys who threatened you tonight?"

Saber's brows slammed into a scowl. "Who threatened you?"

It was my turn to sigh—and figure out how to get Jo-Jo to keep his big mouth shut—but I filled Saber in on Gorman and Kevin.

"I'll check out Kevin Miller," Saber said when I'd covered the highlights, "but Gorman shouldn't be coming near you. Not with a restraining order on him. Damn, you have to be more careful, Cesca. You have to know when to vamp speed away from trouble."

I drew myself up straight. "I will not run from Gorman, Saber. I won't give him the satisfaction."

"Then learn to fly at least enough to evade him if he grabs for you. Seeing you hover over him like an avenging angel would probably have him wetting himself." He paused and speared Jo-Jo with a glare. "We need to start tonight's lesson."

"Yes, sir," Jo-Jo said, shooting to his feet.

"No way," I snapped and stood to face them both.

"But, Princess, we have perfect weather for the lesson."

I stared. "Since when is a hurricane good for flying?"

"It's not a hurricane," Saber admonished. "It's barely a tropical storm."

"And the wind will add lift, my lady."

I planted a hand on my hip. "Mary Poppins and the Flying Nun needed lift, Jo-Jo. I'm supposed to levitate, right?"

"Well, yes, but pure levitating takes more energy. Jumping is one way to, er, jump-start the process, but a good, stiff wind will give you an extra boost while you're learning."

"What about all the bugs and debris swirling in the wind? Shouldn't I wear goggles?" And an apron to protect my clothes.

"We'll stop at the all-night drugstore," Saber said.

I swallowed a growl at Saber and turned back to Jo-Jo.

"What about your act?" I asked, that desperate for a diversion. "You wanted help with the routine and your costume."

"I need to work on my own for a while. Besides, your consort has charged me with teaching you," he said, steadily meeting my gaze, "and teach you I will."

There are times when I want to roll my eyes so far back in my head, I'm sure I'll see my brain. That's one way to have it examined.

And this was one of those times.

High above the wind-whipped whitecaps, I stood quaking in my sneakers on the temporary bridge spanning Matanzas Bay, the one in use while the old Bridge of Lions was being rebuilt. Sure, I was safe on the pedestrian walkway—for now—squarely behind concrete barricades topped with strong metal railings. But I wouldn't be high and dry for long, not if I went through with this lunacy.

"Guys, for the last time, I am *not* taking a flying leap off this bridge. Somebody's watching. I can feel it, and they're going to report me as a jumper."

Saber put an arm around my shoulders and huddled the three of us closer so he didn't have to shout over the wind.

"Cesca, it's nearly two in the morning. There is no traffic right now, so we won't alarm drivers. Plus I called the city police and the sheriff's office to tell them we're conducting an experiment."

"In what? Doing belly busters off the bridge?"

"You're not going to fall, honey. You're going to fly."

"Besides, Highness, you're the one who insisted we practice over water."

"I didn't mean from a million feet in the air." Another strong gust blew, and I death-gripped the railing. "Why can't I jump off something shorter?"

"Like what?" Saber asked.

"Like a curb," I snapped.

"My lady, you have to be high enough to catch the updrafts," Jo-Jo said.

I could tell his patience was waning, but me jump off the bridge? Not in this afterlife.

Saber rubbed his forehead. "I have an idea."

"Oh, goody, another one?"

"Jo-Jo, how much weight can you carry when you fly?"

"Saber," I said, partly objecting to another scheme, and partly to insist that someone watched us.

"Are you thinking I should take the Princess up for a test spin? Like a tandem parachute jump?"

"Exactly. Can you do it?"

Jo-Jo looked uncomfortable. "I can if Highness will allow me the liberty of touching her person."

Both men looked at me.

"Face and conquer your fear, honey," Saber challenged.

I hate it when he's right, and short of making a dash for freedom, I was stuck on the damned bridge. For the moment.

I squared my shoulders. "Fine. How do you want to do this, Jo-Jo?"

"Let's give the piggyback position a go."

He crouched, and Saber gave me a boost onto Jo-Jo's bony back. It was like mounting a malnourished horse. I feared I'd slide right off, but Jo-Jo hooked his arms under my legs.

"Good, Princess. Now put your arms around my neck while I climb up and test my balance with you on my—aargh," he croaked. "Arms. Too. Tight."

I loosened my hold on his neck, then slid off his skinny back when he arched to rub his throat.

Attempt aborted, which was fine by me. I still felt watched, and the watcher was creeping closer.

I peered into the shadows, even used my vamp vision, but saw nothing. I didn't smell anything either—like Gorman's foul breath—but I wouldn't if the lurker was downwind. Should I alert Saber?

"Cesca, pay attention," Saber hollered and tipped his head toward Jo-Jo, who gave his abused neck one last rub.

"By your leave, my lady, I'll hold you in front of me. You'll be able to feel the liftoff better from this position anyway. May I demonstrate?"

I shrugged, and he stepped behind me. His arms around my rib cage, he told me to start walking with my right foot.

"You won't take off without warning me, right?" I yelled over my shoulder.

He shook his head, so I stepped when he did. One. Two. Three.

"Good, Princess. Now we do it for real."

"We're not going to climb on the rails?"

"No. Hold on."

His leg nudged mine.

One step. Gulp.

Two steps. Eek.

Three steps. Panic.

My rubbery legs suddenly locked, and I dug the heels of my tennis shoes into the concrete.

Jo-Jo tripped over me, and we stumbled forward like a couple of stooges.

"Are you all right, Princess?" Jo-Jo asked when we'd righted ourselves, his arm still curled around my waist.

"Fine, and I'm sorry. Really. I'm just positive someone is watching."

At that moment, a flash of golden fur landed smack in front of us, and a brain-rattling *"rrryyyow"* rent the night.

Jo-Jo screamed, *"Aaaiiieeee,"* tightened his hold around me, and vaulted away from Pandora.

Next thing I knew, I was dangling from Jo-Jo's crooked arm, ten feet away from the bridge and a hundred feet over dark, churning water.

NINE

～

I froze, my limbs spread-eagled like the cartoon flying squirrel, my right arm plastered against something warmer than sheer air. As my afterlife flashed before my eyes, one coherent thought persisted: Flying was *so* not like surfing.

On the upside, I wasn't thrashing and flailing in hysterics. No, because I was far too angry.

"Why the *hell* did you do that?" I screamed at Pandora.

To get you off the ground, she answered in my head, paws on the barricade, regarding me with a feline smirk.

"A th-thousand pardons, Princess," Jo-Jo yelled. "I'll put you down as soon as that panther leaves."

"Wait, Cesca, stay calm." Saber held his hands out as if to soothe me, but he was struggling not to laugh. "Jo-Jo, as long as you're out there, you might as well fly a couple of laps around the bridge."

"No, Saber," I yelled. "No lapping."

"Honey, I swear I'll make this up to you. Just do it."

"Just do it? Since when am I a freaking poster girl for Nike?"

"It's the best chance you'll have to get a real feel for flying, Cesca. Seize the opportunity."

"Grrrr," I said, stiffening more when Jo-Jo grunted and his arm began to tremble.

I craned my neck to look up at him. Maybe his face seemed more ashen because of the bridge lights, but his expression of horror was real.

"I-I'm truly sorry for not warning you before I jumped, Highness."

"Forget it. Pandora surprised both of us. I'll deal with her when we land."

Humph, Pandora huffed.

"Does that mean I should do as your consort asks? Fly a few laps?"

"Might as well. Just don't drop me, okay?"

"Never, Highness, but would you kindly remove your elbow from my crotch."

Now I was fuming *and* flaming with embarrassment. Great.

We started slowly, with an easy loop from one end of the bridge to the other. Except for feeling like a piece of luggage under Jo-Jo's arm, the experience wasn't bad. He kept up a patter of vampire flight control tips that helped me relax, and he even talked me into touching down on the roof of a motel on the island side of the bridge.

When he'd readjusted our positions into what he called a skater hold, I thought *levitate* for all I was worth. We took off again to make a short circuit around the bay, and I imagined we were skimming on the wind. Astounding but true, I actually supported my own weight part of the way. Not a solo flight, but it was progress.

Not that I was going to admit the thrill of victory to Pandora—or Saber either. Not with that big told-you-so grin on his face.

As soon as Jo-Jo gently lowered both of us to the bridge walkway, Saber grabbed me for a hug and a smacking kiss.

"I knew you could do it, Cesca. Good work, Jo-Jo."

I smacked Saber back, in the shoulder with my fist.

"We wouldn't have been out there if we hadn't been ambushed. Did you know Pandora was skulking up the bridge?"

Saber crossed his arms. "No, I did not. I would've warned you if a two-hundred-pound cat that I don't trust was about to pounce."

"There is that."

I patted the shoulder I'd hit and turned to eye Pandora, who gazed back with a bored expression. She had morphed to a house cat size and draped herself on the top rail of a barricade a few feet away, nonchalant as you please.

"All right, Pandora," I said with hands on my hips and a rein on my temper. "Why did you scare Jo-Jo?"

"Yeah, that wasn't sporting at all," Jo-Jo scolded. Guess he felt braver with Pandora in her small form.

Pandora shrugged. *It is imperative that you claim this power, and it was merely expedient to startle you both.*

I dismissed her tone and focused on her choice of words.

"Why is it imperative that I learn to fly, and what do you know about it, anyway?"

She leveled me with her golden gaze. *You and Triton must master your individual powers before you may come together.*

"Come together for what?"

Pandora shook her head, rose, and arched her back in a long stretch. *I have said enough, but trust me in this. You must practice your powers, vampire princess. Else Triton and all you love may be lost.*

With that, Pandora sprang from the railing and pranced off toward town.

"Cesca, you want to give us a translation?"

I glanced at Saber. "She said I have to master my powers."

"I've been telling you the same thing, but why is a shape-shifter interested in your powers?"

I started to answer him but thought better of mentioning Triton with Jo-Jo there. "That's where it gets fuzzy."

The rain started as we walked home. It wasn't a downpour, but Jo-Jo decided to fly ahead to his motel, saying he'd never get the stink out of his leather pants if they got too wet.

Saber and I arrived at my cottage soaked and chilled, but a steamy romp in the shower warmed us. Never mind snuggling in my king-size bed.

At just after four in the morning, Saber fell asleep. I spooned with him, listening to the wind rattle palm fronds and blow sheets of rain at the windows.

Saber had noticed I semi-flew on my own and praised me, but hadn't quizzed me again about my conversation with Pandora. That was a relief, because, honestly, I didn't know what to make of it myself.

How were Triton and I supposed to come together—with or without mastering our powers—when he was being all mysterious and stealthy? What powers did he still need to master, and for what purpose should we come together? To defeat whatever bad thing was after Triton? Had to be, because we sure weren't going to come together in any personal way. That ship had sailed a couple of hundred years ago.

And to pose another question, why was Pandora involved with Triton at all? Or with me? She'd shown up in March, the night Gorman had first threatened me, and had kept popping up when least expected until the night she pinned the French Bride killer to the ground. I hadn't seen her in the four months since then, and had stopped expecting to see her.

Now Jo-Jo had shown up, which was, admittedly, a new turning point in my afterlife. A day later, here came Pandora again. Coincidence? I thought not, but what was our connection? Was Pandora my furry, infuriating guardian angel?

Angel. Right. And Jo-Jo would be a star by the next full moon.

When the phone rang at eight on Tuesday morning, I jack-knifed off the sofa, the mystery novel in my hand sailing across the room.

"Cesca, are you making it through the storm all right?" Maggie asked through the phone line static.

I glanced at the dark skies punctuated with jagged lightning.

"I'm snug. How about you?"

"The same, but I'm glad we laid in hurricane supplies. This storm may be upgraded."

Uh-oh. I'd survived storms before, but most of them from the coffin under Maggie's house.

"How bad is it supposed to get?"

"A Category One at the strongest. Come on over if you'll feel more secure here."

"I will if Saber doesn't stick around while I sleep."

"Well, tell him I'm working from home today. I'll leave the back door unlocked in case you two want to dash over here."

"Thanks, Maggie. Is Neil there? Do you want company?"

"No and no, but thanks. If I can reach my supplier in Texas, I might be able to nail down the kitchen tile for that Palatka bungalow project before Neil and I go on our vacation." She paused. "Oh, and Cesca, if you're on the tour schedule for tonight, you'd better check with them before you go out."

"I'm off the schedule until Thursday."

"What? The workaholic is taking two whole days off? What will you do with yourself?"

I laughed. "I don't know yet."

"Well, if you're doing it with Saber, have fun."

We disconnected just as the power flickered, then failed.

I picked up my book, marked my spot, and tiptoed into the bedroom to curl up with Saber.

I awoke at four in the afternoon with the still-gray day looming outside, but the wind and rain seemed to have subsided. When I wandered to the kitchen, Saber was on the phone taking notes and saying "Uh-huh," a lot. Since he used the cordless house unit instead of his cell, I deduced the power was back on.

Must not have been on for long, though. When I reached in the fridge for a Starbloods, the bottle was cool but not as icy cold as I drink it.

I transferred one bottle to the freezer, set the egg timer so

I'd take it out before it froze, and shamelessly listened to Saber's end of the conversation.

"And no one else from the Atlanta nest has left the area? The GPS implants are accounting for every one of them?"

Aha! He must've reached the VPA agent in Atlanta.

He was quiet a moment, then nodded. "All right, thanks. Let me know if you dig up anything else."

Saber disconnected and reached for me, his warm hands bracketing my hips. A little tug and I stood between his legs.

"Sleep well?" he asked as I leaned in for a kiss.

"Mmmm. How long have you been awake?"

"Long enough to get some intel. First, Kevin Miller is exactly who and what he says he is."

"Obsessively annoying but harmless?"

"Yes. As for Vlad's nest, none of Jo-Jo's nestmates have left Atlanta, but we have other irregularities."

"Like what?"

He swept his hand along my upper right arm, over the spot where my GPS tracker lay implanted under the skin. "How much do you know about your tracker?"

I shrugged. "It sends signals so the VPA always knows where I am and when."

"True, but it only registers location changes when you travel more than about three thousand square feet."

I frowned. "You mean my tracker doesn't register anything when I'm going from room to room in my house?"

"If you walked straight from your bedroom to the front yard, the readout might show a blip, but no substantial movement. You go farther than that, and the readout will stamp your movements every three minutes."

"I follow. So what's the irregularity with Vlad's nest?"

"Two Atlanta vamps who should be moving around aren't. Their trackers are giving stationary signals."

"Maybe they're being homebodies."

He took my hand and squeezed. "When we see this with nest vampires, it usually means the vamps wearing those trackers are being punished."

"Oh." I pushed away grim memories of my own punishment, the one that was supposed to have lasted a few uncomfortable days and turned into a few bleak centuries.

"I hope," I said lightly as I sat on Saber's lap, "that Vlad's modern enough not to lock his vamps in a coffin."

"I hope he's not withholding blood too long. A hungry vamp is a dangerous vamp. But," he added, his hand wandering into one of my erogenous zones, "the VPA gal in Atlanta is arranging an in-person visit in the next few days to check on the nest."

"VPA gal? Tsk, tsk. That's sexist, Saber."

"No, it's not. That's how Candy refers to herself to make the vamps think she's just a little Southern belle."

"When she's really a steel magnolia?"

"Honey, Candy Crushman on a rampage makes a vamp attack look like a tea party."

"So visiting the nest won't be dangerous for her?"

"Hardly, especially since her husband Jim will go with her. Crusher is an ex-slayer buddy of mine, and no, he's not a special investigator. More of a mercenary, but he works overseas most of the time."

"Did Candy know about the vamp with silver immunity?"

"No one seems to know about it, but Candy's making it a

high priority to nose around during the on-site visit. She'll check in with me as soon as she knows anything."

"What about the Daytona case? What happened to the man who was bitten?"

"The hospital confirmed he was released early this afternoon, and I had a message from Captain Jackson on the cell. The victim shows up on Ike's surveillance cameras as sitting at the bar for about an hour and leaving in one piece."

"He didn't cuddle up to any vamps while he was there?"

"No, and there aren't any vamps living in Daytona outside Ike's nest. One of his vamps got the victim late Sunday or early Monday morning."

"Makes you wonder just how well Ike has Laurel restrained. Maybe she can fly the nest."

"Doubtful. Besides, I won't get a judge to let me search Ike's residence. I don't have probable cause." He paused. "Are you certain you didn't smell blood in the club or outside?"

"Not even a hint. I smelled something else, but it wasn't blood."

"What kind of something else?" he asked sharply.

"A citrus scent, like oranges or lemons." I shrugged. "That's why I didn't mention it. It was odd, not important."

"I suppose not, but give me the high sign if you sense anything unusual again."

"Again? I'm never going back there."

He smiled. "Not even if Jo-Jo performs at the club?"

"Okay, maybe then." I tapped my chin, considering something else. "Saber, what about Cici?"

"You mean telling Laurel about Jo-Jo?"

"Not even Ike's vamps bought that faerie tale. I think we ought to check it out."

"Let me guess. You want to drag me to Wal-Mart."

I grinned. "You can call it a beer run."

"Fine. We'll wait until the storm moves on."

"Any word on when that'll be?"

"It's picked up speed moving north. You work tonight?"

I gave him a peck on the nose. "Nope, I'm off tonight and tomorrow."

"What about bridge club?"

I'm a fiend for bridge, and Wednesday was our regular night, but most of the ladies were on vacation.

"We're on hold until after Labor Day."

"You mean I have you to myself for two nights running?" he said, nibbling my neck.

"You do—ooh, yes, that spot makes me crazy."

"Good thing I just popped an extra vitamin."

The timer dinged before he carried me out of the kitchen, but I remembered to stow my Starbloods in the fridge for later.

Much later.

After a delightful candlelit romp in my jetted bathtub, Saber wanted to talk real estate, a romantic subject only because he wanted to share the seventeen property listings he'd copied from the Internet. We pored over the printouts and the Sunday real estate section from the *St. Augustine Record* that he'd saved. As we compared features, locations, and prices, a special warmth permeated my heart and soaked into my soul. It was almost as if we were house hunting as a couple, planning a life together.

We'd narrowed his list of first-see choices to twelve when he got the munchies. Since he'd learned to stock my cabinets so there would be food in the house, he helped himself. He'd just set his humongous ham sandwich, a beer, and a glass of sweet tea for me on the coffee table when my doorbell rang.

"Eat," I said, springing up from the couch.

I swung the door open, expecting it to be Maggie checking on us. Jo-Jo stood there instead, quivering with excitement.

"Highness, consort of Highness," he said as I stepped aside to let him in. "Are you two free tomorrow night?"

I glanced at Saber, his mouth full of sandwich. He shrugged.

"What's up tomorrow night?" I asked.

"Open mike night at the Riot," he said, referring to a new comedy club just across the bridge on the island. "It's from nine to ten, and sunset is at eight fourteen. I'll go on last so I have plenty of time to get ready, but I've decided to do it, and, well, I'd like it if you could be there—and Miss Maggie and her gentleman, too. You know, for moral support."

Anxiety twisted my stomach, unfamiliar and unexpected. "What about polishing your act? Didn't you want to practice? Try out your material on us before you go public?"

Whoa, was I worried for him? Darn it, I was. Concerned he'd fall on his face and be crushed. Had Maggie felt like this when I started ghost tour guiding?

"I'm good, Highness," he said with a smile. "Well, maybe not *good*, but I've been practicing in front of the mirror. I think I'm ready to take on an audience again."

That's right. He'd been a performer centuries before I'd been born. He had to know more about it than I did.

"I think we ought to go," Saber said. "You can check out his act for the other gig you lined up for him."

Jo-Jo's eyes went wide. "Highness? You got a job for me?"

"Maybe," I hedged. "It's at a vampire bar in Daytona."

"Wow, really? You said vampires might like my act, but I didn't expect—Wait. Is the owner a vampire?"

"Yes. His name is Ike."

"Ike?" Jo-Jo frowned.

"You know him?" Saber's eyes narrowed, his sandwich abandoned for the moment.

Jo-Jo shook his head. "No, it's just that the name sounds familiar. Like I've heard it somewhere. Are you sure he wants to hire me?"

"I'm sure he doesn't," I said, "but his mortal manager girl-friend talked him into it. Providing, well—"

"That I'm funny?" Jo-Jo bounded for the door. "Don't worry, Princess. I won't let you down."

When the door shut, I plopped beside Saber.

"Did that have a 'famous last words' ring to it?"

"He's grown on you, hasn't he?"

"He's kind of goofy, but yeah. He's the first vampire I've ever liked. What about you?"

"He's the second vampire I've liked." Saber dropped a kiss on my forehead. "I trusted him to teach you to fly."

"You know, if he's a hit, the flying lessons may be over."

We stared at each other a long beat.

"Nah."

* * *

I called Maggie to invite her to Jo-Jo's debut act. As soon as she repeated the invitation to Neil, I heard his "Hell, no, I don't want to watch a vampire comic."

Maggie prevailed simply by reminding him that if Jo-Jo were working the nightclub circuit, he wouldn't be hanging around my place. That changed Neil's tune.

"We'll meet you and Saber there," she assured me.

"And applaud like mad no matter what?"

"You got it."

Except for a drizzle here and there, the storm had passed. Saber and I headed for Wal-Mart to track down Cici.

The task didn't prove difficult. We found her straightening up in the women's clothing section.

She did a double take when I called her name, but she smiled.

"Oh, hey, Prinsceth Thethca, Thaber," she lisped. "You need help finding anything?"

"Actually, Cici, we have a question for you."

"Okay," she said, cautiously.

"Were you at Hot Blooded last Saturday night?"

She blushed. "Yeth, but not for long. I went by to thay hello to the girlth."

"Did you," Saber said gently, "talk to Laurel while you were there?"

"You're joking, right? Laurel wouldn't be caught, well, dead talking to me. Why? Did she accuth me of thomething?"

"No, no," I reassured her. "But it would probably be a good idea to steer clear of the club."

"Why? Ith there trouble?"

"Looks that way," Saber said, and gave me a shoulder bump. "You want to pick up that, ah, thing you wanted while I go get the beer?"

I took the hint. Buy something from the nice girl to distract her from our questions.

I left with another bra top camisole, a pair of shorts, and a little peek into Cici's mind. She had no idea Jo-Jo was in town, so how had Laurel found out about him? Was she spying on me, or did Ike have someone else doing it? Like Jo-Jo himself?

Nope, I'd been in Jo-Jo's head. He might be a dupe, but he wasn't a spy.

On Wednesday afternoon, Saber and I met with his Realtor, Amanda Hogan. The young, blonde, and ultratanned Amanda was skittish with me at first, but was taking me in stride by the time we toured the third property. And she'd stopped eyeing Saber's butt when she thought I wasn't looking. Points for her.

Back at my place, Saber ate while I changed for the comedy club. In deference to Jo-Jo's debut, I wore a turquoise silk jersey dress that crisscrossed under my breasts, paired with silver stiletto sandals. I didn't wear high heels as a rule, because, hey, life is way casual in St. Augustine. But these shoes were Maddie Springer originals, on sale direct from her website and designed to seduce.

My hair is the bane of my afterlife. Long and wavy, and in the humidity I look like Janis Joplin on a bad hair day. Post electric shock. After attacking it with the flatiron, I arranged a French twist and secured the updo with a fancy claw clamp. A bit of eye shadow, powder, and a few sweeps with the mascara wand, and I was ready.

Saber gave a long whistle and look that invited me to take off everything but the sexy heels and stay home. Tempting, but we made it to the comedy club by eight fifty. And, okay, I was glad it was dark enough that the women couldn't ogle Saber, because he was scrumptious in gray slacks and a white shirt.

We snagged a table one row back from the front as Neil and Maggie joined us, and our waitress arrived.

I had my usual sweet tea, heavy on the ice, Saber ordered a beer, and Maggie opted for a frozen margarita, no salt.

Neil ordered a gin and tonic with lime.

"You don't want a double?" Maggie asked.

Neil scowled. "You think he'll be that bad?"

Maggie just patted his arm and turned to me. "Did we miss any acts?"

I shrugged. "We just beat you here, but the open mike part is supposed to start in five minutes."

"Nervous for Jo-Jo?" she asked.

"Terrified."

She grinned as the emcee took the stage. "Good."

I have to admit it. I didn't expect much from the open mike performers, but I underestimated them. My favorites were the mother of five who called her children The Horde, and the thirty-something doing a Beer Bowl sportscast.

Saber and Neil were on their second drinks when the emcee stepped to the microphone to announce the final act and re-mind the audience to tell their friends about the club.

"And now, let me hear you put your hands together for Jo-Jo!"

Jo-Jo took the stage like he owned it, not dressed in the leather pants and poet shirt, but in black jeans and tan button-up shirt. He looked casual, he looked confident, he looked in complete control. And I was a wreck waiting for him to open his mouth.

"Good evening ladies and—"

If he says germs, I'm sliding under the table.

"—gentlemen. Thank you for staying tonight, and I hope you've enjoyed your evening.

"Now, it's probably not obvious, but I'm a vampire."

Titters in the crowd. Good.

"Really. One way you can tell I'm a vampire is that I'm a couple of hundred years old and I still have my hair."

More titters. I glanced at Maggie, who nodded.

"Well, think about it. When was the last time you saw a vampire with hair plugs?"

Jo-Jo's pauses were impeccably timed, and chuckles rippled through the room now. Still, I held my breath.

"You're not convinced, huh? Well, I'd flash my fangs for you, but they fell out a while back when I accidentally bit into something I shouldn't have. A rolling pin."

A snort, some guffaws and giggles.

"See, I was going in to kiss my lady, all romantic-like"—he shifted his feet and reached out on either side of the mike as if to demonstrate an embrace—"when she forcefully reminded me I hadn't taken out the trash."

Jo-Jo made a smacked-in-the-kisser face that shifted the crowd's energy completely into the palm of his comic hand.

"I'm telling you, that woman was serious about her trash day. I tried to find a dentist who'd make dentures with fangs, but no dice. On the bright side, vampire denture cream comes in three full-bodied flavors: mint, cinnamon, and O positive."

Amid an odd groan or two, the room echoed with laughter.

"You've heard about vampire nests, right?" A few in the crowd murmured agreement. "Yeah, they're sort of like a fraternity with fangs. And coeds. And those female vamps? They make us males put the toilet seats down. In the *men's* room. I mean, come on. Who died and put females in charge of toilet seats? It wasn't me."

Jo-Jo paused while the crowd reacted again. Even Neil's lips twitched.

"Most vampires have jobs. Did you know that? It's true. I'm a computer help tech. On the night shift, of course. Some folks think that all night shift techs live in India. I had a call last night from a lady who asked me ten times in three minutes if English was my first language. The next time she asked, I said, 'No, it's my eighth, but I've been speaking it for two hundred years.' She hung up on me, and Bill Gates is gonna be pissed when he finds out. He probably won't send the money he owes me for forwarding all those e-mails."

Jo-Jo twinkled at the audience, and they loved it.

"To wind up for the night, and to demonstrate my vampire prowess"—he waggled his brows and leered at a giggling group of women at the table in front of us—"I'm now going to show you a skill I perfected as a court jester. Maestro?"

He looked to his right, and the emcee tossed three neon yellow tennis balls to him.

"The last time I did this trick," Jo-Jo said, beginning a slow juggle that steadily got faster, "I used swords. Trouble was, I wasn't used to vampire speed. I sort of impaled a crown prince at the head table and had to vamoose out of town." He shook his head. "I haven't hung out with royalty since then. Not until I met St. Augustine's Cesca Marinelli, that is. Or, as I call her, Princess Ci. Give us a royal wave, Ci."

A spotlight blasted our table. Neil groaned, Maggie laughed with a few others, and Saber applauded along with the crowd. Me? I slid down in my seat and plotted revenge.

"All right, folks, time for me to do this trick before Princess Ci busts my balls."

My embarrassment at being singled out melted to amazement when Jo-Jo shifted into vampire gear. The tennis balls suddenly blurred into a yellow halo, as if Jo-Jo were twirling a baton instead of juggling. The audience *ahhhed*, and I felt the room hold its collective breath—even Neil. Then Jo-Jo whooped once, twice, three times, and in another blur of movement, he'd lined the tennis balls at his feet.

He grinned and waved. "Good night, everyone. Hope you enjoyed the show!"

With that, the audience exploded into applause and whistles that lasted so long, Jo-Jo came out for a quick bow before bounding off the stage and heading toward our table.

"Miss Maggie and Mr. Neil, thank you for coming!"

"We enjoyed it, Jo-Jo," Maggie said. "You did good."

"Highness, what did you think?" Eagerness and anxiety mixed in his expression. "Was I good enough to do the gig in Daytona?"

"Good? Hell," a jovial voice boomed from the table behind us, "you've got stage presence, charisma, and a gimmick. I'm going to make you the next hottest comic in the country."

TEN

A middle-aged man with a little paunch and a wide grin came forward to shake Jo-Jo's hand.

"Vince Atlas. I'm a talent agent out of L.A." Vince passed around business cards, the first to Jo-Jo, then one each to the rest of us. "Are you already being represented, Jo-Jo?"

Jo-Jo looked as dazed as I felt and shook his head. "No, sir. This is my first night onstage in a long while."

"I don't know why. You're a natural. Perfect timing. Why haven't you been working?"

Jo-Jo seemed to blush. "I, uh—"

"He came to St. Augustine to get a fresh start," Saber inserted.

"Well, you're fresh, all right. There's not another act like yours in the world, and I know exactly how to capitalize on it. How does that sound?"

"Um, Highness? Saber?"

"Highness?" Vince echoed, his gaze ping-ponging between Jo-Jo and me. "Your Princess Ci is really royalty?"

I shrugged. "Jo-Jo thinks so. If you don't mind my asking, Mr. Atlas—"

"Call me Vince."

"—what is a big Hollywood talent agent doing in a little comedy club in St. Augustine?"

"You mean am I legit? I am. You mind if I sit?"

"Here, take our seats," Maggie said, rising with Neil. "We need to get home. Fine job, Jo-Jo."

Jo-Jo sank into the last chair, and Vince scooted close.

"I'm serious about representing Jo-Jo. I've been an agent for twenty-four years, and you can check my website to see my talent list. As for what I'm doing here, it's my vacation. The wife got too much sun today and stayed in this evening. I decided to stop in here, and I'm sure glad I did. I gotta tell you, I never expected to find an act like yours."

"You do get Jo-Jo is a real vampire, right?" Saber asked.

Vince snorted. "With that display of speed? Figured he had to be that or the real Superman. What about it?"

"Jo-Jo can only work nights," I explained. "He can only travel then, too. Won't that present problems?"

"Not for most club gigs, but it will for TV." He frowned. "Please tell me you can be filmed."

"Yes, sir. Vampires show up on camera."

"Good, then we can work around the interview appearances I have in mind. You do write your own material, correct?"

Jo-Jo glanced at Saber and me. "I had a little help with the routine I did tonight, but, yes, most of it's my work."

"Excellent. I offer a standard contract you can have an at-torney review. Don't have any with me, but I'll have my secretary fax one tomorrow. Will you be here tomorrow night?"

Jo-Jo shook his head. "I don't think so, and I don't know any attorneys."

"I do," Saber said.

"So how do I get you a copy of my contract?" Vince asked.

I spoke up. "I'll come by your hotel tomorrow afternoon to pick up the fax. You can leave it at the front desk if you and your wife will be out."

Vince nodded. "Fair enough. Now, Jo-Jo, I don't want to rush you, but if the contract is agreeable, I'd like to sign you before Sunday. The wife and I leave that day."

"That *is* rushing him," Saber broke in. "Jo-Jo's just getting started. What if he wants to contact other agents?"

"Perfectly good question, but that will take time. I'm prepared to have at least two performances lined up for next week. One in Vegas, one in L.A., and I'm reasonably certain I can have Jo-Jo on Leno in a matter of weeks. I have a contact on his staff."

"Vegas?" Jo-Jo said, brown eyes wide with worship.

"*Leno?*" Saber echoed.

"Next week?" I asked. "Jo-Jo would be leaving that soon?"

Vince nodded. "No point in waiting, is there?"

"Well, except that I want to do the show Highness has lined up in Daytona. I can't cut out on that."

"When is it?" Vince asked me.

I glanced at Saber, who shrugged.

"It wasn't a firm date," I told Vince, "but I'll call the manager to see if Jo-Jo can perform Saturday. That is, if Jo-Jo wants to accept your offer to represent him."

"Your Royalness, forgive my familiarity, but it's Vegas, baby."

The oddest tightness gripped my chest. "Yep, and Jo-Jo will be in the house."

I don't usually phone people after nine in the evening, especially if I don't know them well. It's just not polite. But Jo-Jo and Saber insisted I call Donita, and as it turned out, she didn't mind. She seized the chance to have Jo-Jo do his act at Hot Blooded on Saturday night and said she'd get the advertising rolling.

When I disconnected, Jo-Jo grinned.

"Thank you, Highness. If you and Miss Maggie and Saber here hadn't encouraged me, I don't know what I would have done."

"So you're going to sign with Vince for sure?" I asked.

"If the contract looks good to Saber's lawyer friend, I will. Why not?"

"I don't want you to get taken."

"Highness. Do you know a human who'd try to take a vamp to the cleaners?"

"Good point, but will you feel comfortable in a new place surrounded by humans you don't know?"

"I'll manage. I wonder if Jemina will find out I'm playing Vegas."

Saber laughed. "You want some payback, huh?"

"Oh, yeah."

"Send her a clipping when you get a rave review."

"I want her to see me on TV, too. Can you imagine it? Me on *Jay Leno*?" He paused. "I wonder if Vince'll get me on *Oprah*."

The reverence in his voice when he said *Oprah* had me imagining a choir of angelic voices singing the name. Was this how I'd sounded to Maggie? Not about Oprah, but had I been that agog when I landed the tour guide job I wanted so badly?

"Just don't forget the little people when you're rich and famous," Saber said. "And do not, under any circumstances, mention that you taught Cesca to fly."

Jo-Jo blinked. "But I haven't finished that task yet, and I need to." He looked at me. "You're close to being ready to fly on your own, Highness. We just need a few more sessions. Would you like to practice now?"

From Saber's satisfied expression, he obviously wasn't going to object. I looked back to Jo-Jo's eager face.

"Don't you want to savor your success tonight?"

"I am."

I glanced at the clock on my desk. Almost midnight. "Don't you have to go to work soon on the computer help line?"

"I can be a little late. Besides, I'll have to resign if I'm as busy as Vince says I'll be."

I started to ask, "Don't you want to give me a break?" but I know when not to waste my breath.

As it turned out, I needed every bit of breath I could draw.

Oh, the lessons in the backyard went well enough, even if the ground was still wet and spongy from the tropical storm deluge on Tuesday. I used vamp hearing to be sure Hugh and Selma Lister were really asleep. Judging by the snores I detected coming from two bedrooms, my neighbors were out cold. So was everyone else on the block except for the woman with a new baby who lived on the street behind us.

This night's flying lesson went a little better than the last one, and Jo-Jo praised my progress. I still couldn't get the hang of a walking takeoff, but I levitated a few inches higher than before.

I'd just started jump-and-hover practice and was a new personal best of three feet off the ground, when Triton's voice screamed in my head.

Hit the ground. Now!

Focus shattered. Breath stopped. Time warped.

I fell, my legs folding on impact, and a bullet zinged through the air where I had just hovered to hit the still rain-soaked yard with a spit.

"Sniper! Move!" Saber yelled, his Glock in his hand faster than I could see him draw.

Sluggish with shock, I rolled toward the corner of Maggie's house.

Phfft, spit, phfft, spit.

Second and third shots whizzed close to my head, as Saber fired rounds into the oak tree in Maggie's front yard, directly over the gate. The acrid smell of gunshots hung in the air.

Then silence.

One beat. Two.

I lay in the dewy grass, trembling with reaction, afraid to move, afraid to stay in the open.

"Cesca," Saber hissed. "Are you hit?"

I looked up to see him shove Jo-Jo toward my cottage, then duck behind the tiki bar. I also watched lights blink on at every neighbor's house. My mouth was too dry to speak, so I shook my head.

"The shooter may circle around. Run for it while I cover you."

I pushed to a crouch, determined that my trembling limbs would hold me. When Saber nodded, I tore across the yard fast enough to leave a contrail and dove through the door Jo-Jo held open. Saber tumbled in behind me.

While Jo-Jo huddled on the floor, wild-eyed, Saber grabbed me. I clung to him, shaking so hard I bit my tongue. Then I heard Hugh Lister cursing. Oddly, that bit of normalcy calmed me.

Sirens wailed closer, and the house phone rang.

"Answer it, but stay low," Saber said.

"What the hell is going on?" Neil snapped as soon as I said hello.

"Someone shot at us. Saber said it's a sniper."

"Where, for God's sake?"

"The huge oak on the gate side of the front yard."

"I'll take a look out the windows while you talk to Mags."

"Is anyone hurt?" That's Maggie, cutting to the chase.

I willed my voice to be steady and matter-of-fact. No point in worrying her. I was spooked enough for both of us.

"No one's hurt. Don't tell Neil, but Jo-Jo was giving me another flying lesson when it happened."

"Any threats from Gorman lately?"

"Yeah, I saw him Tuesday night after my tour, but I don't think it's him."

"Why not?"

"I didn't smell garlic and jalapeño breath on the wind."

"You didn't sense this coming at all, did you?"

"No." I was seriously freaked about that.

"Be sure to tell the cops about Gorman, and, honey, keep up those flight lessons. Sounds like you might need 'em."

I didn't bother to tell Maggie it was falling that saved me, not flying.

The St. Augustine police were on the scene for an hour and recovered three .22-caliber slugs that had been imbedded in the grass. Silver slugs. Made for a vampire, but effective on any old body.

Teams of police persons spread through the neighborhood taking statements. One cop questioned Maggie and Neil, and another talked to Hugh and Selma Lister. Oh, yes, Hugh had barged through the jasmine hedge in a rage, ready to burn us out there and then, and damn the arson charge. Well, burn me out anyway. Maggie might've gotten off the hook because Hugh didn't seem to want to mess with Neil.

Maggie hugged me when the cops dismissed her. Neil just glared. Then the cops questioned us again about what we'd been doing in the yard. Saber said we were saying good night to Jo-Jo. When asked if we had any enemies, the answers took longer.

I mentioned Gorman but didn't for a minute think he'd taken the potshot. For starters, he wasn't a young, nimble man. I couldn't see him climbing the oak tree, much less getting away. Still, I knew the cops would roust him from bed and check the arsenal they knew he owned.

Jo-Jo mentioned Vlad, but what were the city cops to do about an ancient vamp in Atlanta? Nada.

Saber mentioned the problems in Daytona, but Ike wouldn't be caught dead in a tree, and I couldn't see him sending a hit-vamp after me. Now, Laurel? I wouldn't put a thing past her, but Ike had her on domestic drudge duty, and it hadn't sounded like he was releasing her from punishment anytime soon.

So who was the sniper?

Where was Pandora?

How had Triton known about the danger?

Though he was still shaken when the cops finally left, Jo-Jo stirred himself to leave when Saber offered him a ride.

"I hate to ask this, Princess, but can you still pick up Vince's contract?"

"I'll do it," I assured him.

"Thank you, Graciousness. Oh, and I'm giving you two last lessons on Thursday and Friday after your tours."

I sighed. "Jo-Jo, there's no need."

"I beg to differ, Highness. If you could have truly flown tonight, you might have caught the shooter."

That thought made me shiver to my toes.

"He's right, Cesca."

"Guys, we can't practice outside without being targets."

"We can if whoever it was doesn't know where to find us," Jo-Jo said. "There's a little neighborhood park near the comedy club. No one will expect us to be there."

Saber nodded. "We'll meet you there. Cesca, what time are your next two tours?"

"Both at nine."

"Then we'll meet Jo-Jo at eleven. You'll practice for an hour, maybe less, and we'll get out of there."

He enfolded me in his arms and kissed me on the cheek.

"And, if you can find that damned cat who's supposed to be protecting you, tell her I want her on patrol. Both nights."

"Aren't you coming back after you take Jo-Jo to the motel?"

Mouth tight, he shook his head. "First, I'm dropping in on Ike and company. Then I'm going home to check the online GPS readouts of every vamp in my territory."

"Why?"

"Because no one but a ninja or a vampire could've gotten out of that tree without detection."

He didn't have to tell me it wasn't a ninja.

ELEVEN

I fought feeling abandoned when Saber left with Jo-Jo. I knew he had to go, but my heart still pounded two beats too fast, and I couldn't munch ice fast enough to ease my dry mouth. Mostly, I wished Saber had been there to hold me.

Take control, my rational voice said as I crunched another ice cube. Be the affect, not the effect.

Stupid voice didn't know how close it had come to being permanently silenced.

If Triton hadn't warned me, I could be dead. If I hadn't listened to the warning, I could be dead. If the shooter's aim had been better, I could be forever dead.

Wait. Why wasn't the sniper a better shot? For that matter, why would a vamp use a rifle at all? Vampires didn't rely on firearms. They killed up close and disgustingly personal.

Which either meant this vamp couldn't kill me up close or didn't want to be identified.

Damn it all, I hadn't survived over two centuries in that crummy coffin to be killed by a sneaky sniper. I'd listen to my rational voice and take charge.

To that end, I closed all the drapes, reset the alarm, and even checked the escape hatch in my closet to be sure I hadn't blocked it with boxes. Nope. The closet system shoe rack swung away at a touch to reveal the escape tunnel behind it. The hatch moved smoothly and silently and sealed completely.

Not that I thought the shooter was hanging around. In fact, Hugh Lister posed more of a threat. Yep, if I tuned in with vampire hearing, I could hear Hugh swearing viciously enough to peel the enamel off his teeth. Selma? She blessed to the heavens and muttered something about a long cruise and her damn vodka.

Since I couldn't do anything about the Listers, I decided to dial up Triton on the telepathic airwaves. He'd darned well better answer my call.

I went to my desk and plucked the chain and mermaid charm from the tiki mug. Then I quieted and centered myself, the charm in my left hand. This time, the white noise buzz passed quickly into the song of ocean waves, and Triton's mental door opened a slit.

"How did you know about the sniper?" I whispered.

The cat. Be alert and aware.

"But where is she?"

Triton's mental door vanished, but Pandora's thoughts poured in.

Princess Vampire, I am nearby once again.

"Are you all right?"

I am well. You must wear the talisman so I may be fully attuned to you.

"Is that what happened tonight? You couldn't find me?"

Pandora was silent for so long, I thought she'd cut the connection.

I was diverted by another signal.

"Like what? The mother ship?"

I regretted being snarky when I sensed her confusion. "Never mind. Did you see the shooter?"

I arrived too late. I know only it was a vampire. Triton will try to learn more.

"Peachy, and will one of you please tell me when you get the scoop? Saber would like to catch this guy, you know. Oh, and he wants you to patrol when I practice flying tomorrow night. Can you do it?"

Wear the mermaid, and I shall find you.

"Uh, Pandora. About the charm."

Silence.

"Pandora?"

The panther had left the building. I was getting more than a little fed up with these secretive shape-shifters and their cryptic messages.

I stared at the charm in my hand but hesitated to slip the steel chain over my head. Why? Because radio signal or not, I didn't want my wearing Triton's talisman to be an issue between Saber and me. Options. I needed options.

I could stick the charm inside my bra. The old lady who had last owned Maggie's Victorian house had spoken to her granddaughter about carrying mad money in her bra. Of course, at the time I'd still been buried in the forgotten basement, so I hadn't understood what mad money was. Or what a bra was, for that matter.

I could put the charm and chain in a tiny plastic jewelry bag, and wear that inside my bra. Would plastic interfere with the signal?

The heck with options. I needed a decision.

I settled on putting the charm in a scrap of drapery material and fastened it with mini safety pins. There. That I could stuff in my bra. Place it under one boob, and Saber would never be the wiser. It was padded enough not to stick or scratch me, and just uncomfortable enough that I'd remember to remove it before Saber and I made love.

Speaking of Saber, was he already home and on his computer looking up vampire GPS records? I glanced at the dolphin clock on my desk. Two in the morning. Probably not. He might still be at Ike's club.

I wished I could help Saber investigate, but realized I could do some research on Jo-Jo's would-be agent. That might be dull enough to lull my heartbeat back to normal.

After thirty minutes, I'd read all I could find on Vince Atlas in cyber land. He was, indeed, the real deal, and even represented some actors and actresses I'd heard of. A shocker since I watch mostly HGTV and classic TV shows and movies. There were Darlene Dickens and Jonathan Barlow, young stars of the new office comedy *Time Card*, and then there was Shane Steele. Shane was a hunka-hunka burning blond who'd appeared in two action movies I'd watched with Saber.

If Jo-Jo decided to sign the contract with Vince—and I knew he would—he'd be in great company.

* * *

I awoke at three on Thursday afternoon, showered, and checked messages while I downed my daily Starbloods. Saber had called to tell me he'd contacted the attorney to look at Jo-Jo's contract. Randy Tate's office was just a mile from the Island Inn where Vince and his wife were staying. Saber didn't report anything about the sniper, or his drop-in on Ike and company, but told me he'd see me later.

By four thirty, I'd finished running errands—Jo-Jo's and my own—so I drove through Davis Shores checking out houses Saber might be interested in seeing. In the process, I found the neighborhood park Jo-Jo had mentioned. Except for a decorative well, the park was an expanse of grass lined with live oaks and palms. Here we'd spot a human sniper with one eye closed, but a vampire shooter was a wild card. I resolved to be more alert tonight, even with Pandora on the prowl.

Traffic back across the temporary Bridge of Lions was heavy on Thursdays due to the summer concerts held in the Plaza de la Constitución. And, of course, the drawbridge delayed me, too. Which was all right. I had over three hours to change into my costume, and I might just stop in at the concert before my tour began. Music always lifts one's spirits, right?

Lawn chairs and coolers cluttered the plaza by eight that night, the concertgoers tapping their feet to the bluegrass music. I listened awhile, people-watched, and thought about how different things were now than they had been when I was young.

Oh, the plaza had been here forever, with Matanzas Bay on the east, and the Government House on the west. Townspeople gathered to visit the market, hear the latest proclamations, and exchange gossip. The women gossiped here, anyway. The men crowded into taverns to hear the news sailors brought from ports around the world.

At eight thirty, I left the plaza to meet my tour group. I wandered up Cathedral Place, past the bank building where I'd lived with Maggie in her condo penthouse on the sixth floor. We had good times there, but I was happy we lived in separate homes now. Much as I missed our late-night talks, having men in both our lives called for more privacy.

As I strode north on St. George Street, it occurred to me that I'd never had private space in my old life. My parents' household and those of our neighbors had bustled with activity. Home had echoed with my mother's scolding, with the noise of my boisterous brothers, and later, with the voices of their wives and children. A comfortable sort of chaos, but confining.

The only times I'd known quiet were those when I'd snagged one of my father's boats and headed to the island. Sometimes I'd play in the waves, other times I'd sit on the beach and stargaze. I made getaways with or without Triton, but more often with him. Those were carefree times, and, though I was ticked at Triton right now, I had loved him then.

Maggie said a woman never forgot her first love, and she was right. But Saber was my first in more important ways than Triton could be. I didn't agree with Saber on every topic under the Florida sun, but I could talk with him or share quiet time with him. We certainly had no problems between the sheets.

Well, *that* thought dispelled my melancholy, and so did seeing Jag Queen Millie waiting for me.

"Cesca!" She grabbed me in a fierce hug. "Thank God

you're in one piece! Kay heard from her hairdresser that there was a shooting at your place last night. What in the world happened?"

"Someone took potshots at us from a tree and got away."

Millie tut-tutted. "I'll bet it was that nasty Gorman character giving you trouble again. But, my dear, should you be out in the open with this armed nut running around?"

"I'm sure the tour patrons will be safe, Millie. I refused to hide from Gorman the last time, and I won't hide from him or anyone else this time."

"That's the spirit. Now, Cesca," she said with a jerk of her head, "who is that strange skinny man with all the cameras and gadgets?"

I didn't have to look to know Millie was talking about Kevin Miller, but I glanced at him anyway. He held one of his precious meters and wove his way through the fifteen other tourists waiting for me to start.

"He's a post-graduate-school ghostbuster," I told her as I bent to retrieve the lantern from the substation cabinet.

"Well, he certainly is odd. He's been telling all and sundry that he's about to crack your code for connecting with ghosts and make a killing. What is that supposed to mean?"

I straightened fast enough to make myself dizzy. Make a killing? Could Saber's intel be wrong? Could Kevin be the shooter? He was young, wiry, and had to be strong to carry that equipment like a pack mule. Maybe those high-tech gadgets fit together to make a .22 rifle, just like in a James Bond movie.

As I watched, Kevin tripped on a cobblestone, then tiptoe-danced his lanky frame around three couples in the effort not to mow them down.

Okay, if those gadgets fit together to make a rifle, it would be more like Maxwell Smart than James Bond. Still, Pandora had warned me of betrayal and treachery. Despite his earnest eyes and guileless grin, was Kevin a killer in geek clothing?

"Cesca!" Millie said near my ear.

I flinched. "He's a little odd but harmless. Are you taking the tour tonight, Millie?"

"No, dear, but I didn't come just to grill you about the shooting either. Fact is," she said with a faint blush, "I met a new gentleman friend for a drink earlier. Dan was walking me to the parking garage when I heard that Kevin person blabbing."

"Is your friend still here?"

Millie nodded at a man in his sixties sporting navy cotton slacks, a sky blue shirt, and a head of white hair a movie star would envy. He gazed at Millie with an endearingly besotted expression.

"I'd introduce you to Dan, but I think it's rather early in our acquaintance for him to meet my friends. I don't want to pressure him, if you know what I mean."

I chuckled. "He doesn't know about the Jag Queens yet?"

"I need to break that to him soon, don't I? By the way, will you be able to make the preseason game?"

"Not this time." I patted Millie's arm. "You go be with your gentleman, Millie. I'll talk to you soon."

Millie and Dan walked off arm in arm, and I dove into my opening spiel.

"Welcome to the Old Coast Ghost Walk. I'm Cesca Marinelli, born here in St. Augustine in 1780."

"That was during the British period, wasn't it?"

"Exactly," I answered the studious-looking woman. "The Peace of Paris returned Florida to Spain in 1783, which marked the second Spanish period. Of course, the city was over two hundred years old by that time, and the ghost population only grew from there.

"Now, if you'll start toward the city gates and hand me your tickets as you go by, we'll begin our tour with the Huguenot Cemetery. Oh, and if you feel a ghostly presence at the gates, say hi to Elizabeth."

The group moved out, passing me their tickets. Kevin came last, fumbling a meter as he searched his pockets.

"Hi, Ms. Marinelli. Can you hold this a minute?"

He shoved the gadget in my hand, and when the meter immediately screeched, he grabbed it back and peered at the screen. "Wow, wicked awesome EMF reading."

"Anything for science," I said dryly. "Find your ticket?"

"Uh, no."

"Never mind. Let's go."

"The Huguenot Cemetery," I said when I caught up with my tourists, "was established in 1821 to accommodate those who died from the yellow fever epidemic that swept through St. Augustine. The last burial here took place in 1884, and most who are interred here are Protestants. During Spanish rule, only Catholics were buried inside the city proper."

As we approached, three ghosts waited for us, two who looked positively gleeful. I also spotted Gorman on the opposite side of the stone-fenced cemetery but ignored him to launch into the stories of Judge Stickney, and of Erastus Nye, John Lyman, and John Gifford Hull.

"Erastus and the two Johns are said to have come to St. Augustine from the north shortly before their deaths, and all were buried side by side, their tombstones nearly identical." I didn't mention that the three could be pranksters, too. I didn't want to influence an experience anyone might have.

While Kevin muttered excitedly over his equipment, I told the stories of graveyard lore, stories I only told once a week and only because they were required. They hit disturbingly close to home.

"Especially in the height of plagues such as yellow fever, the dead were buried quickly to prevent further spread of the disease. However, not everyone who was buried was quite dead.

"In some cases, victims presented all the outward signs of death but regained consciousness after being buried. We know this because, when coffins were later moved, claw marks were evident inside the lids. The victims had desperately attempted to free themselves."

Several people in the crowd visibly shuddered, me right along with them. The residual energy of victims buried alive and clawing to escape made me sick with horror.

"Thus, those who died of certain illnesses," I continued, "began being buried with a string tied to one hand. That string was also tied to a bell at ground level. Families, friends, or those hired to do the job began keeping watch in graveyards at night. If a bell rang, the person interred was quickly unearthed and freed. From this practice, the phrases *graveyard shift* and *saved by the bell* are said to have come into use."

As I shepherded my group to the rest of the sights, Kevin

seemed to grow more subdued. That is, until we reached the south end of town near the plaza then moved to the bay front. Kevin said a litany of *ohmygods* as he filmed, enough to spook even the hovering Gorman.

At eleven o'clock that night, with the lighthouse beam sweeping the sky, Saber and I arrived at the park to find Pandora in her house cat form lounging on the rim of the well. No Jo-Jo.

"You didn't frighten Jo-Jo away, did you?" I asked her.

Pandora snorted.

"I take it that's a no. Has she patrolled the area?"

"Why don't you ask her?"

Saber frowned. "Cesca, I don't hold conversations with werecreatures."

"Pandora isn't a were. She's—"

"A magical shape-shifter, I know." He gave Pandora the eye. "All right. Did you see anything suspicious?"

No, and I admire this man for speaking to me.

"She says no, but thanks you for talking to her directly."

"You're welcome."

"Who's welcome for whaaa—" Jo-Jo said, flying in from behind us, but faltering in his landing when he saw Pandora.

If a cat could roll its eyes, Pandora did.

"It's okay. Pandora is our lookout tonight."

"Uh-huh. Just as long as she stays that size. By the way, I got a call from Vince tonight. He has me booked to open for a band at the Hard Rock Hotel in Vegas on Wednesday. Can you believe it?"

"That's great, Jo-Jo," I said. "Congratulations."

"You'll have Jemina eating crow in no time," Saber added. "Just don't gamble away your paycheck."

"That's no problem. I don't have the face to bluff." He grinned and rubbed his hands together. "All right, Highness, let's start with jumping levitation since we had to cut that short last night."

Pandora hopped off the well and trotted around the park, stopping now and then to sniff the grass or the air. Was that just a cat thing, or was she detecting trouble?

I jumped and hovered, then practiced standing levitation. I didn't get off the ground much in either exercise, and tripped over myself trying those walking takeoffs. I knew it was all in my head, but I kept hearing those *phfft* sounds of bullets whizzing by me the night before.

Forty-five minutes into the lesson, Saber's cell phone rang, startling us all. He flipped the phone open, barked, "Saber," then listened.

The last of my pitiful concentration was shot as soon as he asked, "How many of them are dead?"

TWELVE

Saber walked away from us, the cell phone vacuum-sealed to his ear.

Which didn't mean I couldn't turn on the vamp hearing and eavesdrop, but I didn't.

"Should we sink a fang in it and call it done?"

When I must've looked blank, Jo-Jo added, "The flight lesson, Highness. We're done, right?"

"Right. Is that a new line for your comedy act?"

"That depends. You like it?"

I wagged my hand in the so-so sign.

He glanced at Saber. "Same time, same place tomorrow?"

"Unless I call you, yes. And thanks, Jo-Jo."

He gave me a little bow, turned, and executed a perfect walking takeoff. I didn't care about hovering, but I sure would save a lot of gas money if I could do that kind of flying.

On the other hand, I couldn't see me flying to the beach with my surfboard. That would just be weird.

Yes, I was distracting myself from listening in on Saber, but I didn't have to be good for long.

"Right, Candy," Saber said as he walked toward me again. "I'll call you back from Cesca's as soon as we do a sweep."

Saber flipped his phone shut, and Pandora loped to join us. "Trouble?"

"Candy and Crusher went to see Vlad, but they were ambushed on the way out."

My breath hitched. "Are they all right? I mean, I guess they are since Candy called you, but—"

"We'll talk about it at home." He looked down at Pandora. "This is a stretch for me, but I need you to ride back with us and sweep the neighborhood. Will you do that?"

Pandora chuffed and trotted toward the SUV.

Saber grabbed my hand. "Let's go."

We drove up and down every block in my neighborhood so Pandora could alert us to any lurking danger. When she gave me the mental thumbs-up, Saber parked at the curb in front of Maggie's and hustled me inside the cottage. He even asked Pandora into the house to scope my place for bugs. Listening devices, he'd clarified in case Pandora thought he meant stray water beetles.

Saber brought his own bug-detecting equipment from his car. Pandora didn't say a word—or rather think a thought—while she and Saber worked their way through my house. Within ten minutes, Saber declared the cottage clean. Then he went to the kitchen to get Candy on the phone.

Pandora insisted on leaving. *I will patrol,* she said in my head as she stood at the door. I let her out, and she grew to full panther size as she padded across the lawn. Five months ago, it had freaked me out to see her do that trick. Heck, five months ago, Pandora herself had freaked me. Had my perception of normal changed or what?

When I joined Saber in the kitchen, he not only had Candy on the line, he'd turned the phone on speaker. We huddled over the handset resting on my retro table.

"Candy, tell me everything now. I want Cesca to hear this from the beginning."

"Cesca, this is Candy Crushman," she said with a Southern drawl. "My husband Jim and I did a drop-in on Vlad and his nest tonight. Somehow they expected us."

"So you didn't arrange to see them?" I asked. My VPA handler always called me to schedule a visit. Then again, I went to see him most of the time, not the other way around.

"Did I make an appointment, you mean? No. The goal was to catch them off guard, but they weren't surprised. And weren't remotely cordial either."

"What happened?" Saber asked.

"We observed a hell of a lot of tension in the nest, and, when we asked who was being punished, the tension amped. Vlad said two vamps were being restrained, and admitted one was this Marco dude you asked us to look for."

"Did Vlad say why they were in lockdown or when they'd be released?"

"Nope, only that they were learnin' not to defy him."

"What about Marco being immune to silver? Did you have the chance to ask about that?"

"Yeah, and we got stonewalled. Vlad shook his head at us like we were particularly stupid or gullible to believe such a tale. He said it was impossible, but Saber—" She pronounced it *Say-buh*. "You know how vamps can go utterly still?"

"Yeah."

"The energy in that room went from tense to dead still when I asked about the silver immunity."

"Shit," Saber said, running a hand through his hair. "I don't suppose Vlad showed you where he's imprisoned the vamps."

"Hell, Saber, he wouldn't have shown me the bathroom if I'd threatened to pee on his carpet. He barked at a female called Jemina to show us out, and—"

"Wait, Candy," I interrupted, a quick glance at Saber. "Did you say Jemina?"

"Do you know her?"

"No, but she was Jo-Jo's girlfriend. And his partner back in his vaudeville days."

"That is one edgy vamp. Her movements were jerky, like she was bein' controlled by a junkie puppet master needin' a fix. Soon as she closed the metal door, she locked it, and we were jumped in the parkin' lot not ten seconds later."

"By how many?" Saber asked.

"Only two. Jim had his highest-grade silver knife and took 'em down before they did too much damage. We have new scars, and we're gonna be sore as hell tomorrow, but we're okay."

I had a mental flash of slashed arms and oozing blood, and a sweet, coppery smell. My stomach heaved, but I willed myself to hold it together.

"Did Crusher kill them both?"

"Oh, yeah, with silver bullets to the brain. We called the disposal team to take them to our morgue so we can ID 'em and put 'em in the system as exterminated."

"Candy, I hate to say this," I began, still puzzling over part of the vision, "but it doesn't seem like those guys fought hard."

"Like they meant to kill us, you mean?" she said. "You're right, but how did you know?"

"I'm a psychic empath. As you described the attack, I saw a few pieces of it happen, as if I were watching a movie trailer."

"Well, you're dead on, Cesca. Pardon the pun. Jim and I thought the same thing. It was a sacrifice fly, a diversion. Otherwise, vamps would've come pourin' out of Vlad's place."

"Instead, Vlad let them die."

We were all silent a moment. I wondered if Saber and Candy knew what Vlad had accomplished by sacrificing two of his people. Normand had done something like that once.

"Candy," Saber said, breaking into my thoughts, "I don't suppose you've had a team go sweep your office for bugs yet."

"Not yet, but it's on the list. Cesca's place is clean?"

"Yeah, and so is my cell phone. I sweep my house every few days, and I'll do it again tomorrow."

"I don't know what the hell is goin' on, Saber, but I'm keepin' an eye on the tracker readouts of every vamp in that nest. Anything looks the least bit suspicious, and I'm shuttin' those suckers down."

"I understand, Candy, but please call me first if it comes to that. Also let me know if any of the readouts show another vamp moving this way."

"You still think it was a vamp who took those shots at y'all last night?"

"I know it was," I answered, then mouthed *Pandora* at Saber.

"Good enough. Crusher says to call if you need backup."

Saber disconnected, and we stared at each other for a long moment before he leaned back in his chair.

"Pandora confirmed the sniper was a vamp?"

I nodded. "Sorry I forgot to tell you. She didn't get a description."

"Damn. If those vampires had wanted Candy and Crusher dead, they would be. Vlad couldn't afford to bring the whole VPA down on him, though."

"So he sent vamps who were loyal enough to him to die. Normand did that, too."

"How often?"

I shook my head. "Just once that I know of."

"Tell me about it," Saber said, taking my hand.

"Marco's father pitched a fit that his son had been taken and turned. I'm not sure how the *comandante* of the *castillo* got involved, but he demanded retribution. Normand gave him the vamp who had supposedly turned Marco, and the *comandante* had the vampire publicly executed. They displayed the decapitated, sun-fried body for days."

Saber frowned. "Why did the commander of the fort care about the son of a mere soldier?"

"According to Marco, his dad had been more than a soldier back in Spain. Marco bragged that his father and grandfather had been silversmiths, but that they'd been falsely accused of something. He never said what."

"Sounds far-fetched for a skilled artisan to turn soldier."

"Yes, except that Marco had links of silver chain he said his father made in a workshop at his house. And rumor in the

Quarter was that his father gave small tokens crafted in silver to the governor."

"What did you think?"

I grinned. "That Marco was a liar and a thief. I couldn't believe he never got caught swiping the things he'd show off."

"That's another chapter that never made it into the city's historic records." He sat back in his chair. "Let's go back to the ambush. Did you see anything else in your vision?"

"No, and I couldn't see Vlad or anyone else when Candy talked about them. I just felt—" I paused to test the impression before I spoke the words. "I felt like I did in Normand's court. Oppressed. Closed in. Controlled."

Saber shrugged. "That's the norm for vampire nests. Except for a few that are organized like companies or clubs."

"Jo-Jo's fraternities with fangs?"

He sent me a tired smile and rubbed the back of his neck.

"Look, before I forget, the Florida vamps are all present and accounted for. Tracker readouts show most of them moving around a fair amount."

"What about Laurel's tracker?"

"Her readouts have been stationary for a few days, but they would be if she's confined to Ike's residence. The odd thing is that they also flatline like a heart monitor would do."

"Did mine do that when it stopped working in March?"

"Yes, but only for ten seconds. Then your signal stopped entirely. Laurel's flatlines for an hour or two at a time then starts working again, so I'm guessing it's an electrical short."

I frowned. I'm no expert in electricity, but there was a clue here. I felt it.

"Saber, electricity makes a sound, doesn't it?"

"One that's usually too low or high for a human to hear."

"I don't think vampires hear it either. I didn't hear my tracker go bad."

"Where are you going with this?"

"The night the sniper shot at us, Pandora told me she'd been distracted by another signal. That she couldn't find me."

"When you were home?"

"I know, but I had the charm in a mug by my laptop, so that could cause interference. Plus, if a flatlining tracker emits an obnoxious beep that Pandora could hear, the sound could confuse her, couldn't it?"

"So you think Laurel could've been the sniper?"

I shrugged. "I can't see her up a tree, and I doubt she's a card-carrying NRA member, but cell phone signals don't seem to bother Pandora. What else could?"

"A whole list of things, I imagine, but I'll order Laurel's tracker records for the past few months to see if there's a pattern, and tell Dave Corey to order a new tracker for her."

"Good luck getting Laurel to have it implanted. She's nasty to vampires. Imagine what she's like with the average human."

"Überbitch."

"On wheels. I hope she's still in Ike's doghouse on Saturday. It sure would be nice if she wasn't at the club for Jo-Jo's act."

Saber chuckled. "You aren't a princess. You're the queen of avoidance."

"Well, Laurel is a royal pain."

"Honey, you energy-sucked her once. You can do it again."

I shook my head. "Not and free her afterward. Nope, if I have to energy-siphon Laurel that much again, I'll have to kill her. I don't think I can do that."

"When it comes down to life and death, you'll be surprised what you can do."

One advantage to being buried all that time was that I'd developed focus. After Saber went to sleep, I used that skill to block thoughts of everything except my design homework. I worked steadily until seven, then slipped into bed with Saber on the happy thought that we'd be house hunting again later.

I was raring to go Friday afternoon, but Saber had to leave a message for Jo-Jo before we left. Saber's attorney friend had given his seal of approval to Vince's contract terms and had checked on any complaints filed by former clients. There were none. Looked like Jo-Jo had fallen into a great deal.

Saber wasn't as lucky. By six Friday evening, we'd seen eight houses in four neighborhoods. The three affordable ones needed major updating, but Saber and I could do some of the labor. I'd learned to use a few basic power tools when I'd hung around Maggie's construction crew while they worked on her Victorian house and my cottage. The men and women might've been amused at having a vampire pelting them with questions, but they taught me to cut and install crown molding and do other carpentry projects. Also, we could contact Maggie's contractor for help with major things like plumbing and electrical work.

When it was clear to Amanda that Saber wasn't ready to make any offers, she went to her car to make a cell call, then asked us to see one more property.

"This one is on the island, a bit south of where you said you want to be, but I promise you it's special."

She said "special" with an odd glitter in her eyes. Something more than Realtor-fee fever, but why did she lob that comment at me instead of Saber?

We followed Amanda south on A1A, past where the road narrowed to two lanes. She talked on her cell phone during the entire drive, and when she turned east ahead of us, Saber muttered a curse.

"Has she lost her way or been out in the sun too long?"

"What's wrong?"

"She's out of her little blonde mind if she thinks I can afford a house on the ocean side of the highway. I sure can't afford a house with an ocean view."

"Maybe it's just an ocean peek."

He wasn't amused and was even less so when he pulled off the worn blacktop. He stared out the windshield and gaped.

"What the *hell* is that?"

From what I could see of the shape and window style, *that* was a 1950s bungalow. A tiny, ramshackle bungalow sitting amid a sandbox of dune weeds, overgrown shrubs, and vines that crawled up the exterior walls and onto the shallow-pitched roof.

On the upside, the house sat smack in the middle of what had to be several ocean front lots. Contrary to all good sense and reason, I fell in love with it.

"Oh, Saber, talk about a clean slate!"

"It's an eyesore," he growled back. "I'm surprised the neighbors haven't torched it."

"They can't. There are laws against fires on the beach."

He leveled a look at me. "We are not getting out of the car. I don't care what Amanda says. It's not even safe to go look in the windows. The vines will strangle us if the snakes don't get us first."

"Come on, Saber. Think of it as an adventure."

"I'm thinking it's a waste of time."

"But we're here."

"So are the rattlers and brown recluse spiders. Not to mention sand fleas."

I snorted. "You've killed werewolves and vampires. What's a little wildlife compared to that?"

He gave me his stony cop face. I threw up my hands.

"All right. But can I at least get some pictures for my design class?"

"You brought your camera?"

"No, I was hoping I could use yours."

"Remind me to take that damn thing out of my car." He sighed. "Okay, a few pictures, and we're outta here."

I leaned over to kiss him on the cheek, then twisted to fish his digital camera from the backseat floorboard. "Right, and we'll stop by CVS on the way home so I can put the photos on a CD. It won't take but a minute."

"Cesca, it's Friday, and it's tourist season. It'll take more than a minute."

"Fine, then you can get calamine lotion for your sand flea bites while I get the CD. Come on, let's go."

We met Amanda on a mangled flagstone path leading to the front door.

"Sorry about the wait. A colleague was double-checking some facts on the property for me. Well, do you recognize it?"

"As what?" Saber snapped. "A perfect bombing range?"

Amanda kept her sales smile pinned in place. "I know it doesn't look like much from the outside—"

"Amanda, it's a wreck."

"Actually, Saber," I said, "now that we're closer, some of the exterior paint doesn't look that bad."

"Don't help," he shot back. "Now look, Amanda—"

This time she interrupted him. "The house comes with three lots, and I promise it's better inside."

"So was the city of Pompeii when they dug it out, but I wouldn't want to live there."

"The house is one bedroom, one bath," Amanda went on as she picked her way toward the door, "but the living area is generous, and the entire back of the house is an enclosed porch facing the ocean, accessible through both the kitchen and living area."

"I'm betting that's because the walls have collapsed," Saber groused.

"Five minutes," I said. "Pictures and we're gone."

Saber gave me a martyred grimace but came along quietly when I took his hand. Amanda opened the door with relative ease, considering the bush partly blocking it, and then we stepped into the gloom inside.

The ceiling was higher than I expected, with exposed beams. The hardwood floors? Well, dusty was being generous, but they looked like oak and were solid. No obvious rot. No roof, wall, or floor cave-ins. The dingy white walls looked like salvaged wood planks nailed over drywall. I glanced at Saber's granite face and started snapping pictures.

Two slightly warped dark wood doors to the right of the living room were open. One was the bedroom, the other a small bathroom with filthy fixtures. I snapped off more shots of both rooms and gingerly opened the closet door. Not a bad size for a shoebox house, and no band of mutant spiders assaulted me.

"Now back here is the kitchen. It's small, of course, but you could expand. And here's the fabulous porch with the view. Isn't it perfect?"

Though the view was marred by salt air–spotted windows, even Saber sucked in a breath at the magnificent expanse of ocean. I got photos of the grungy kitchen, the porch, and then the view.

"Well, what do you think?" Amanda asked, her bright eyes darting between us but not with uncertainty.

More like this was a done deal.

"Is the view the way you remember it, Ms. Marinelli?"

Remember it? Saber was right. Amanda had been in the sun too long if she thought I'd ever been here, and she'd completely lost her wits if she thought she could sell him on this place.

"I don't know what this property is priced at," Saber said, "but I can't afford it."

The agent tilted her head, a tiny crease forming between her eyes. "But Mr. Saber, you're preapproved. You can afford to tear this house down and start all over again."

"Not and buy even one of these lots. They have to sell for five hundred thousand apiece."

"Oh, but the property isn't for sale, Mr. Saber."

He blinked. "If the property isn't for sale, why the hell did you bring us here?"

She turned her wide, blue-eyed gaze on me. "He doesn't know, does he?"

"Know what? Amanda, is this place for sale, or isn't it?"

"That would depend on you, Ms. Marinelli. You see, you already own it."

THIRTEEN

I wanted to stick a finger in my ear and wiggle it, because I must've heard wrong.

"Amanda, what did you just say?"

"I said you own these three lots and the house. Surely you got the offers to buy the land in the mail. There have been two of them in the last year."

I'd received a lot of offers since I'd been unearthed, all right. Offers to buy life, health, and disability insurance, refinance my nonexistent home, and win a cruise if I'd just take a short tour at a new golf course luxury condo community. An offer to buy property *I* owned?

I shook my head. "No, Amanda. You must have me confused with someone else."

"But I don't. My boss was the real-estate agent for one of the clients who wanted your property. She ordered an exhaustive title search, and you're the surviving owner."

"Surviving?"

I must've paled, because Saber put an arm around me.

"Would you like to sit down to hear this?" Amanda glanced around the porch as if she expected a chair to materialize.

"Just get to the point," Saber said.

"Well, this is a bit irregular, but do you know who Jesse Fish was?"

"The Fish Island guy," I said, and elaborated for Saber. "When St. Augustine changed hands from the Spanish to the British and back to the Spanish again, Jesse Fish acted as a quasi real estate agent and arbitrated land ownership claims. He also supposedly owned most of Anastasia Island and parts of the downtown area besides."

"Not supposedly. He *did* own the island by virtue of a Spanish land grant conferred in 1795."

"Jesse Fish died in 1790," I said.

"Really? Well, his son must've received the grant."

"The point, Amanda?" Saber reminded her.

She drew a deep breath. "In 1798, a Jesse Fish sold one hundred acres of Anastasia Island to Patrizio Dante Marinelli."

My vision blurred, and a buzz chainsawed in my ears.

Patrizio Marinelli. Papa? I shook my head, hoping it would clear. The buzzing only grew louder.

Amanda went blithely on. "The title was in Mr. Marinelli's name as well as yours, with full rights of survivorship."

"Do you mean to say that Cesca's father bought this land for her?"

Amanda shrugged. "Back then, women didn't own land."

"We understand that, but how could the land still be hers?

She was just eighteen. That's over two hundred years worth of taxes that had to be paid."

"And there were land ownership squabbles," I added faintly. "When Florida became a United States territory, land grants weren't always honored."

"This one was," Amanda insisted. "The records show Mr. Marinelli paid the taxes until 1802. At that time the land was transferred in perpetual trust to—let me see."

Amanda pulled a stenographer's spiral from her red briefcase while fine tremors ripped my muscles.

"Ah, here it is. Delphinus and Company first held the land in trust."

The tremors spread to my legs, and I locked my knees to stay upright. Triton. As he brought back greater treasures from the sea each time he shape-shifted, Triton had joked about forming Delphinus and Company. He was Delphinus; I was company.

"Of course," Amanda continued, "the first business was bought out by another one, and that one absorbed into yet another, and so on, but it was surprisingly easy to trace back. I assure you, the taxes have been paid without fail, and the land is legally yours."

My mouth was sand-in-the-summer dry, but I forced myself to speak. "Amanda, are you absolutely sure about this?"

"I saw the photocopy of the original deed. Or maybe it was a copy of microfiche, but the record is complete right down to the date of purchase. August second of seventeen ninety-eight."

My knees wobbled, and my throat constricted. Memories churned like storm waves.

"Saber," I choked out.

That was all I had to say. Bless the man, he told Amanda we'd be in touch, then got me out of that house and into his car before cold tears tracked down my face.

I think Saber took my icy hands in his. I think he murmured, "Tell me." I could only stare out the windshield at the ocean and remember.

Papa and I went sailing, not in his merchant vessel but in a small craft he'd salvaged. The one he used to teach my brothers and me to sail, and the one I took out with Triton when we were sixteen.

The summer day was fine, and we cut through the sparkling blue Atlantic waters heading south, with Anastasia Island to starboard. I finished tying off the lines and went to stand beside Papa at the wheel.

"Why do you not marry, my girl?"

I braced myself for the kind of scold Mama gave me. It did not come.

"Figlia piccola."

Little daughter, he called me, so he must not be too angry.

"Are you too much in love with Triton to choose another?"

I was, but I denied it.

"Does marriage hold fear then? Has a man tried to hurt you?"

Oh, my, but I blushed that il mio papa would ask me such a thing! He told me not to be missish, and demanded the truth.

I would not have a man I could have no respect or affection for, I told him. Instead, I should stay home and care for my parents. Papa laughed at that and warned me not to let mama hear me say it. She did not want an old maid of a daughter.

Papa was quiet a long time. A while later, we spotted the bow and tall mast of a wrecked ship on the beach, the mast jutting toward the sky at a drunken angle. Papa shook his head and muttered a prayer.

Sometimes a man does not reach safe port, he said. A father must secure the future of his daughters while he may, even a willful, independent one that refused to marry.

He smiled at me, his gentle, teasing smile. Then he pinched my chin and told me to look sharp. We sailed home speaking of nothing more than the coming rough weather he felt in his bones.

I blinked away the past to find Saber watching me steadily, his cobalt eyes filled with compassion.

"Your father bought the land to insure your future," he said, his voice soothing. "Your dowry."

I nodded and wiped tears from my cheeks with trembling fingers. "Papa could have sold it back to Mr. Fish after I was caught by the vampires. Or sold it before he moved the family from St. Augustine. Papa must have still loved me, even when Mama cursed my name."

"He also trusted Triton to keep the land for you. Delphinus means dolphin. That is Triton, isn't it?"

I sniffed, fumbled for the tissue Saber held out to me, and blew my nose. "Yes, and I'm going to kill that man if he ever shows his face. Slowly and painfully kill him."

Saber chuckled. "That's the spirit. Ready to go home?"

I blinked away the last of my tears and nodded, but I knew we'd have to discuss the land issue later. Not to mention Triton's role in it. For now, I was happy for the reprieve.

* * *

Saber watched the news while I changed into my Minorcan costume for the ghost tour. Yes, I know a few days ago I'd decided the costume was too hot to wear in the summer. That was then. Today, raw emotions and melancholy had left me chilled.

Saber asked if I wanted to take the night off—from tour guiding and from the flying session. I agreed to let him cancel the flight lesson, but insisted on doing my tour. I loved my job, and I even loved the ghosts along the route.

I didn't love seeing my Covenant stalker, Victor Gorman, waiting at the tour substation by the waterwheel. Nor was I wild about spotting my personal paranormal investigator, Kevin Miller, either. The creep and the geek.

I *so* wasn't in the mood for any more drama today.

"Vampire," Gorman roared as I drew near.

He was loud enough to drive the dead into hiding, never mind snagging the attention of my ghost walk patrons and anyone else within earshot.

"What's this crap about that loony tunes blood-suckin' buddy a yours bein' a comic?"

"You mean Jo-Jo?" I asked, oh so calmly.

"I don't care about his name. What the hell is he gonna be doin' in Daytona? My connections tell me there's advertisin' up all over town."

"If you know about the ads, then you know he's doing a show at Hot Blooded. Saturday, for one night only," I said a little louder for the sake of our listening audience. "Then he'll be playing Vegas and Los Angeles."

"You can't be serious."

"Oh, but I am. He's already been signed by a high-powered Hollywood talent agent."

Gorman snorted. "Yeah? Who?"

"Me."

I spun to find Vince Atlas eyeing Gorman as if he were diseased. I hadn't seen Vince in the crowd, but his timing was perfect.

"Jo-Jo is going to be a household name," Vince said, turning on the showmanship. "If you want to see him for a reasonable price, catch him at Hot Blooded."

"I don't want to see a vampire comic. That's just stupid."

"Stupid is as stupid does." Vince flashed a grin and turned to me. "Princess Ci, please come meet my wife."

"It's Cesca, Vince."

"Cesca, then. I've told Jessica all about you and your nice young man. And my new rising star Jo-Jo, of course."

"Wait a minute," Gorman snarled. "I ain't done."

"Done doing what?" I asked.

The way Gorman was grinding his teeth, he'd be gumming pudding by next week.

"I'm warnin' you. The Covenant ain't standin' for this."

"Gorman, Jo-Jo's leaving town to go on tour, and things will get back to normal. I thought you'd be happy."

"Well, yeah, but what about them others? We don't want our town overrun by a bunch of—"

"Evil pervert bloodsuckers, I know. Believe what you want, but there is no plot to make St. Augustine the vampire capital of the world."

"Besides," Kevin said as he bopped up to poke an EMF

meter at my bodice, "Ms. Marinelli already told you she can't control where vampires live."

"Kevin," I warned, "do not shove that thing at me."

"I just need to get tonight's baseline reading, and then I need to show you the piece of video I got last night."

"Not right now, please." I turned to Vince. "I'd love to meet your wife, but I must get the tour started. Maybe we can chat after I finish?"

He nodded. "If not tonight, we can share a table for Jo-Jo's performance tomorrow."

"I'll look forward to it," I said, and faced Gorman as Vince walked away.

"Listen, I've been civil to you, but you're violating the restraining order, and we both know it. You've said your piece, so I suggest you go now. And Kevin," I continued without giving Gorman a chance to respond, "I'll see your video later."

With that, I retrieved my lantern and stepped into the crowd.

"Welcome to Old Coast Ghost Tours, everyone. I'll collect your tickets as we begin our tour by passing through the city gates."

That galvanized the group. They surged toward me to hand over their tickets, and the tour was on.

The evening was a huge success, partly because Gorman had taken the hint and left. Mostly because the ghosts came out to play. After multiple sightings at the Huguenot Cemetery, I herded my group to the Tolomato Cemetery. There the Bridal Ghost made herself visible, and at least five light orbs zipped and dipped to the ooohs and aaahs of the crowd. My group felt cold spots all over the old town, and some tourists reported being touched on the shoulder or arm, yet no one became distraught by the phenomenon.

Kevin didn't get in anyone's way, thanks to two cute, curvy brunettes who latched on to him. I heard them introduce themselves as Leah and Caro, and within fifteen minutes, Kevin was allowing them to help take temperature readings and shoot video.

After the tour, I met Vince's wife, Jessica. Petite and auburn-haired, I liked her immediately, but the three of us only spoke long enough for me to give Vince Donita's name, and to arrange for me to take Jo-Jo to Ike's club. Vince and Jessica would get to the club early enough to talk to Donita for a few minutes, and would save a table for four.

Leah and Caro still monopolized Kevin so completely, I thought for sure I'd be able to slip quietly home. He caught me as I put the lantern away.

"Ms. Marinelli, I really need you to see this. I've never captured anything quite like it, and I need to know if it means something to you. Please?"

Since the girls flanked him, I figured I could be quick. "Okay, let's see what you have."

Kevin opened the lid of a portable DVD player, and clicked Play. Sharp images showed me in my Regency gown on last night's tour. The shots all seemed to have been taken in the plaza, and I didn't see anything unusual until a white outline appeared behind my left shoulder as I gestured toward the cathedral in the background. The figure had a distinct head and torso but no facial features. A minute later, the white figure had gone, and a dark, amorphous shadow hovered over my right shoulder.

Prickles stabbed the back of my neck where my hair rose as I watched the shadow press toward me, the edges of the image curling almost as if it were embracing me. Suddenly, the dark mass fractured and faded.

Kevin kept the video running and both images showed up two more times as I moved the group to another landmark in the plaza, and then to the Spanish Military Hospital. The only difference was that when they appeared again, the black figure hovered longer than the white one.

"What do you make of that?" Kevin asked. "Are they ghosts you recognize?"

I fought a shiver because I didn't want Kevin to think me a wimp. "They're energies or entities, but they aren't true ghosts or any spirit I recognize. I never felt them last night."

"I think," Caro volunteered, "they're, like, ghostly versions of those cartoon angels and devils. One on each shoulder."

"The dark one seems to be what we call a shadow man," Kevin said. "They're not generally harmful, but no one knows why they show up as dark instead of light."

"What about the white form? Is that an angel?" Leah asked.

Kevin shrugged. "Who knows? I took more video of Ms. Marinelli tonight, so I'll see if they show up again." He closed the lid and snapped it shut. "When is your next tour?"

"Sunday," I answered before I thought to lie.

"Good. I'll be here."

"And we'll come back to help you," Caro said, tucking a hand into Kevin's arm.

Leah nodded and claimed Kevin's other side. "Right. That is, if it's okay with you, Kevvy."

Kevvy?

Okay, I was outta there. Even a down and dirty talk with Saber about Triton and the land trust beat listening to that syrup.

The main drag of San Marco Avenue was light on traffic. I was halfway home but dawdled at a lit shop window to look at a display of blown glass bowls. I don't know what made me turn, but Pandora, in her huge house cat form, came out of nowhere at a dead run and threw herself on my chest.

I staggered back, heard a *thwit*, and then the sound of shattering glass. A beat later, an alarm went off.

Behind the building, Pandora said in my head.

When I didn't move immediately, she nipped me.

Run.

I stumbled once, then used vamp speed. When I reached the back of the building, I stopped, pressed my back into the nubby surface of a brick wall, and wondered what the hell was happening. Another sniper? The sound I'd heard was different from the gunshots of the other night, but I was no expert. I was the only person I knew who didn't own a gun.

The first police sirens wailed as Pandora trotted around the corner of the building.

Follow me, she commanded and headed behind another building to come out on a street behind San Marco.

She didn't morph into panther size, I guess so as not to scare the bejeebers out of anyone who happened to see us. Of course, her house cat size was as big as a bobcat. That was intimidating enough.

"What happened back there?" I asked in a whisper as we hurried along the shadowed streets.

The man with the scarred face shot an arrow at you.

"Gorman?"

Pandora glanced over her shoulder as if to say *Duh*.

"He's never pulled so much as a pop gun on me. Why try to kill me now?"

Pandora shook her head. *This I do not know, but you must tell your man.*

Oh goody. Another thing for Saber to feel good about.

Pandora stopped so fast, I nearly plowed into her haunches. *You will tell your man,* she said, her amber eyes narrowing on me. *There are dangers enough, and you must eliminate those threats you can.*

She was saying more than the words I heard in my head. I knew it, but I was tired of the coded messages.

"Are you talking about whatever Triton is hiding from?"

You will learn what you need to know in due time.

She cocked her head toward the bay and twitched her ears, then paced off again.

We reached Maggie's front yard just as Saber stormed through the gate. He checked his steps, looked hard at Pandora, then settled his gaze on me.

"I heard the sirens. What happened?"

"Gorman shot an arrow at me but broke a shop window."

Saber clenched his fists. "Pandora saved you?"

"She knocked me out of the way."

Saber nodded at her. "Good work. Get her in the house and stand guard until I get back."

Pandora trotted toward the cottage. I stepped closer to Saber.

"Get back from where? You're not going after Gorman."

"No. I'm calling the cops from a pay phone to give them an anonymous tip that Gorman broke the window. Any more questions?"

I bit my lip. "Can I have a hug before you go?"

"God, yes."

He grabbed me fast and hard in a hug that threatened to pop the stuffing out of me, but I clung to him just as tightly. I was about to tell him to forget the call and take me inside—take me, period—when Pandora gave a throaty chuff.

Saber eased me away and touched his forehead to mine.

"I'll be gone ten minutes, and I want to slip into something more comfortable when I get back."

"S-slip into what?"

"You."

FOURTEEN

Saber cupped the back of my head, pressed a scorching kiss to my mouth, then let me go and sprinted to his car.

"Ten minutes," he called softly.

I took off for my cottage, my keys in one hand, working the buttons of my costume with the other. My blouse was open before I hit the door.

Lock it, Pandora said from her perch on the tiki bar.

I nodded. "Thanks, Pandora. Later."

Eight minutes.

I tossed my clothes off on the way through the living room to the bathroom. I didn't care where they landed. I needed a shower. I was sick of being shot at and ticked at being in the middle of Triton's skullduggery. I wanted my calm, normal afterlife back, damn it. And I wanted Saber.

I flipped the shower on hot, squashed my hair into a shower cap, and stepped under the pulsating spray.

Five minutes.

Creamy body wash. Coconut scent. I inhaled the aroma as I spread the slick liquid on my shoulders, down my arms, over my aching breasts and the quivering muscles of my belly. The last vestiges of fear swirled down the drain.

Two minutes.

I shut off the water, ripped the cap off my hair—and the shower door burst open.

A scream died in my throat.

Deke stood there, naked and aroused, his cobalt eyes dark with fevered desire.

He stepped into the shower stall, and I backed into the glass tile. Very slowly, his gaze dropped to my breasts, and every trickle of water on my body sizzled. With a fingertip, he reached to catch a ripe droplet on my nipple, then raised the drop to his mouth.

One. Long. Minute.

"Hi, honey. I'm early."

"I'm ready," I whispered.

He lifted me, pressed me against the shower wall, and I wrapped my legs around his waist. When he slipped into my wet warmth, my muscles closed tight around him as if to hold him near forever. Each stroke of his shaft built pain-pleasure friction, caressed needs in my heart that had no name. The wave of climax climbed until I hovered on the crest. I pressed Deke deeper, screamed his name. His shout of release echoed mine, and my body sang with power, my heart with fierce love.

A coma. A multiple orgasm, sex-sated, blissful coma. I didn't want to move again for at least a thousand years.

Saber, though, decided he was hungry and pulled on navy blue boxers to go fix a sandwich. Hey, I support whatever keeps my man at peak strength and stamina.

When I dragged myself out of bed, donned a sleep shirt, and joined him in the kitchen, I found my bra with the foam cups lying on the turquoise tabletop.

"I knew I was flinging my clothes left and right, but I didn't think I threw anything this far."

He put a glass of sweet tea on the table and sat down in front of his half-eaten sandwich.

"You didn't throw your bra this far. I stepped on it and got stabbed by this."

He lifted one bra cup to reveal Triton's mermaid charm underneath. He dropped it in my hand and raised a brow.

Uh-oh. Was Saber upset? He said he wasn't jealous, exactly, but he could've fooled me. The charm gave my palm a mild jolt, and I let it clatter to the table.

"Why was that in a scrap of fabric?" he asked with a hint of his cop voice.

I sighed. "Remember when we were talking about Laurel's tracker flatlining? I told you Pandora said she was diverted by another signal."

"Go on."

"She also said the charm acts like a homing device for her and told me to wear it. I put the charm in the fabric pouch for padding, then put the pouch in my bra."

"Why not just wear it as a necklace?"

I raked my hair back. "Because I didn't want you to think I was wearing it for Triton's sake."

He didn't smile, but I felt his energy shift. "Noted and appreciated, but your safety is what matters. Come here."

He picked up the chain and began easing it over my head when I flinched. "Wait."

"Did I catch your hair?"

"No, but this thing buzzes with static energy when I hold it. In the cloth, it didn't do that."

"You're afraid it will keep buzzing when it's touching your skin, huh? Let's see."

He finished arranging the chain, then picked up the charm and dropped it down the inside of my sleep shirt. I held my breath, waiting for the charm to go spazzy with energy, but it didn't. No static buzz, no static shock. Not even the sound of ocean waves.

"Well? How is it?"

I twitched my shoulders to see if anything happened. Nope. Nothing but a little bump between my breasts.

"Fine, but are you sure it won't bother you if I wear it?"

He wagged his eyebrows. "As long as I'm the only one diving for mermaid treasure, I don't care. Now, do you want to know what I found out about your land while you were out getting shot at and giving me gray hair?"

I crossed my eyes at him, but the effect was lost since he was already hoofing it into the living room. I leaned around the doorframe to ogle his boxer-clad butt as he scooped a stack of papers from my desk.

He handed me a tome. "Take a look."

"Don't I get a hint what to look for?"

"You'll see it."

He took a swig from his plastic bottle of root beer and waited expectantly. I growled under my breath and began scanning the pages. Legalese wasn't my strong point, but only the first two pages were full of legal jargon. The third page contained a list of names and dates, and I spotted the pattern immediately.

"Is this it? That Triton moved locations and changed the name of his company every twenty years?"

"Twenty-two years in one case," Saber corrected. "And he didn't just change the name, he absorbed each old company into each new one. A new twist on corporate takeovers."

"He didn't disguise the names much. The list starts with Delphinus and Company and ends with Trey Delphis Antiquities out of California. He might as well have put a neon sign on his trail."

"Since you were right about the land squabbles, I think he did it so ownership would be easy to trace. Look." He scooted his chair closer to mine and thumbed through the stack to pull out another sheet. "I summarized this, but the transactions show you started with the equivalent of one hundred acres. As the island developed progressively southward, Triton sold off pieces."

I followed Saber's finger down the column of dates. "I see it. Most of these sales were in the late 1970s and '80s."

"Then another chunk in the early 1990s. I figure as the property values rose, Triton sold land and put the proceeds in trust to help pay the taxes."

"That's good. At least it won't take a Fort Knox fortune to pay him back." I looked over at him. "Is there any land left other than the three lots?"

"No, but I have to hand it to him. He must've studied the

plots, because he not only saved beachfront land for you, he kept the part where an access street dead-ends. You have a wide buffer between your property and the next one."

"Score points for Triton." I sipped on my tea and leafed through more papers but didn't see what I was hunting for.

"Did you find out who built the house?"

"You mean that shack? No. Those records aren't online."

"I guess it doesn't matter who built it, but what am I going to do about it?"

Saber snorted. "Wait for the next storm to blow it down."

"Come on, be serious. Now that I know about"—I waved a hand at the papers—"all this, I can't ignore it. If nothing else, I owe it to the neighbors to spiff up the house."

He pushed his plate away and crossed his arms on the table. "I have a feeling you want to make that place a project."

"Well, the thought had occurred. It would look fantastic on my design résumé. Plus, you're looking for a house, and that one is just sitting there."

"No, Cesca. No way."

"You wouldn't have to buy it. You could rent it. Cheap. And then it would be occupied."

"It's barely tourable, never mind livable."

"But it could be if I fixed it up and expanded. I could build an office for you, and another bathroom. Or I could put on a second story, make the whole upstairs a master bedroom suite."

"Even if the county will approve any plan other than razing the place, as soon as you improve that property, your taxes and wind and flood insurance will be astronomical."

"Maybe not. Besides, even if you don't want to live there, I'll be able to move away from Maggie in four years."

He shrugged. "Being that you haven't bitten a human in centuries, the VPA would probably approve you to move whenever you wanted."

I raised a brow. "Really?"

"Yes, but you've just decorated this place exactly like you want it. Why trade down?"

I gazed around my funky retro kitchen. I *had* put months of time and effort into decorating the cottage, and I loved it. Too, the cottage was twice as big as the beach house, so no way would my things fit in the smaller place. Besides, I loved being close to Maggie, and I could walk to my job.

The rub was that I didn't own the cottage. Maggie did. I was glad to pay her rent. I insisted on it, in fact. But someday, I wanted my own space. Why not turn the sow's ear of a shack into— Well, okay, maybe making it a silk purse palace was stretching the laws of probability, but the beach house could look a lot better.

"You have a point," I admitted, and saw him relax a little. "But, even like it is, I could use the house to stow my board and surfing gear. Besides, I'm itching to tear out all those bushes and vines just to get a better idea of what the house could look like. With vampire strength, I could demo the landscape in the flash of a fang."

He grinned. "Yeah, you could. I'll even help you when I can. But," he said, holding up his hand when I squealed with excitement, "I'm not living there. In fact, I'm thinking of buying Neil's house."

I blinked. "No kidding? When did you see his place?"

"When I picked up the fireworks for the party last week.

For the price he said he's asking, it's in better shape than anything Amanda's shown me."

"Saber, that's great."

"We'll see if it works out," he said around a yawn.

I got up and took his arm. "Come on, let's get you to bed."

"I need to ask you about one more thing."

"Ask me," I said, leading him through the kitchen door, "while we walk."

"Do you know where Triton is right now?"

"No. I've tried to talk to him telepathically, but he's as mysterious as Pandora. He's in hiding from some big, bad evil, but I never get a sense of where he's holed up."

"Have he or Pandora given you anything solid about what's going on? Anything other than that vague message about betrayal and treachery?"

"No, just that there's danger. Why?"

"You've been shot at twice in a week, and you ask why?"

"Oh. There is that."

"I don't suppose you'd wear a Kevlar vest until people stop shooting at you."

"A Kevlar vest over a bra top camisole? That would get me shot by the fashion police."

"Cesca, you need to take this seriously."

"I am, but you know it takes silver directly in the heart or brain to kill a vampire."

"Or a beheading," he added grimly.

"No worries about that. I see a sword, and I'm gone so fast, I'm a mere memory."

"That's exactly what I'm afraid of."

*   *   *

I cleaned the kitchen, then looked over the rest of the pages Saber had printed for me. I didn't understand 90 percent of it, but that was okay. I kept going back to the list of Triton's companies and the places he'd lived. The list started with Cuba and the Florida Keys, then showed him in New Orleans and several coastal cities in Texas, including Galveston. He surfaced in south Florida again for a while, even in St. Augustine in the 1930s. After that, he shifted to cities all along the West Coast.

The man knew how to diversify, too. At one time he'd owned interests in shipping, assaying, even timber and land companies. But his main businesses seemed to have been antiques of one kind or another.

And now he was in hiding. Saber wondered why and from what, and so did I. I sure wished somebody would give me a clue sooner rather than later.

I crawled into bed earlier than usual and slept until four when the phone rang.

"'Lo," I muttered into the cordless unit.

"I woke you, huh?" Saber said, chuckling.

"Mmmm. What's up?"

"Two things. First, I heard from Detective Balch."

"Oh, yeah?" Balch worked for the St. Augustine Police Department and had been in on the French Bride case. "Dare I hope they caught Gorman?"

"They did, though Balch said they can't charge him with anything but destruction of property unless a little bird wants to come forward. Then they can hold him for attempted murder."

"He'd still get out on bail, right?"

"Depends on his lawyer and the judge."

"Then pressing charges is more trouble than it's worth. What's the other thing?"

"I just toured Neil's house. Cesca, this is the one."

"You're sure?" I asked, coming fully alert. "You know what they say about friends buying things from friends."

"I know, but Maggie helped him update the place, so it's good. Oh, and Maggie was there, so I mentioned Jo-Jo's gig tonight. In case she wanted to twist Neil's arm again."

"And?"

"She said they're leaving early tomorrow for two weeks in Savannah. Did you know that?"

Head smack. I'd forgotten all about their trip.

"I knew, I just lost track of time. Are you coming back this afternoon?"

"No. Now that the house looks like a deal, I need to get things rolling to sell my place. Oh, and Neil gave me a key so I can show you the house while they're gone." He paused. "You're bringing Jo-Jo down to Daytona tonight, right?"

"Unless he's decided to fly."

"Either way, put out the mental call for Pandora to cover your back. I'll meet you at the club at ten."

As soon as I ended the call with Saber, I phoned Maggie. Neil answered, and except when the waves were really bitchin', I'd never heard him so psyched.

"Hey, Fresca. I sold my house to Deke today."

"I know. Congratulations. What time are you and Maggie leaving tomorrow?"

"I'll let her tell you."

"Cesca, what's up?" Maggie asked.

"Saber reminded me about your Savannah trip. Can I come over in"—I glanced at the alarm clock I'd bought for Saber's sake—"half an hour? You can show me what needs taking care of while you're gone."

"You're on, and plan to stay for sweet tea."

I showered, dressed, and tossed off my afternoon Starbloods, then spent an hour with Maggie. She had a list of instructions for watering plants both inside and out but said she'd set the thermostat, alarm, and timer for the lights before she left. She'd also put a hold on the newspapers and mail, but had a back-order on cabinet hardware that might be delivered while she was gone. I'd check the front porch for packages daily.

Maggie also told me the neighbors were agog because the Listers had gone on a cruise. Selma had dragged Hugh out of the house, him cursing, her blessing.

The subject switched to wedding plans over my sweet tea and her iced coffee. Neil wandered in to hint they were going to dinner to celebrate selling his house.

I ironed my outfit for the evening at Hot Blooded and generally puttered until it was time to dress. My navy blue Capris, taupe bra top, and taupe cotton jacket were perfect—nice, but not too dressy. No way was I wearing the killer heels tonight, not if I might be going toe-to-toe with Laurel. A ponytail was a touch too sporty for the evening, so I tamed my hair as best I could with the flatiron and left it loose.

Pandora nearly scared me out of my sandals when she *rrryyow*ed from the hood of my truck.

"Geez, Pandora, wear a bell or something."

She gave me a feline smirk. *I must go with you.*

"Are you expecting trouble at the club?"

I must be nearby to stand watch.

"And that's all you're saying, huh?" I opened the driver's-side door. "Fine, get in, but please don't scare Jo-Jo again."

No, another time would be a bore.

By nine o'clock, we were headed to Daytona in my SSR, Pandora so quiet on the back floorboard, I don't think Jo-Jo knew she was in the truck. Then again, Jo-Jo was such a ball of nerves, I'm not sure he knew his name.

"What if Wednesday was a fluke?" he asked for the fifth time in ten miles.

"It wasn't a fluke," I assured him yet again. "You've had the talent all along. You just needed to update your material and gain confidence."

"But this is all happening so fast. Getting an agent, having gigs in Las Vegas and L.A. What if it all craters because I haven't suffered for my art long enough?"

"Jo-Jo, you've waited decades to get back into show biz."

He grinned. "You're right. That's long enough."

Good thing Jo-Jo calmed down after that. I wasn't nervous for him, but I was a ball of dread about seeing Laurel. I put out the call to every deity I could think of that she'd still be banned from Hot Blooded.

The parking lot was jammed—a good sign, I hoped—but I found a spot near the Dumpster. I also saw Saber get out of his SUV, and breathed a sigh of relief that he'd beat us here. Pandora hopped out and scuttled away, presumably to patrol.

Donita, dressed in dark brown slacks and shimmery salmon-colored blouse, met us just outside the club's back entrance.

"Thank you for doing a show for us, Jo-Jo," she said when I introduced them. "I've spoken with your agent, and seated him at a ringside table. Your drinks are on the house tonight, of course," she said to Saber and me.

Donita smiled and said all the right words, but she was strung as tight as a garrote. As soon as we crossed into the shadowed back hall of the club, I knew why. Laurel was back. Out of sight, but ranting so loudly, the whole club could probably hear her.

"This is a vampire bar, Lord Ike," she railed from a room somewhere above us. "Mortals should walk the edge of their worst nightmares and darkest fantasies here, not be entertained by a comic. That twit of a manager is turning Hot Blooded into a club just like any other in Daytona."

A masculine voice answered her, speaking too quietly for me to catch the words, but I heard the clacking beads of human bone that Laurel wore in her cornrows.

I wrinkled my nose at the clacking and at the odor of oranges permeating the hall.

"Where is Laurel?" I whispered to Donita.

She sighed and ran a hand through her curls. "In Ike's office. His door faces the stairs. She went up just as I went out to meet you."

I looked up the partly open staircase. Yes, the smell was a little stronger there.

"A thousand pardons," Laurel screeched, "but I must speak. Having a comic perform here is bad enough, but he brings that pitiful excuse of a vampire bitch Francesca with him. She will infiltrate your territory, Lord Ike. She will take your nest for her own. Surely you must see that."

Again, we heard Ike's voice, indistinct but rumbling. It didn't sound like his happy voice, if he had one. Tempted as I was to turn up the vamp hearing and listen in, I didn't. Not out of respect but because Saber distracted me.

"When did Ike let her out of solitary?" he asked Donita.

"Thursday." Donita shrugged apologetically and turned to Jo-Jo. "I'm sorry for this. Let me take you to your dressing room and make you comfortable."

But Jo-Jo didn't move. His facial muscles had drawn tight, making his thin face look almost skeletal.

"Jo-Jo," I said, lightly touching his arm.

He startled.

"What's up, Jo-Jo?" Saber asked, his cop face sliding into place. "You look like you recognize Laurel's voice."

"I do. She sounds like my ex-girlfriend. On steroids. I think I just got nervous again."

Donita smiled. "Come on. The dressing room isn't lavish, but it's quiet. And really, everyone but Laurel is excited you're here."

That stretched the truth like a whale in a bikini.

Once Jo-Jo was settled, Donita showed us through an unmarked door. I didn't recall seeing it during the raid, but the door led to the club proper and wasn't far from the front row of tables where Vince and Jessica Atlas sat.

I introduced Jessica Atlas to Saber, then Vince asked Donita a question that allowed Saber and me to talk.

We kept our voices extra low because, in spite of the blaring music, vampires have bat ears.

"Jo-Jo's reaction to hearing Laurel's voice was more than he let on, wasn't it?" I said.

Saber nodded. "He's a sucky liar."

"Do you think it's important?"

"I don't know, but remember those GPS tracker records I ordered on Laurel? They prove she's been in Atlanta at least once a month since mid-April."

"Did Jo-Jo actually meet her at Vlad's, do you think? Or did he overhear her talking?"

"I suppose he could have recognized her voice alone. God knows, she isn't quiet."

"What do we do now?"

"Keep an eye on the vamps in here until we can have a discussion with Jo-Jo."

"Gotcha. By the way, I smell that funny citrus odor again. It was stronger in the back hall than it is in here."

Our drinks arrived, served by Suzy, the vamp who'd worn the cheerleader outfit when we were here last. Tonight, in jeans and a plain T-shirt, she looked like she wanted to say something, but the music faded, and a spotlight lit a wooden stage skirted with bloodred fabric.

Saber and I exchanged a loaded glance when Ike himself literally and slowly flew over the crowd to land on the stage. He bowed to the shocked audience and stepped up to the standing microphone.

"Good evening, ladies and gentlemen," he said, his inflection part Alfred Hitchcock, part Vincent Price. "Welcome to Hot Blooded, where you may walk the edge of danger and delight. Tonight we present Jo-Jo the Jester."

The two didn't shake hands when Jo-Jo trotted up the stage steps, but that wasn't unusual. Vamps didn't observe that bit of human tradition. No, what surprised me was the long, measuring look Jo-Jo gave Ike.

Then Jo-Jo turned to the mike and launched into his routine. He used the same material he had for open-mike night, but expanded it to poke more fun at vampire life. He had the crowd in his pocket from the beginning, and they never wavered, even when he told a clunker joke. Vince jotted notes on every audience reaction. To coach Jo-Jo later?

Surprisingly, most of the vampires seemed to enjoy Jo-Jo's show. Tower actually cracked a smile at the denture cream line, and Suzy and Coach laughed along with the humans when Jo-Jo told a vampire football joke.

Ike and Laurel stood near the long bar, yet apart from each other. Laurel exuded such barely controlled anger, the bone beads in her hair vibrated. Ike appeared to ignore her, and his expression remained impassive. Until, that is, Jo-Jo clowned about hanging out in St. Augustine with Princess Ci, and calling me all the silly royal names he'd annoyed me with since we'd met. Ike was most definitely not amused then, but neither was I. At least Jo-Jo didn't mention our flight lessons.

When Jo-Jo went into his final juggling bit, the crowd went wild with whistles and applause. Judging by Vince's grin, the act was a hit again.

Jo-Jo worked his way to our table, stopping to schmooze here and there. Ike, on the other hand, made a beeline for me.

"Princess Vampire, a few words, if you please?"

I didn't please. Ike's energy made my skin crawl and sting as if being bitten by an army of fire ants.

Still, I was civil. "Certainly, Ike. Saber, you want to stretch your legs with us?"

Ike led us into the back hall through the door we'd used earlier, and Laurel slammed in right behind us.

"You." She charged at me, fangs out, bone beads clacking in her cornrows like a Halloween skeleton in a high wind. "I will kill you for bringing mockery upon Lord Ike."

My heart had lodged in my throat, but I stood still and siphoned just a touch of her energy. Well, that and fanned my hand between us.

"Geez, Laurel, back off. You smell like lemon Pledge."

That surprised her, and she retreated a scant inch. Enough to see remnant silver burns on her wrists, and sense them on her ankles. I sucked off a tad more energy for good measure.

"Now," I said mildly, "what is your problem?"

"She speaks," Ike bit out, "of Jo-Jo mocking the vampire way of life. It is not a matter for humor."

I kept my eyes on Laurel, watching, waiting for her next move as I answered. "News flash, guys. In America, everything is fodder for humor."

"Mortals should fear us," Laurel hissed in my face. "We are superior in every way."

"You know, that superior race attitude didn't work out real well for Hitler. Besides, you might want to remember that Saber's standing right there."

"Bitch," Laurel shrieked.

She raised a hand to slap me, but I saw it and moved faster.

I blocked her arm, swept her legs out from under her, and put her on her back on the tile floor in under two seconds.

The moment she was down, Saber was there, pressing the barrel of his semiautomatic into Laurel's forehead, trembling with the effort of holding his fire.

FIFTEEN

~ ~

I'd seen Saber in full cop mode, but this was slayer mode.

"Don't. Even. Twitch," he said, low and deadly. When Laurel froze, Saber slanted a hard look at Ike. "Do you control her, or do I exterminate her here and now?"

Ike divided his black gaze between Saber and me, his thin lips clamped into a white line. With an audible hiss of breath, he finally spoke to Laurel.

"Go to my office and wait," he commanded.

Saber hesitated, then eased back, but kept his weapon steady on her heart until Laurel rose and streaked down the hall and up the stairs. Even then, he didn't relax. He stood guard, weapon trained on the partially open stairwell.

"I will not forget this display of force in my territory," Ike growled.

"I'm not forgetting it either," Saber snapped. "One more violation, and you cross Laurel off your roster of nestmates."

"Laurel may have an unruly temper, but she is correct in her suspicions. The Princess Vampire seeks to take over my nest."

I unclenched my fists and shook my head at him. "Ike, Ike, Ike. Let me make this perfectly clear. I wouldn't take your nest or your territory if you handed it to me on a platinum platter."

"And yet the comic conveys a different message when he calls you those names. Royalness, Highness, Magnificence."

"Weren't you paying attention out there? He didn't just call me those names, he created jokes out of them. He's mocking his own past as a court jester."

Ike narrowed his eyes as if weighing the truth of what I said. "He did not seek to plant the idea that my vampires should swear loyalty to you?"

"Hardly. That was part of the act, not a plot."

"Still, I will not allow him to perform at Hot Blooded again."

"*Allow* him?" I laughed. "Ike, Jo-Jo's booked in Vegas. You won't be able to *afford* him again. Now, are we done?"

The connecting door to the club opened then, and Jo-Jo stuck his head in.

"Oh, hey, am I interrupting?"

Ike pursed his lips, but waved Jo-Jo in.

"Vince and his wife are leaving," Jo-Jo said, eyeing Saber as he holstered his weapon. "Are you ready to go, PC, or do you want to stay awhile?"

"PC?" Ike echoed. "Does that not mean politically correct?"

"Well, yeah, but it's also short for Princess Ci."

I rolled my eyes. "Give it a rest, Jo-Jo."

"Why?" he asked, looking genuinely confused.

"Never mind," I said as the club door opened again.

This time Donita slipped into the hall. She blinked to see us standing there but recovered quickly when Ike held out his hand to her.

"Do you know where Laurel is?" Donita asked him.

"She is in my office."

"Oh. Can you send her down? I need you to sign Jo-Jo's check, and, uh—"

"It would be better if she were not present?"

"Yes. I'm sorry."

"It is no matter."

Ike turned his head toward the stairs, and I knew he sent Laurel the mind message to go to the bar by the front staircase. Scary how I read not only his intention but clearly saw the images he projected without even trying. I so did not want to be in Ike's head.

In a moment, we all heard Laurel's footsteps above us, a stomping, petulant child.

Donita kissed Ike's cheek. "Thanks. I've already written the check and recorded it. You just need to sign it."

Ike inclined his head. "Jo-Jo, would you care to accompany me to collect your fee?"

I didn't like Ike's tone, but Jo-Jo nodded. "Lead on."

When Ike and Jo-Jo reached the top of the stairs, Donita leaned in close to us.

"Mr. Saber," she said softly, "could I talk with you for a moment outside? I need to be sure that we're private."

Saber arched a brow at me.

"Go on. I'll see if Jo-Jo left anything in the dressing room."

I slipped into what looked like a break room for the employees. A few chairs and a worn couch crowded the space, but it seemed clean. A bathroom was to the right, so I peered in there. Jo-Jo didn't seem to have left anything, but I heard voices through an air vent. From the cadence, one of the voices was Ike's.

I did what any snoop would do. I turned on my vamp hearing and eavesdropped.

". . . I will kill you," Ike said. "Do you understand?"

"I'm poking fun at my life as a vampire, not yours. Why should you care?" Jo-Jo countered. "Besides, I know who the real power is behind you, Ike. If you don't want to find yourself permanently replaced, back off."

"You dare to threaten me?" Ike roared.

"I dare. I know what your silent partner is like, and I know who's been kissing up to him. You'd do well to take care of that nice Donita and leave me, the Princess Francesca, and all those she cares for alone." Footsteps tracked overhead and a door opened. "Watch your back, Ike."

I got a flash of Ike's fear in my head, and jerked back from the vent to see my own astonished expression reflected in the medicine cabinet mirror.

Someone else was controlling Ike, and Jo-Jo knew who it was? I couldn't wait to wring every last detail from him.

I scurried back to the hall and stood at the bottom of the staircase just as Jo-Jo descended. He looked as serious as he had brandishing my fake sword a few nights ago.

"I'm ready to split when you are."

We found Donita and Saber coming from the parking lot as we went out. Donita thanked Jo-Jo again and wished him the best. Saber reminded me he'd pick me up Sunday to see Neil's house and gave me a chaste kiss good night. Darn it on the chaste part.

Then again, Pandora was waiting to hop into the back floorboard, and I was itching to pump Jo-Jo for information. Saber would just distract me.

I let Jo-Jo chatter about the act, how pleased Vince was, and how Vince had arranged for them to fly to L.A. by charter jet tomorrow night.

"Just think. Me, in the jet set. Of course, I could fly out there myself, but it would take a couple of nights. And it's too far to take luggage or my laptop."

I did a double take. "Wait. You could fly all the way to California? Like the kind of flying you're teaching me?"

"Yeah, but, boy, would my arms be tired."

"That joke sucks," I said, but felt my lips twitch.

"Hey, you walked right into it." The highway lights illuminated his grin. "By the way, I'm not that tired. You want one last flying lesson? We could practice in your cottage so nobody can take potshots at us."

I agreed because, if nothing else, I hadn't given up the fantasy of levitating with Saber during sex.

However, that thought didn't deter me from quizzing him.

"So, did you recognize Laurel tonight?"

"Laurel?"

"The cornrow queen. Have you seen her before?"

"No, Highness."

"Then you've heard her voice, and you recognized it, right? You might as well tell me. I heard you in Ike's office."

"Heard what, Your Royal Beauteousness?"

"Can the crap. Who's the power behind Ike, and where have you seen—or heard—Laurel before tonight?"

Jo-Jo squirmed in the passenger seat. "Princess, I don't think it's safe for you to know."

"If you tell me, you'll have to kill me?"

"Never, but someone else may."

"Jo-Jo, don't make me stop this car. Spill."

He heaved a sigh and bit his lip. "All right, but please don't let Ike know you know."

"Duh, like I would."

"All right. Laurel has been in Vlad's court. I didn't see her clearly, so, truly, I did not recognize her."

I believed him, if for no other reason than that he'd lapsed into his odd mixture of formal and casual speech. "Go on."

"I did not overhear the entire exchange, but Vlad seemed to be giving Laurel messages or instructions."

"About what? How to run the club? The nest?"

"There was something about tributes. Payments like we who live with Vlad make. Perhaps Ike gives some of the club earnings to Vlad."

"Geez, if Vlad demands tributes, he really does run his nest like a fiefdom."

"Yes, and Ike's nest would be an extension of Vlad's."

I thought a moment. "Jo-Jo, was it just Laurel and Vlad you overheard? Were they the only two in the meeting?"

"Well, no. Marco was there."

"Did he do any of the talking?"

"Other than agreeing with Vlad, I don't think so. But the guy is a complete sycophant, so that wasn't unusual."

I drummed my fingers on the steering wheel. "Okay, let me

get this straight. You think Vlad is the power behind Ike, and that Laurel is the go-between?"

"Yes. Ike didn't deny that there is a power behind him."

"Did he look shocked that you knew?"

Jo-Jo nodded slowly. "Yes, he was shocked. And angry."

"And probably embarrassed. What about that threat you made? That Ike could be permanently replaced, and he should watch his back?"

"It is only the truth. If Vlad is indeed backing Ike, Vlad could just as easily withdraw his backing."

"And give it to someone else? Like Laurel or Marco?"

Jo-Jo shrugged. "He might support a female as a nest leader, but he is old-fashioned."

"You mean he's a chauvinist."

"That would be Vlad."

"Okay, so let's think. Some vamps live in nests, but others live independently. Is that right?"

"Right."

"And maybe all vamps who live in nests contribute to the household, as it were. Ike's vamps probably do the same thing, come to think of it."

"I'm with you."

"Then what difference does it make if Vlad *is* the power behind Ike?"

Jo-Jo shrugged. "I don't suppose it makes any real difference. If Ike is paying fair tribute, and stays submissive to Vlad, there's no special reason to get rid of him."

"Hmmm. Then I wonder why Ike is frightened."

Jo-Jo stiffened. "I did not tell you he was fearful, my lady."

"You didn't have to."

*   *   *

Pandora hopped out of my truck at home without Jo-Jo ever knowing she had hitched with us. I wondered if any of what Jo-Jo and I had discussed about Ike and Vlad meant squat to Pandora. Or related to Triton's being in hiding. I couldn't see how either vamp would be a big, bad threat to the shape-shifters, but if Pandora had gleaned useful information, more power to her.

The indoor flying lesson with Jo-Jo was short and, well, short. Ten-foot ceilings aren't exactly the friendly skies. I levitated perhaps six inches off the floor, and jump-hovered an entire foot on four tries out of ten. I was still a bust in the walk-fly event, but even Olympians have their specialties. Jo-Jo gave me the rah-rah talk and urged me to keep practicing.

"You must own your power, Princess," he told me. "You can do this and more."

"Like what?" I huffed a breath of frustration. "What the hell else am I supposed to be able to do?"

"You don't know, Highness?"

I sighed. "The crazy killer we caught in March ranted about me coming into my powers when I was no longer, um—"

"A virgin?"

I blushed, but I wanted answers. Answers that maybe only another vampire could give me.

"Right, but here's the thing. I didn't wake up and, bam, I was the proud owner of superpowers. I mean, is there a checklist of powers I should know about?"

"Honestly, Highness, I've heard those of the House of Normand could kill with a mere thought."

I snorted. "I never saw Normand do it. You don't know *any*thing about instant powers?"

Jo-Jo frowned. "Flying is standard. Enthralling and unenthralling. Strength and speed, of course." He shrugged. "The virgin myth aside, most of the powers just take an effort of will. You want them to awaken, and they do."

Ah, no wonder. When it came to vamp power, I spent enough time in denial to make it a second home.

"Did I answer your question, Princess?"

"More than you know. Do you want a ride to the regional airport tomorrow night?"

"Vince and Jessica insisted on driving me." Now Jo-Jo blushed lightly. "Princess, I know I've been kind of a pain, but thank you for everything. I owe you."

"Just become rich and famous and rub it in Jemina's face."

I was brushing my teeth at four on Sunday afternoon, when Saber strolled into the bathroom jingling a set of keys.

"You ready to go see Neil's house?"

"Your house," I corrected, giving him a toothpaste grin. "Did you call an agent in Daytona yesterday?"

"Yep. She came over to see the place, and we settled on an asking price."

"Did she mention staging?"

"She did, and I told her my lady friend is an HGTV freak who would help with that. You *will* help, right?"

"I'll do anything but clean toilets and windows."

He kissed my mint-fresh mouth, and twenty-five minutes later we pulled into the driveway of a light yellow cinder block one-story house landscaped mainly with tall palms, azaleas, and sea grapes. The wood trim was cocoa, and a large, slightly bowed front window marked the house as circa 1940s or '50s. Inside, though, the floor plan was wonderfully open, and I saw Maggie's touch everywhere. In the living-dining room, contemporary-style crown molding and thick baseboards in white set off warm mocha walls. The kitchen boasted granite countertops and stainless steel appliances, and it looked onto a deck with a hot tub and a beautiful fenced backyard.

The laundry room was in the two-car garage, but Saber didn't mind that. A fair-sized full bath was down the hall, plus two good-sized secondary bedrooms and a large master suite. The bathrooms were fully renovated, too, with warm slate tile.

I guess I'd been quieter than I thought throughout the tour, because Saber caught me in his arms before we left the master suite.

"Well, what do you think?"

I grinned and kissed him. "You're right, it's perfect."

"You're not ticked that I don't want to live in your beach house?"

"The way you feel about spiders and snakes and vines? Honey, you couldn't *handle* the beach house."

He was so jovial on the way back to my place, I almost hated to bring up business. But, hey, Triton was still in hiding, a sniper was still on the loose, and something was rotten in Ike's nest.

"Saber, what did Donita talk with you about last night?"

"Just about her concern that Laurel is out of control."

"Not breaking news, but she may be more out of control than Donita knows."

"Give."

I filled him in about eavesdropping and told him Jo-Jo's theory that Vlad was backing Ike.

Saber smacked the steering wheel with his hand. "Damn it. If that's true, I need to get a task force together to clean house."

"Why?"

"Nests are limited in size specifically so no one vamp or group of vamps can set up a major power base. It's like the difference between a small business and a conglomerate. The more power one vamp wields, the more lawless he can be."

"So keeping the nests small is a sort of damage control?"

"Exactly. How accurate do you think Jo-Jo's theory is?"

I shrugged. "It made sense. Maybe you should talk to him before he leaves tonight."

"Are you taking him to the airport?"

"He's riding with Vince, but you could go to the motel or call him."

He lifted a brow. "Do you work tonight?"

"Yep, at eight."

"Then I'm sticking with you."

Sunday night seemed even hotter and muggier than it had been during the day, so I wore my lighter emerald Regency gown for work. Kevin Miller was there again, and so were Caro and Leah, carrying part of his equipment.

Saber raised a brow at them and whispered, "When did Kevin pick up the groupies?"

"On Friday's tour. Cute, aren't they?"

"If they keep him from bugging you, they have my vote."

Only ten other tourists were there, and they appeared to know each other well. The highlight was Gorman's absence.

Turned out that the ten people who knew each other were

fans of the *Ghost Hunters* television series. They not only asked Kevin what he was doing, they documented their personal experiences and helped ask questions to elicit spirit answers via electronic voice phenomenon—EVP. Kevin just might've been a bigger attraction than the ghosts, and he promised to post the night's findings on his MySpace page.

Saber fell back partway through the tour to make a call. I presumed it was to Jo-Jo, especially when I heard Saber say, "Break a leg."

Most of the group left at nine forty-five. Kevin, Leah, and Caro stayed, Kevin insisting that I see the video he'd taken on Friday night.

A shiver shot up my spine as Kevin ran the video showing a shadow rise from the ground behind me on the screen. In the same frame, a dog I didn't remember seeing in the plaza raised its hackles and growled until the owner jerked on its leash.

"You didn't sense that presence?" Kevin asked me.

"No, but it gives me goose bumps now."

Saber frowned at Kevin. "Is it harmful?"

"I don't know. I've sent it to one of my professors for her opinion, but she may not be back from vacation yet." He fast-forwarded to another scene, this one taken on the bay front showing the white mist floating over my head.

"I still think," Leah said, "that's a good force of some kind. Maybe not an angel, but good."

Kevin closed the DVD player and stuffed it in one of the bags he carried. "Ms. Marinelli, I know you tell the tour groups that the ghosts here aren't malevolent."

"I say that because it's true. Fay is as cranky as all get out, and our ghosts might pull pranks, but none of them are out-right hostile."

"But you are a sensitive. Are there places that bother you to go into? Like the old drugstore?"

I shuddered. "The Spanish hospital is difficult."

"So you see or sense the spirits there, and they bother you, for whatever reason."

"That's fair to say. Why?"

"It's just odd that you have some recognition of the other ghosts in town but don't feel either of these energies that are strong enough to be showing up on video."

"Odd? Kevin, I think it's downright weird and totally creepy that I can't sense these things, but I can't explain it."

"Well, I asked both of those energies questions, and my EMF meter beeped at least one of the times I asked. Maybe I'll get some EVPs."

"Better get started on that before the"—Saber paused—"spirits erase anything.

"Oh, right." Kevin turned abruptly and herded Caro and Leah down St. George Street.

"Nice job getting rid of them," I said. "Any reason why?"

He nodded at the tour substation, and Pandora emerged from the shadows.

"Trouble?" Saber asked her.

Go home, I heard in my head.

Pandora didn't say more, but she didn't have to. Not after she leaped to the cottage roof in full panther size to keep watch.

I changed into jeans, a scoop neck T-shirt, and tennis shoes, and then occupied myself by folding laundry, even though my hands shook. We didn't question why Pandora wanted us at the cottage, but waiting for the unknown was maddening.

Saber watched the news, took out the trash and recycling for me, and paced to manage his stress.

At one forty Monday morning his cell phone rang. He put it on speaker so I could hear firsthand.

"Saber, Captain Jackson. Where are you?"

"St. Augustine."

"Get to the vampire club. I've got a mess on my hands."

"Human victims?"

"No. Ike's dead. Damn near decapitated, and that Laurel bitch is ballistic."

SIXTEEN

Police cars and crime scene tape cordoned off Hot Blooded and most of the block. Pandora, who was waiting on my patio for us after the call, paced in the backseat of Saber's SUV as he looked for a parking space. He found one a block from the club, grabbed some gear from the cargo area, and stuffed the items in his windbreaker pockets.

We wove our way through the crowd of gawkers drawn by the flashing cruiser lights. Jackson must've given orders to let us both in, because the officer at the police checkpoint ticked my name off the list without so much as a glance.

I will scout, Pandora said in my head and trotted off before I had a chance to respond.

We found Jackson standing behind an older model white car, a grayish color to his black skin.

"Saber," he said, then nodded at me. "The body's in the car, but you may not want Francesca to see it."

"No problem," I told him, holding up my hands, and backing up a step as both men donned rubber gloves.

I thought I saw Pandora skulking under the front bumper of the car but didn't worry she'd get in the way.

Thankfully, Ike's body hadn't released the kinds of fluids in death that a human's would have. The smell of his relatively small amount of blood loss made me queasy enough. Overhearing Jackson murmur to Saber about Ike's position in the car, and his head hanging by a thread of tissue, gave me all too vivid a picture of the crime scene.

Jackson called for an evidence technician, and a short woman in a jumpsuit hurried forward. I heard the snap of a paper bag, something dropped inside it, and then more murmuring before the men and evidence tech headed for me. The woman carried the grocery-sized bag and stood a little apart.

"Here's the rundown," Jackson said. "The officer who was first on scene was on routine patrol when he heard screams from the parking lot. He found Donita Ward, aged thirty-five, on the ground just outside her passenger door, in hysterics."

"Where is she now?" Saber asked, stripping off the gloves.

Jackson tipped his head toward an EVAC unit. The back ambulance door yawned open, and I made out the figure sitting just inside huddled in a blanket. She was so terribly still.

"Is she all right?" I asked Jackson.

"She's in shock. The first officer got a preliminary statement, but it's pretty garbled. You can talk to her," he added, anticipating my next question, "but Saber suggested we have you look at something first."

Saber handed me a mask and hairnet. "I want you to look

at what appears to be the murder weapon," he said. "You might want to wear a mask to cut the odor a little."

I didn't think a mask would help—not being as gaggy as I am about blood—but the hairnet would cut the chance of me contaminating the evidence.

"Okay, I'm ready," I said through the mask.

Jackson motioned for the woman and pulled a humongous flashlight from a holder on his belt. The tech opened the bag, Jackson shined the light inside, and Saber put a steadying hand on my back.

I looked down at the long, wickedly curved knife. The handle was intricately carved and had the patina of antique ivory. Two bands of metal crisscrossed the ivory. My stomach heaved from the smell of blood smeared on the blade near the hilt, but my nose twitched from two other odors.

"The blade is silver," I said, meeting Saber's gaze over my mask. "It makes my nose itch."

"Like an allergy?" Jackson asked.

"Yes. I don't think there's a super-high silver content, but it's high enough. The bands may be silver, too."

"Don't take this wrong, but Saber says the smell of blood bothers you. You sure that's not causing the itch?"

"Blood scent makes me dizzy and nauseous. The itchy nose is definitely a reaction to silver."

"Do you recognize the weapon? The carvings look familiar?"

"It looks like a half-size scimitar, but I'm no expert on weapons. Neil might be able to give an opinion."

"Who is Neil?"

"An anthropologist for the state of Florida. He lives in St. Augustine."

Jackson nodded. "Once we see about lifting prints, we'll have a number of experts look at it. Anything else you noticed?"

I hesitated because I really didn't want to smell the bag again. But Ike *had* been murdered, and I had the bad feeling Donita was going to be a suspect.

I leaned closer to the bag and sniffed. Yep, it wasn't my imagination. I smelled the faintest trace of citrus.

I stood back, away from the bag, and ripped off the mask. "Citrus, Saber. There's a citrus smell coming from the knife, and it's the same scent I smelled in the club and on Laurel."

"Laurel, the psycho vamp?" Jackson asked.

"The same," Saber said, his lips set in a grim line. "I should've executed her Saturday night."

"You couldn't kill her in cold blood. Besides, the cleaning solution scent should've faded by now."

"Would you two fill me in here? What happened Saturday?"

Saber shifted away from the evidence tech, and Jackson dismissed her with a nod.

"Cesca is picking up an odor that's out of place. She smelled it last week when we served the warrant, and again Saturday when we were here to see a comic perform. Specifically, she smelled the scent on Laurel."

"Citrus? That's common enough."

"I know," I said, nodding. "It's in everything from perfume to bathroom cleaners. The morning you served the warrant, I thought it came from an air freshener system."

"Did you ask if Ike had one?"

I looked at Saber, then shrugged. "With all that's happened, we forgot."

"Okay, so, go on. Why does this matter?"

"We're not sure it does," Saber admitted. "Look, if a normal vampire smells at all, it's of only two things. Blood and sex. They don't bother to cover up either one."

"Which means," I added, "that unless someone is making artificial blood in a Florida orange flavor, the citrus smell is out of place."

Jackson almost cracked a grin. "You say Laurel had this scent on her on Saturday?"

"Yes, but Ike had been making her clean the residence. I figured the smell was from a cleaning product on her skin. But why would it be on this knife?"

"Could it be in the blood instead?"

I frowned and thought about that. When Normand had served dinner, had I ever smelled what the servant du jour had eaten the day before? Probably not, since I'd buried my nose in the servants' skin as I drank. That way I blocked the smell of blood, which blocked a smidge of the taste.

"I doubt the scent is coming from Ike's blood. Even if he ate food, I don't see Ike being the orange juice type."

Jackson shrugged. "It was worth asking. Now, here's another question. If you're right about the silver content, does that narrow the field to a human killer?"

Again, Saber and I exchanged a glance.

"Ten days ago, I would have answered an unqualified yes," Saber said. "Since then, we've learned about one vampire who appears to be immune to silver."

"I take it that vamp isn't in the club?"

"He's in Atlanta. Or we're reasonably certain he's still there, but I'll have to check it out."

"In the meantime, we need to question the vamps inside." Jackson ran a hand over his military short hair and eyed me. "How about taking a whiff of the vampires while we question them? You can smell for blood and this citrus odor."

"Not the most appealing offer I've had all night, but I'll do it on one condition."

"Which is?"

I looked at Saber. "Will you shoot first and ask questions later if Laurel gets in my face again?"

"Hell, I won't even ask questions later, but I have a condition, too. If you pull Laurel's aura, you drain her into submission. Clear?"

"Crystal."

"Good." He took my elbow. "Let's go see what we can get out of Donita before we go in."

Saber and Jackson let me approach first, and I spotted Pandora under the ambulance.

"Donita, it's Cesca," I said as I sat beside her. "Can you hear me?"

A full minute passed before she blinked and slowly turned her head to look at me.

"Donita, what happened?"

"I'm going on a trip today," she said, her voice soft and scratchy. "To meet my girlfriends. We do this every year."

I nodded. "Go on."

"I-I went to his office. To tell him I was leaving. He wasn't there."

Her hands clenched into trembling fists, and I laid my hand over hers. I meant the touch to be only comforting, not to get sucked into an instant mind connection, not to see Ike through her eyes, not to feel her pain. When the vision rose like a rogue wave, I could do nothing but ride it to the end.

"I unlocked my car. I got in. I saw him."

Through her mind's eye and emotions, I saw him, too. Propped with his back to the passenger door. Blood spatter on the windshield and dashboard, and a trickle on his white shirt. His head tilted back to expose the obscene wound. Brown eyes open, staring. Surprise, disbelief, then stark terror ripped through me, and I found myself in Donita tumbling out of the car and onto the pavement, keening in horror.

A fierce squeeze of my hand jerked me back to the moment. Donita's nails dug into my skin.

"Francesca," she whispered. "I didn't get to say good-bye."

Tears tracked down her face then, and Saber hunkered down to ease her hands from mine.

"Donita, did you see or hear anything when you came outside? Was anyone near your car?"

"Nothing."

"Do you know who could have done this?"

"Laurel was always angry, always pushing."

"Yes, you told me Saturday you were worried that she was out of control. Did she argue with Ike again?"

"She wanted him to fire me. To stop seeing me."

"And what did Ike say?"

Her lips tightened. "He told her to mind her own business, not his. I was ready to quit just to have some peace."

"Do you think Laurel killed Ike?"

"I don't know. I just don't know. God, I'm so cold."

"Just one more thing. Does the club have some sort of an air freshening system?"

The question jarred Donita. "What does that have to do with someone killing Ike?"

Saber shrugged. "Probably nothing. Just a loose end."

Donita shook her head. "There's nothing but central heat and air conditioning that I know of."

"All right. The paramedics need to take you to the hospital now, but Cesca and I will check on you later."

"Can we call anyone for you?" I asked. "Your girlfriends?"

"No, I'll do it."

She wouldn't call them, though. I was still just connected enough to hear that she didn't care about anything at the moment. Who could blame her?

Jackson, who'd stood by and listened, motioned to an officer as the paramedics helped Donita onto a gurney. I knew he was putting the man on hospital guard duty, but I didn't object. Sure, it was ludicrous to think Donita could've taken out a vampire, but she'd been his lover, and she'd found the body. That gave her two tickets to suspect city.

We headed for the club's back entrance, Jackson in the lead. I didn't see Pandora, but supposed she was on shape-shifter stealth reconnaissance.

"I doubt we'll get anything useful," Jackson was saying, "but we've seized the computer to check the security feed. I figured you should be here when we questioned the vamps, so my guys took statements from the humans."

"I suppose no one saw a thing," Saber said.

"Not that they'd admit to."

"Have you released them?"

"Yeah, even the waitstaff. We'll have to question them away from the club, because they're too frightened to say a word against a vampire."

When we stepped into the club proper, it was obvious that humans weren't the only ones who seemed frightened into silence.

Tower and Zena, Coach, Suzy, and Ray—the Antonio Banderas look-alike vamp who had been Ike's attorney—sat at a table in the center of the room. Suzy dabbed her eyes with a napkin, and Ray looked grim, but the rest were deadpan and dead still. That is, except when Laurel, dressed like a slutty biker vamp, brushed behind them as she paced. Then I saw the tiniest twitch of an eye or tightening of a mouth. Ike's vamps might not be grieving him, but they didn't look overjoyed that he was forever dead, either.

Charles and Miranda weren't present, but then they had likely gone back to their jobs at Ike's residence after Laurel was released from punishment. I wondered if Jackson had thought to search the lair.

I'd scanned the men Jackson had fanned out around the room when my skin prickled and I knew Laurel had spotted us.

"Fires of hell," she screeched, startling half of Jackson's people into drawing their weapons. "Ike told you two never to come here again."

From twenty feet away, she flowed across the room in a one-second rush, but I was ready. I pulled hard at her aura, her life force, took it into myself and held it. Laurel, though, stopped fast enough to send a whiplash of energy through the air and through me. I held what I'd already taken and pulled again.

"No!" She threw up a hand and backed up a few paces, her mocha skin gleaming with a fine sheen, bone beads in her corn-rows clacking. "You will not humiliate me again, bitch."

"I don't want to humiliate you, Laurel." Which was true, since I'd just as soon see her shipped to the Antarctic. "I don't want you in my face."

"And I do not wish you in this club." Her flat black eyes narrowed. "Why are you here?"

"They're assisting in the investigation," Jackson said.

Laurel flipped a hand. "Arrest Ike's little whore and be done with it."

"Come on, Laurel," Saber said as he strolled toward the table of vamps. "Donita didn't kill your boss."

Laurel spun on Saber, those damn beads clacking again. "And you presume that why? Because she is a weakling human? Fool. She ensnared the affections of Lord Ike by trickery. She could easily have killed him the same way."

"You don't believe that, do you, Tower?" Saber asked.

Jackson and I had taken advantage of Laurel's distraction to approach the table of vamps from the other side, but no one missed Tower jerk in his chair.

"Lady Laurel is the new mistress," the ebony-skinned Tower said carefully.

"*Lady* Laurel?" I blurted.

She moved closer to the vamps she now ruled.

"It is not so exalted a title as yours, Princess Ci," she drawled snidely, "but it is a customary one."

"It's also one more reason to move you to the top of the suspect list," Saber said.

"What do you mean?"

He caught my gaze and jerked his head ever so slightly. *Smell the vamps.* I sensed his message more than heard him, and began a slow pace behind each chair, pausing to sniff, while Saber kept pressure on Laurel.

"How long have you been plotting to kill Ike, Laurel? Since he punished you, or longer than that?"

"You are accusing *me*? Ike's second-in-command? I was sworn to protect him."

"You were also supposed to follow his orders, not question them."

"I advised my lord, as was my duty."

"Come off it, Laurel. You fought with Ike over Donita. You were so jealous, you reeked of it."

I completed my circle around the table, and stood behind Suzy as Laurel drew herself tall.

"You are mistaken. I saw that changing the club would not be in Lord Ike's best interest."

"And, since he wouldn't dump Donita, you decided to run the club without him."

"You plan to arrest me?"

Saber turned to me and arched his brow.

"Suzy." I lightly touched her shoulder.

She startled and let out a small squeal. "Yes?"

"Has Laurel changed her clothes tonight?"

"N-no. She never changes once she's dressed for the night."

I met Saber's gaze. "I don't smell Ike's blood or anything else on any of them. Not citrus, not even sex."

Saber looked puzzled, and Jackson scowled. I could've sworn something furtive crossed Laurel's face, but then she laughed.

"Did you hear, my nestmates? The great vampire princess came here to smell us like a dog."

"Arf, arf," I said. "Now you can thank me."

"Why should I lower myself to do that?"

"Because, unfortunately, I just cleared your spiteful self of murder charges."

Laurel gave me a slow blink. "You dare to speak to me like that?"

I shrugged, and Laurel moved.

Saber shouted even as I sucked her energy like a mega Hoover. This time she didn't block me soon enough. I had her. She faltered, and Saber was on her like lightning, forcing her to the floor, straddling her leather-clad butt. Jackson had drawn his weapon but kept it trained on the unmoving vamps.

"Laurel, vampire of the Daytona Beach nest," Saber said over her thrashing and the crash of beads in her hair. "You're under arrest on suspicion of conspiracy to commit murder. As a duly sworn VPA agent of the United States, I declare you a Rampant, subject to immediate arrest and execution. You have the right to remain silent. You have the right to mediation."

He jerked her arms back and slapped silver-laced handcuffs on her almost faster than I could see. I expected her to scream when the silver touched her skin. She didn't. She hissed and spat, and cursed us all while Saber gave her the executioner version of the Miranda warning, but she didn't seem to react to the touch of silver.

A knot formed deep in my gut.

"Saber, hold on a minute."

He glanced over as I knelt beside him. "What?"

I peered at Laurel's wrists twisting in the handcuffs. They were reddening, but because of her struggle or the silver?

"The cuffs should be burning her."

"They are burning, bitch," Laurel gritted out, "but I will not show weakness before my nest."

A chair scraped on the wood floor behind us. Jackson called out, and Saber whirled with his semiautomatic in hand.

I spun, too, crouched and ready to suck energy again, but Ray held out his hands.

"Please, I mean no harm."

No one eased off. Not Jackson, not his contingent of cops, not Saber.

"If I may speak?" Ray said, arms spread.

I gave him a curt nod.

"You know that I am an attorney, but I also have some modest knowledge of medicine. I created a salve for Laurel's silver burns that also contains anesthetic properties."

"You mean it numbs her skin?" I glanced at Saber. Had Ray made the salve Saber had given me?

"Yes, Princess. The salve creates a barrier to pain, which may be why she is tolerating the handcuffs, but the silver is seeping into her system."

"If that's all you have to say," Jackson growled.

Ray cut him off. "It is not. Saber, could you perhaps allow Laurel to stand?"

Saber grabbed the back of her sleeveless leather vest and hauled her to her feet. I stood, too, moving so I could keep an eye on Ike's former bodyguards, Zena and Tower. If anyone objected to taking Laurel out of here, they were my top choices.

Laurel stood proud, chin up, black eyes holding scorn. "Ray, you will see to my release, of course."

Ray slowly shook his head. "I think it is best that you go peacefully, Laurel. You see, Ike willed his worldly possessions and properties to me. I am now in command."

I wasn't the only one to suck in a shocked breath. Laurel's eyes narrowed, and her mocha skin flushed as if she were burning with the fever of bloodlust.

Which, in that moment, I guess she was.

"I will go free," Laurel snarled. "Then we will see who holds this nest."

"Yeah, yeah," Saber said, keeping a tight hand on her jacket. "Jackson, I take it there's a vamp cell available in lockup?"

Jackson lowered his weapon with only a slight tremble in his hand. "There is. I've got special transport waiting, too. I'll radio them to pull up out front, but you'll have to come down to book her in."

Saber nodded and began marching Laurel toward the front door, grasping the back of her jacket in his left hand, his semiautomatic pointed at her back in the other. Jackson covered Saber, but there was no need. The more steps Laurel took away from them, the more the vamps at the table relaxed.

A cop near the door held it open. Through the opening, I saw the cop car pull up to the curb. Saber propelled Laurel over the threshold to the sidewalk and toward the cruiser, everything under control.

Until two steps later.

A *whoosh* of movement too fast to track, a back breeze through the door, and Laurel and Saber were gone.

SEVENTEEN

The club echoed with my feral cry, terror for Saber crushing every coherent thought save one. If Laurel had hurt him, I would kill her.

I found myself outside, but she was gone. Vanished. Saber sprawled on the sidewalk against the building, pale and still.

I moved in a fog of fear, fell to my knees at his side. I ran my hands over his face, down the buttons of his shirt, across his chest. An inhale, an exhale. Thank the deities, he lived, but how badly was he hurt? When I picked up his left hand, he moaned.

"Saber, how bad is it?"

A very brown hand covered mine and held me still.

"It will be best," Ray said, "if you do not pull on his wrist. I am fairly certain it is broken."

"Oh, Saber, I'm sorry," I whispered, tearing up as I sensed Jackson standing over us.

Ray cradled Saber's lower arm and laid it on his chest, then probed his head and collarbone with gentle fingers.

Saber's eyes snapped open. He gazed blankly at me, then at Ray.

"What the hell?" he ground out, struggling to sit.

Ray restrained him with a touch.

"Saber, be still, please." I said. "You were body slammed into the wall."

"It's just my wrist, and a bump on the head," he said irritably. "Damn it, Laurel got away, didn't she?"

"More like she was whisked away." I patted his thigh, more to comfort me than him. "You couldn't have stopped it."

"A hit like that," Jackson said from behind me, "you're lucky you didn't break your back."

"Be better than the paperwork I'll have to fill out for losing a prisoner."

Ray snorted. "He will live."

I gave him a grateful smile. "I need to get him to the ER."

"I've called for another ambulance," Jackson said.

But Saber insisted on standing, and Ray carefully hoisted Saber to his feet. I tucked myself into his good side, or what I thought was the one less injured. Since he groaned and shuffled sideways a step, I figured his ribs had suffered from meeting the cinder block wall. Did he have internal injuries? Damn, where was that EVAC unit?

Saber gripped my shoulder, then looked at Ray and Jackson. "Any clue who snatched Laurel?"

The cop and the vamp shook their heads.

"Cesca?"

"Other than it had to be a vampire, just one. You smell like an orange."

"I do?" He let go of me to lift his shirt by the buttons and sniff. "Shit. Who the hell is this?"

Saber insisted that Jackson try to get evidence from his shirt. When Ray helped remove the shirt, I'd bitten my lip to keep from crying over the bruises and scrapes on Saber's back and arms.

Jackson had patted my shoulder in comfort—huge points to him for touching me. As soon as the EMTs had loaded Saber into the ambulance, I'd taken off at a dead run for Saber's SUV to meet him at the hospital.

Pandora sat on the hood of Saber's car.

I will stay on the scent while you see to your man.

"The orange scent?" I asked, clicking the unlock button.

Yes, and I will alert Triton to the trouble.

"Well, bring reinforcements, will you? We'll be at Saber's place."

She hopped to the pavement. *Keep wearing the charm. I will find you.*

Three hours later, Saber's arm was in a cast from his hand to the middle of his forearm, the cast in a blue and white sling. We'd filled Saber's prescription at a twenty-four-hour Walgreens. Next stop, his condo, where I'd help him clean up, give him a pain pill, and tuck him into bed.

"Nice place," I said when he told me to turn into the driveway of a building near the Intracoastal. A very nice building. Five stories, balconies on every floor, built in the 1970s or '80s.

"I bought the place a long time ago. Cheap," he muttered as he hit the button of a remote control device.

The security gate slid open, and my tight-lipped-with-pain darling guided me to an under-the-building parking place, pointing out the location of the elevator we passed. With his pain meds in hand, I helped him into the elevator.

"Hit five," he said.

"Oooh, the penthouse floor," I said lightly. "I bet it has a great view."

Saber just grunted, and I held his good hand until I unlocked the door to his condo.

He had a corner unit, and dawn was just creeping through huge plate glass windows on the west and north walls of the living room. I only glanced at the view as I supported Saber down a hall, and I eased him onto his king-size bed.

"Lie still a minute. I'll be right back."

Light from another huge window in the bedroom lit my way to the bathroom. I groped for the light switch and flipped it on. Wow, no wonder Saber wanted Neil's house. The decor was so similar, Maggie might've been at work here. I grabbed a fresh tan washcloth from a brushed nickel towel rack, wet the cloth with warm water from one of the two sinks, and wheeled back to the bedroom.

"Here," I said as I sat next to him on the bed, "let me clean you up before I strip you."

"Now that sounds like a plan." He waggled his brows at me, but halfheartedly.

"Rein in your libido, lover. You need to take a pain pill and sleep."

"No, I need to find out who killed Ike, who grabbed Laurel, and what the hell might happen next."

"And what oranges have to do with our mystery vampire." I dabbed away dirt smudges the ER hadn't cleaned. "Pandora is tracking the scent. Right now, we can't do more."

"I can. I can search the VPA records and try to make more sense of this."

"Those records list some personal info on vamps, don't they? Habits, companions, and whatnot?"

Since I was patting the washcloth on a cut near his lip, he merely nodded.

"Then I'll get on your computer. Root around in the records, and see what I can find."

He caught my hand. "The records aren't in an area of the site you can access."

"Well, um, actually, they are."

"You memorized my codes?"

Since he was giving me his "Lucy, you got some 'splainin' to do" glare—the look that made him seem very Latino and all the hotter—I just shrugged.

He sighed. "Do it, then, and leave the printouts on my desk. I'll get on them tomorrow."

"Nuh-uh. You're going to rest tomorrow. Doctor's orders."

"We'll see." He squeezed my hand. "Did you see Donita in the ER?"

"No. She must've been taken to another hospital. That or she'd already been released."

"Doubtful, but it doesn't matter. We'll catch up with her later."

"Do you think she's in danger?"

"From Laurel?"

"Or the nest."

"Again, doubtful. But we need to question her and the vampires—thoroughly this time."

"We will. Can I ask a question before I get your pill?"

"You want to know if those are blackout drapes? Yes, they are. I got them because of my odd hours, but you'll be fine sleeping in here next to me. In my bed, for a change."

I grinned. "Good to know, since I didn't bring my super sunblock, but I have a different question."

"Fire away."

"What do you know about Ray?"

"He was Ike's friend and attorney, and he joined the nest in April or May. Why?"

"Other than I'm still trying to wrap my head around Ike having a friend, never mind an attorney, why did he help you tonight?"

"To make points? Show he'll be a kinder, gentler head of the nest?"

"Maybe, but I have this feeling it's more than that."

"Did you read him?"

"Not him, just his manner. He's very different from the other vamps."

Saber's gaze narrowed. "How?"

"They seem, well, aimless, I guess is the word. They don't have much personality zing. Except for Suzy. And maybe Charles and Miranda."

Saber shrugged. "Many vamps are simply satisfied to have the protection of a nest."

"I'll have to take your word for it." I bit my lip. "You are going to let me be there when you question them, right?"

"You don't have to work?"

"If I'm on the schedule, I'll take time off."

"You don't have to do that," he said, shrugging out of the sling. "The vamps aren't a threat to me."

"Maybe not, but I might be able to read something from them that will speed up the investigation."

"It's worth a shot."

His eyelids drooped, and I kissed him lightly on the mouth. "While I'm here nursing you, I can start staging your condo for a fast sale."

I gave him his pill, got him stripped to his boxers, and tucked him in. From a chair on the other side of the bed, I kept watch until his breathing evened.

I was still hopped up on adrenaline, too restless to concentrate on the computer, so I burned worry energy by touring the Spartan but updated condo. Cherrywood floors stretched through every room save the tiled bathrooms, and the overall style was modern. A couch and two chairs in the living room took advantage of the view. A coffee table, a side table, and two lamps rounded out the furnishings.

The living room opened to a kitchen dominated by sleek black appliances and the same light brown countertop that Saber had in the bathrooms. A long bar separated the kitchen from the dining room, and there was room for a dining set, but Saber didn't have one.

I found the second, smaller bedroom that Saber used for his office, where tall bookshelves lined one wall. A desk on the opposite wall held Saber's laptop, a printer, and some loose papers.

The condo's paint job seemed fresh, and everything was neat and relatively new, so the staging list I jotted on a pad from Saber's desk was short. A dining set, some art, and a few more accessories, and the condo would be ready to show. Unless Saber's Realtor wanted something else done. I'd check with Saber before I went shopping.

I peeked in on Saber and smiled to find him lightly snoring. With a swift kiss on his forehead, I moved to the next order of business. Researching the VPA records.

Ice clinked in my glass of water as I went back to Saber's office. Good thing I didn't have a mouthful of anything because, as soon as I sat in his desk chair, my breath caught.

Three small picture frames with black trim sat to one side of the desk, partly hidden by the printer. One held a photo of me coming out of the ocean lugging my surfboard. He must've taken the picture during our first official date when we'd taken a picnic to the beach and Saber had insisted on watching me surf. That he had the photo on his desk made me go warm and mushy inside.

Another frame displayed a photo of two couples standing side by side in their Sunday best. One couple looked to be in their fifties, the other in their twenties or thirties. The younger woman held a baby in her arms, and the photo had been taken outside a church with palm trees in the background. The two men were near clones, so I figured them for father and son. Was Saber the baby? Nah. The ladies' hats were from the 1940s.

The last photo made me smile. A boy, maybe three years old, was dressed in a cowboy outfit complete with a white hat, and a six-shooter like those I'd seen in old Westerns. The child stood in front of a Christmas tree, blond furniture I thought was from the 1940s showing in the edges of the shot. Little Deke Saber? I'd seen that fierce expression before. It was eerily similar to his cop face, in fact.

Something written at the bottom of the photo looked to be in Saber's firm, slanted handwriting. I turned the frame toward the brightening light outside to read the script. *Remember, 1951.*

Nineteen fifty-one? If the little cowboy was Saber, and he was three in the picture, that would make Saber—

No. It couldn't be. We'd celebrated his birthday on April fifth, and though I hadn't asked his age because I didn't want to feel like an ancient cradle-robbing hag, he couldn't be much over thirty-six. Not with his washboard abs, tight butt, and a whole list of muscle groups that *so* were not sagging.

The photo must have been of Saber's dad, and the other one of his grandparents and great grandparents. Had to be. Right?

I chewed on my lip as I replaced the frame. I considered going to the bedroom to look for Saber's driver's license, but a glance out the window at the growing day changed my mind. I had research to do, about two hours to do it, and I'd promised Saber printouts of all the data I could find.

I logged into the protected part of the VPA site with Saber's user name and password and pulled up every file on everyone in Ike's nest, starting with Ike himself.

Born in the late 1860s, Ike was reportedly the product of a black mother and Chinese father, and had resided in California until some point in his mid-twenties. The facts pretty well fizzled after that, other than to note Ike had been in Florida since 1955, and in Daytona by 1979.

Miranda and Charles were listed as being one hundred and twenty and twenty-one years old, respectively. Both had been born in Devonshire, England, had met while serving on an earl's domestic staff. They'd been married and had one adult child at the time they were turned in their early forties.

Coach, the guy who looked thirty, was ninety in combined human and vampire years. He'd been turned in 1949, and had really been a football coach, though the records didn't say where. Suzy was forty-five and had been turned at age nineteen while in college. Again, the records didn't reveal where Suzy had gone to school, but her favorite food had been a Frito pie served with a Dr Pepper. Ooookay.

The information on Tower and Zena was sketchy, but they were listed as being over three hundred years old. The record did mention that Tower had known Laurel for many of those years, and I wondered how close they might have been. Would Tower aid and abet Laurel if she came to him for help?

Ray's fact sheet held the most information. At close to two hundred thirty, he was a few years older than me and was of direct Spanish descent. He had, in fact, lived in Alta California in the days that made me think of Zorro. He had studied medicine in the 1800s, law in the early 1900s, and still held his license to practice law. Had Ray known Ike back on the West Coast in the old days? Was Ray Ike's sire?

I pulled up Laurel's information last. A former slave, she'd been turned in 1863 while escaping in the Underground Railroad system, and had lived in the North until the late 1980s. She'd come south gradually, joining nests, then moving on. She hooked up with Ike ten years ago.

The records didn't list any known regular companions for Laurel, or for any vamps in Ike's nest—except each other.

I left the printouts on the desk and then almost went back into the VPA files to research Saber. I wanted to. My hands poised over the keyboard, but a glance at the clock changed my mind. It was nine thirty in the morning, and I was fading.

Instead, I e-mailed Old Coast Ghost Tours to tell them to take me off the schedule for the next three days. Probably more time than I needed, but I'd been working almost nonstop for months. I could use the break. And, yes, I did feel the tiniest bit guilty for the short notice, but I squashed it. I'd filled in dozens of times for other guides. Someone else could jolly well fill in for me.

With a last glance at the photos, I tiptoed into the bedroom to close the blackout drapes, quietly opened drawers until I found what I wanted, and traded my jeans and top for one of Saber's T-shirts.

As I crawled into bed, I kept wondering about the boy in the picture. Should I ask Saber about it? Could I admit to being that nosy? Would he tell me about it on his own?

Should, could, would swirled in my head for only a few minutes before I drifted to sleep.

I bolted out of bed at three in the afternoon, just as soon as I realized Saber wasn't in bed with me. I charged down the hall toward the living room, only to come to a whiplash halt at the office doorway.

"Where's the fire?" Saber flashed a tired grin.

He was dressed in shorts and a short-sleeved button-up shirt, sans his sling. He looked worn but not unwell.

I sagged against the door casing, my heart still racing. "Geez, Saber, I was worried you'd gone out."

"I did, but only for some Starbloods. It's in the fridge."

"You drove with your cast? On pain meds? Saber, I could've picked up Starbloods later. And where's your sling? You're supposed to keep your arm elevated so it doesn't swell."

He looked at his swathed arm where it rested on the desktop. "It is elevated."

"It's supposed to be higher than your heart."

He slouched down in the desk chair until he was in danger of sliding out of it. "How's that?"

My lips twitched, but I shook my head. "Not good enough. Come on, at least lie on the couch."

"Don't you want to hear my report?"

"Absolutely," I said, marching over to him. "But you can tell me in the living room."

I went to take his good arm to get him moving, but that close to the desk, I couldn't help but glance at the photos. When I looked at Saber, he met my gaze in silence, and I saw the wheels spinning in his head. Then the moment passed.

"I'll come peacefully as long as you'll leave that shirt on." He winked. "It's making me hot."

I laughed as he wanted me to do, and settled him on the couch with pillows from the bedroom. (Note to self: Add throw pillows to the shopping list). After downing the Starbloods he'd made a special trip to buy, I cleaned my teeth to a minty fresh shine and rejoined Saber for my briefing.

"Good work on the research last night," he said when I plopped in the chair opposite him and tucked my legs under me. "I've learned a little more this afternoon, and we just might catch a break."

"Well, don't leave me in suspense. What did you get?"

"First, I called Jackson. The carving on the weapon is too intricate to give him a good print, and the techs haven't found unaccounted for hair or skin or anything else I can compare with DNA samples the VPA keeps."

"Any word about the carvings on the knife?"

"Nada. Jackson sent an e-mail with some good shots of it, and I forwarded those to Neil."

"I doubt Neil's checking his mail."

"He's checking. He gave me his cell number in case anything came up with the house, so I gave him a heads-up."

"Can I see the photos?"

He passed five sheets of paper across the coffee table, and I quickly examined each one.

"Does the style look familiar?"

"They're not particularly Spanish, Italian, British, or anything else I'd recognize." I looked up at him. "If Neil can't give you any leads, will Jackson send these to other experts?"

Saber took the papers I passed back. "Yes, but I also e-mailed these to Jo-Jo on the chance he might recognize the weapon itself."

"You mean recognize it as belonging to Atlanta Marco?"

"Makes sense to ask. If Jo-Jo can verify it's Marco's, then we can tie the murder weapon to him."

"But if Marco is out of Atlanta, shouldn't his tracker readouts show that?"

"Yep, which is why I've also talked with Candy again."

I blinked. "You have been busy. Exactly how long have you been up?"

"A while. You want to hear what Candy said?"

"I do. Is Marco in Atlanta or not?"

"He is. Maybe. Candy and Crusher are putting a task force together. That may take a day or two, but they'll go back to Vlad's and demand a little habeas corpus action."

I read and watch enough mysteries to know what that

means. "They're going to get Vlad to turn Marco over to them?"

"They're going to find out if Marco is really there at all. His tracker still indicates he is, but he's been stationary for ten days. We're thinking he's removed the tracker."

"And just left it at Vlad's place? I thought there was a body mass sensor or some kind of fail-safe in the trackers."

"There is, but Marco could've gotten around that by implanting it in someone else."

That thought made the Starbloods sour in my stomach.

"Candy can't raid Vlad's nest any sooner?"

"She can't do that and ensure the team's safety, much less meet their objective. They need to go in full out this time."

"What about Laurel's tracker records? Is the GPS working?"

"She's completely off the radar as of last night. The tracker has been removed. The past records show that the flatline signal started six weeks ago, while she was in Atlanta. So, besides making Ike's payoffs to Vlad, she was up to something else. What, we don't know."

"So, she knows immune-to-silver Marco, too, and she knew Jo-Jo was in town almost before we did, though I don't understand how she pulled that off."

"It was Jo-Jo, indirectly."

"What?"

"I'm pretty sure his computer and cell phone were bugged. I told him to check out my theory first chance he gets. I also suspect that Vlad has had someone hack into the VPA site."

"Did you tell Candy? The VPA should get security upgrades, like, fast."

He nodded. "I told her we need to upgrade the trackers, too, but let's go back to what we know. Assume for a minute that Laurel wants to take over Ike's nest. Especially after Ike hooks up with Donita. Laurel causes problems but doesn't swing the rest of the vamps to her side, so she gets Vlad to send backup."

"Enter Marco the muscle." I paused and frowned. "But if he killed Ike, why snatch Laurel?"

"He needs her for some reason."

I nodded. "Saber, are we sure the other vamps weren't involved in Ike's murder? Or even Donita?"

"You have doubts about Donita?"

"Not really, but I want to talk to her."

"We'll hit her place early, then go to Ike's residence so we'll be there when the gang wakes up."

"Fine, but you need to rest before we go."

Saber grimaced. "Actually, what I need is a shower and shave. Can you tape a plastic bag over my arm?"

"As long as you put the sling back on afterward."

Fifteen minutes later, Saber had shaved, and I had his cast wrapped tight in a white kitchen trash bag. Then, of course, he couldn't reach his back, or wash his hair, so I got in the shower stall with him. My little voice kept nattering about something, but I tuned it out when our slippery bodies rubbed each other in all the *oh, there* places. We barely toweled off before we kissed each other to bed.

Ten minutes after Saber drifted to sleep, I heard what my little voice had been telling me in the shower.

The scrapes and bruises that had been on Saber's back and arms last night weren't there now. They had healed. Overnight.

That just wasn't possible. Not for a human.

A bone-deep hum started in my solar plexus and spread to my chest, as if every cell vibrated with . . . what? Not fear. Anger? Betrayal? Hurt?

I lay stiff beside Saber, not wanting to disturb him yet dying to lift the sheet from his arm to see if I was right. To see if the nicks and dings in his bronze skin had truly healed. The blackout drapes were still drawn against the Western sun, but I could see with vamp vision. If I had the courage to look.

I didn't. I lay quietly, trembling and remembering.

Like book pages being fanned, images flipped through my memory. Saber moving incredibly fast to tackle Laurel last night. Pulling his gun on her Saturday night before I could blink. Firing on the sniper before I saw him draw his gun. None of those movements had been quite preternatural, yet they seemed speedier than a human could manage.

The tremors shook my body like a severe case of chills now, and I couldn't stop the whimper that gripped my throat.

Saber shifted. Next thing I knew, his tanned hand lay on the sheet over my belly.

"You saw the photos."

I cut my gaze to his and tried to breathe. "I did."

"You never wondered how I had over a thousand kills?"

I let out a little sob. "I thought you were very driven."

Saber snorted. "You would be right."

"What happened?"

My whisper was more ragged than I wanted it to be, and Saber's cobalt eyes turned nearly black in the dim light.

"My father and grandfather were slayers, but they moved often to protect the family. To protect me." He paused, swallowed. "I overheard them talking about a turf war between the vamps and the werewolves one night. I was ten. When they left to do their jobs, I followed them.

"I stayed a safe distance away, and I watched the bloodbath that killed my grandfather and wounded my father. When I thought everyone was gone, I went to help. That's when a vamp and a were attacked again."

My gut seized. "They killed your dad?"

"They tortured him. They cut me, and then themselves, and mingled our blood. Then they forced me to suck their wounds and swallow the blood."

"While your dad watched." I saw it unfold in his memory as if on a fuzzy movie screen.

"They told my father to remember that what he despised was now in me, that I was now a blood brother to them. Shit, it was the only time I ever knew a vamp and a were to cooperate."

I gritted my teeth against the pain rolling off the boy in the vision. "Your father recovered?"

Saber gave a shuddering sigh and met my gaze. "Yes. He trained me, and he kept an eye on me for changes, but there weren't any. Dad never treated me like something he hated."

Since looking into his eyes had broken the mind connection, I had to ask. "Is he still living?"

He shook his head, a tiny movement. "My parents died ten years ago."

"I take it the werewolf and vampire who did that to you are also dead."

"They are."

I held the silence for a moment. "Does anyone else know?"

"Like the vamps or the VPA?" He shrugged. "I think Ike

knew something was different, but he never mentioned it. The VPA knows, and my government records have been altered."

"Meaning what? You have a fake ID that makes you younger instead of older?"

"Exactly." He hesitated, then said, "I always planned to tell you, I just didn't know how. How pissed are you?"

As soon as he asked, my body relaxed. "Not too much. I'm not quite the cradle robber I thought I was, and that's good."

"But?"

"But, if you're not a vampire or a werecreature, what—" I broke off, not sure that I wanted to know.

"What am I?" Saber smiled, but it didn't reach his eyes. "I'm human with enhancements. My senses are heightened, though not as keen as yours. I have more strength and speed, and I'm immune to vamp enthrallment. I heal quickly and age slowly."

"So you'll be around for a while yet?"

He began kneading my belly with his warm hand. "As long as you want me."

I let the last big pieces of confusion fall away. This was still Saber. The man I loved.

"Promise me one thing."

"No more secrets?"

"No more cracks about bonfire birthday cakes."

He smiled and moved his hand south until he cupped my mound and squeezed. Oh. So. Slowly.

"The only fire . . ." he crooned, his voice a wicked invitation.

I squirmed under his probing fingers.

"That I'll mention again . . ."

My breathing grew heavy as wet heat flooded me.

"Is the one right here."

EIGHTEEN

At six fifteen that evening, Saber and I sat with Donita in her modest home on a quiet residential street. Eyes red and puffy, she curled up at one end of an overstuffed couch, hugging her knees. A lost waif.

Judging from the tissues littering the carpet, Donita had been in the same place since she came home. If she'd entertained Ike here, I could see why she'd avoid the bedroom.

"I'm sorry about your arm," she told Saber for the second time since she'd let us in. "I can't believe Laurel got away."

I'd made him wear the sling. Fast healer or not, a broken wrist took a human time to mend. Besides, it might make one of the vamps we'd visit later underestimate him.

"Captain Jackson told me he saw you earlier," Saber said.

"Y-yes. H-he told me the police would keep my car for a while." She shuddered and swallowed. "I don't want it. I don't even want to be in this house anymore."

"We know this is hard," I said, "but anything you can tell us will help. How long had you been with Ike?"

"Only since late May. A client wanted to see the club, so I took her." She stopped and plowed her fingers through the short curls that lay wilted on her head. "Ike hardly ever came downstairs to the club proper while I knew him, but he came down that evening."

"Was he doing anything special?" Saber asked. "Checking the bar or talking with customers?"

"No. He came down the main staircase. You know, the one at the front wall of the club. I saw him right away, and I remember he sort of glanced over the crowd until he looked right at me."

"You started seeing him after that?" I prompted.

"I went back every night for a week. I was nervous as hell, but there was something about him." She twisted her hands. "I talked a lot about what I did, and what I might do for his business. He finally said he'd hire me if I'd have a late date with him."

"How did Laurel react?" Saber asked.

"She'd interrupt us while we talked, make catty remarks. I figured she was jealous, but her attitude got worse when I suggested that Ike make some changes in the club. She started stirring up trouble with the others, and that jewelry she asked me to pawn for her? She said they were things from old boyfriends. She blew up when you didn't arrest me."

"I believe you, but back up. What changes did you suggest that Ike make to the club?"

"I wanted the on-site sex and biting stopped. Even behind closed doors and consensual, I felt it was dangerous."

Saber's cop face was firmly in place now. "What did you see to make you think that?"

She pressed her lips together. "Laurel. The men she bit were still, ah, out of it at closing time. She just laughed and said they weren't strong enough for her, and that she'd done nothing wrong. But it bothered me, you know?"

Saber nodded. "When did Ike agree to change the policy?"

"After he talked to Ray. Ike didn't tell me what Ray said, but I guess he agreed with me. Ike stopped the sex and biting just before the end of July."

"Did you," Saber pressed, "see the picture of the man who was bitten and robbed?"

"The one from last week? No, but I wouldn't be surprised if Laurel caught the guy outside and bit him, just to thumb her nose at Ike."

"That makes sense," I said, "but how do you know it wasn't another vamp who bit that man?"

She shrugged. "None of the others wiped out their partners. The few vamps that were having sex with patrons came out of the rooms with the people they took in. Never alone like Laurel. And none of the people were savagely bitten, except Laurel's men."

"What did Laurel do when Ike changed the club policy?"

"She raved that Ike was making them all run tame instead of seizing their birthright of fear and blood."

I shivered. That sounded like Laurel's battle cry, all right, and now she was out running rogue.

"You told us last night," Saber said, "that Laurel was pressuring Ike to fire you and break off your relationship."

Donita sighed. "I'd pretty much made up my mind to quit. The job wasn't worth the hassle."

"Would you have stopped seeing Ike, too?"

"I don't know. I didn't expect we'd last forever, but I never thought—" Her breath hitched on a strangled sob.

I passed the tissue box.

"If you had told Ike you were quitting," Saber said slowly, "how do you think he would've reacted?"

Donita swiped at her nose and took a deep breath. "Honestly? I think he would've told Laurel to can it or leave. He was fed up with her and her rants."

"One more thing," Saber said. "Was Laurel seeing anyone steadily? Was she out of town much?"

"She was out of town a few times, but I never heard her mention dating. She didn't even hang out with the other vamps."

"Good enough. Thanks for seeing us."

Saber rose, but I lingered another minute.

"Do you have someone to stay with? Someone to help you get through this?"

She shook her head. "I can't leave while I'm a suspect. Jackson made that very clear. Maybe when I'm free, I'll move out of Daytona. Go someplace completely different where . . ." Her voice trailed off.

Where she could forget, I thought as we left. But she wouldn't forget. Those moments with Ike's dead body were indelibly etched on her psyche and would haunt her dreams for a lifetime.

Ike's residence was actually north of Daytona and way off the main road. The sprawling two-story house sat on several acres of land, with a split rail fence around the outer border. Between the fence and what seemed to be a barn in ruins, the place looked like it might have been the main house of a working ranch at one time. I did a double take at the rocking chairs on the long, wide front porch.

I glanced at Saber. "Is the place supposed to look like a retirement home for old fanged folks?"

"Maybe it's a Donita touch."

"Maybe, but I can't see Ike kicking back out here."

"We can. We'll be able to hear Ray and the gang when they first wake."

Since we arrived before sunset, we didn't expect anyone to be stirring yet. That's why I jumped a foot when the door opened as Saber and I stepped onto the porch.

Ray stood in the shadow of the doorway, lips twitching.

"Forgive me if I startled you, Princess."

I waved a hand. "I'm just surprised to see you up. Are you a day-walker?"

"Not as you are. I wake half an hour before full dark."

"Ahh," I said, my heart still tripping over itself. Startle factor aside, Ray's looks alone cranked a woman's heart rate.

Ray smiled, as if he knew what I was thinking, but turned to Saber. "You are here to question us?"

"Thought I'd catch you all before you left for the club."

"The club is temporarily closed," he said as we entered the house. "It is a time for mourning."

"It's a time," Saber drawled, "to figure out who's loyal to you and who isn't."

Ray inclined his head. "That, too. Come into the parlor."

Said the spider to the fly? Maybe not, because the place

didn't look creepy. In fact, with all the black leather furniture and cow horns mounted on the wall, it looked like a cross between a kinky bachelor pad and a roundup.

Cow horns in a vampire nest? Geez.

"Please, sit," Ray invited. "We can talk until my nestmates have awakened."

He dropped into a wide chair with the boneless grace that reminded me of Pandora. Which made me wonder where Pandora was, and if she was all right.

"Now," Ray said, elbows propped on the armchair and fingers tented, "what do you need to know?"

"Why did you move from the South Beach nest to Ike's?"

"Because Ike invited me." A flicker of emotion I couldn't define crossed his face, and he leaned forward. "The truth is that Ike noticed a change in Laurel in the spring. He wanted to know why she was behaving so secretively, so he hired me to investigate."

"Like a private detective?" I blurted.

Ray smiled. "I have done many kinds of work, and, yes, I have been an investigator. I moved into the nest as a cover."

"Did you find out what Laurel was up to?" Saber asked.

"Not entirely." He paused as if considering what—or how much—to tell us. "She began going to Atlanta as Ike's emissary but began staying longer each time. We assumed she was having an affair. However, when she returned, she was always more on edge, more—"

"Bitchy?" I supplied.

Ray gave an expressive shrug. "Good sex should have had a more positive effect."

"Did you follow her?" Saber asked.

"I attempted to. She must have sensed me, because I never confirmed who she was meeting."

"We're fairly certain we know who she met, but when was the last time you remember Laurel going to Atlanta?"

"The end of July or first of August."

Saber and I exchanged a glance. *Yeah, that fit.*

"Did Ike have Laurel or anyone else spying on Cesca?"

"Not that I knew of, and I knew everything of importance."

"What about Laurel's punishment? Was she really shackled?"

"For four nights, with silver cuffs and chains. Ike wrapped her wrists and ankles in gauze so he didn't damage her too severely, but she was secured in the shackles."

"Can we see them?" Saber pressed.

Ray gave us each a long stare. "Why is this important to investigating Ike's murder?"

"A number of reasons," Saber sidestepped. "Can we see the shackles Ike used on Laurel?"

Ray cocked his head as if listening, then rose. "I will show you, but you must finish your inspection before the others are fully awake."

From the parlor he led us down a hall with two half flights of stairs at the end. One flight led up, the other down. I caught the scent of oranges from the space below.

"What's down there?" I asked Ray.

"Laurel's quarters, but the shackles are in Ike's rooms. Up here."

He preceded us to the landing at the top of the stairs, hit a light switch, and opened the door to a huge suite done in black and white. The furnishings weren't remarkable other than they were sleek black, edgily modern, and expensive. The bed sat in the middle of the room and was draped in black satin. The bathroom I peeked in was small, more mainstream in decor, but with black towels. When I wandered to the sitting area near a stone fireplace, my nose started itching.

"Are the silver chains stored here?" I asked.

Ray nodded. "In the trunk against the wall. Ike wore special rubber gloves to handle them."

I rubbed my nose as Saber went to the chest and opened it.

With his good hand, he lifted out two sets of cuffs attached to sturdy chains, one at a time. The shackles were the kind prisoners wore with longer chains to allow a modicum more movement. Saber draped one set of shackles over the lip of the trunk, examined them in turn, and then held the locks up to the light.

"Ike didn't notice these shackle locks had been tampered with?"

"What? But Ike had the only keys." Ray edged marginally closer. "Where do you see this tampering?"

"Scratch marks. They're faint, and they could be older than they look, but I'd lay odds they're new."

"You suspect that Laurel picked the locks?" Ray asked.

"That's one theory."

Saber dropped the cuffs and chains back in the chest and closed it as I turned to Ray.

"Will you let me see Laurel's room for just a minute?"

He huffed a breath, clearly impatient, but gave me a short nod.

"Saber, are you finished here? The others will not care if you are in Laurel's rooms, but Ike's—"

"I'm done. Let's go."

As soon as Ray opened Laurel's door, even he and Saber smelled the tang of oranges. The furniture was a mishmash of antiques and just plain old pieces, but the carved canopy double bed on the far wall could've belonged to an honest-to-gosh storybook princess.

I followed my nose to the bathroom first, looking for the source of the smell. No bathroom cleaners stored under the vanity. No orange-scented shampoo or conditioner or soap, but one green towel hanging on a rack smelled of it.

"Ray, do you have any paper grocery bags?"

He frowned. "I do not know, but I can ask Miranda."

"Ask me what?"

I gave a "Yeep," and Saber darn near had his weapon drawn as we spun to see Miranda bracing an empty laundry basket on her matronly hip.

"Oh, my, I'm sorry, Master Ray," she said quickly, her British accent strong.

He waved a hand. "It is no matter, Miranda. Are the others all awake now?"

"Yes, sir."

"Please let them know that I need them in the parlor shortly. Oh, and do you have some paper bags the Princess and Saber may take with them?"

She bobbed her head, curtsied, and hustled out of the room.

A curtsy to the master of the house? Now that was British, but I only let it bemuse me for a moment.

"Thanks, Ray," I said as I scooted by him on one side of the door, Saber on the other.

Next I went to the bed, where the scent seemed to be the

strongest. The half-burned candle was vanilla, but the sheets reeked of oranges and sex. Not two words I'd have thought of in the same sentence.

I glanced at Saber standing at the footboard. "You need to take the sheets, too."

Miranda bustled back in just then with a small stack of Publix grocery bags. "Will these do?"

"Yes, thank you," I said with a smile as she handed me the bags. "I'm sure glad you take paper instead of plastic."

She sniffed. "If anyone should care about the earth, vampires should. We're here long enough."

I couldn't help grinning. "You're right. Miranda, when did you last clean this room?"

"Nearly two weeks ago, ma'am. Is anything amiss?"

"No, no. Just wondering. Thank you."

"Miranda, you may join the others in the parlor now. We will be there shortly. Correct, Saber? Princess?"

"We'll be there in a jiffy," I answered for both of us.

Ray lounged against the doorjamb and watched in silence while we bundled the bedding into several bags, Saber helping one-handed because of the sling. In the bath, I put the towel in yet another bag, folded the tops of the bag over twice to semi-seal them, and gathered them all to carry out. I wanted Saber's good hand free, just in case Ray's vamps took exception to us being in the house.

As we headed toward the door, Ray straightened and held out his hand.

"A moment. I have cooperated, and I will allow you to question the others, but you must tell me why taking these things is important to the investigation."

Saber straightened the strap of his sling. "Here's the short version. We know that Ike was paying protection money to Vlad. We know that Laurel was making runs to Atlanta for Ike. We know that there is a vampire in Vlad's nest who is reported to be immune to silver."

Ray inhaled, hissing air into his lungs. "That is not possible."

"Apparently, it is," I said. "But, wait, there's more. Laurel knew things she shouldn't have known. Like that Jo-Jo was in St. Augustine darn near before we'd met him."

"She also gave Donita jewelry to pawn," Saber said. "Items that tourists who had been in the club reported missing. They didn't have memories of being robbed but remembered leaving the club with their jewelry and not having it the next day."

"And you believe Laurel was behind this?"

Saber took a deep breath. "We believe that Laurel helped murder Ike so she could take over the nest. We strongly suspect that the vamp with immunity to silver is helping her."

Ray eyed us steadily. "You realize how fantastic this purported immunity sounds."

"We know," I admitted. "But Laurel didn't escape by herself last night. She has a vamp accomplice who wasn't at the club. That leaves us with Miranda and Charles, and it doesn't make sense that either of them is involved."

"No. No, it does not." Ray locked gazes with Saber. "What will you do about Vlad?"

"Shut him down. Having a network of nests violates the rules, and I'll hunt the bastard myself if I have to."

"So the minor nests will no longer be forced to pay tribute to the major ones?"

"The word is going out to VPA agents all over the country. Major nest leaders will be audited."

Ray raised a brow. "By the VPA?"

"Worse," I said. "The IRS."

Ray smiled with a touch of the sparkle I'd seen in his dark eyes when we first met. Then he shook his head and sobered.

"I must tell you so that you may warn others. There is a madness among the major nest leaders, as if they all have been infected with the same disease. And it is growing worse. It is the other reason I left South Beach."

A madness? Shudders ripped through me, along with a dread I didn't understand. The paper bags I clutched rattled and snapped as I shivered.

"Someone walking over your grave, Princess?"

I fisted the bags tighter. "You might say that."

"If you sense *la oscuridad*, then you must prepare to fight it with *la luz*."

"The darkness and the light? Ray, could you go for clear instead of cryptic here?"

He opened his mouth, then shut it. "When the time is right, you will understand. Come, the rest are becoming edgy."

"I hate this woo-woo crap," I muttered to Saber on the way back to the parlor.

He chuckled softly. "Right, this from the psychic vampire."

I glared, but without real ire. To tell the truth, Ray's reference to the darkness made me think of the weird dark shape Kevin had captured on digital video.

Our interviews with the other vampires didn't take long. No one knew squat about Laurel's love life, and no one had seen her bring "company" home. Yes, Laurel had tried to stir them against Donita, but they confessed to being increasingly afraid of Laurel. The madness having a trickle-down effect?

When Saber asked if the no sex, no biting policy made anyone angry, they told us it only ticked Laurel. Miranda and Charles had each other, of course, and couldn't give a flipping fang about club policies. The rest of them were relieved. Why? It turned out that Coach, Tower, and Suzy were seeing the three blood bunnies, Claire, Barb, and Tessa. The blonde Amazon Zena? She was seeing the club's day manager, a divorced forty-year old with a child.

Mama Zena? Yikes! Talk about scaring small children.

Before we left, Saber cautioned them all that Laurel could be extremely dangerous and to be on their individual and collective guards. That duty discharged, we left.

In the car, Saber phoned Jackson to report he was bringing evidence into the station. Jackson said he'd wait for us, and that he'd call an evidence tech to take samples from us to account for any extra hairs, skin, and whatnot. Miranda was likely the only other vamp to darken Laurel's bedroom door, and her DNA would be on file with the VPA. Hers and Ray's.

We gave our samples, then talked with Jackson in the break room about our theory that, although Laurel probably didn't kill Ike herself, she was an accessory to murder. Saber also shared that the VPA agents in Atlanta were storming Vlad's nest, and that we were waiting to hear the results.

"You're positive Donita Ward had nothing to do with it?"

"Captain," I said, "Laurel tried to make it look like Donita had robbed those tourists. Setting Donita up for murder would be a cinch, especially with a vampire accomplice."

"I can't say I disagree, I just wish this case weren't so

damned messy." He tapped his pen on the table where his cup of coffee sat cold. "I'll call her tomorrow. Let her know she's no longer a suspect."

We left the station at ten and, because Saber's stomach was making volcanic hunger noises, we stopped at an IHOP and got an isolated booth in the back. He ordered a huge breakfast: eggs, bacon, ham, sausage, hash brown potatoes, toast, and a side of pancakes. I had sweet tea heavy on the ice, and, though he let me pick at his pancakes, he glowered if my fork inched anywhere near the hash browns.

I finally put down my fork, crossed my arms on the table, and gave him the evil eye.

"All right, let's have it. What is bugging you?"

With the last bite of hash browns halfway to his mouth, he startled and glanced up. "What?"

"You're getting all broody on me. Are you worried about the results if the police have to run a DNA test on your samples?"

"Why would I worry about that?"

"You know. The mixed blood thing."

"It doesn't show in my DNA."

"Oh. What about tonight? We did good questioning Donita and the vampires, didn't we?"

"Yes, but Laurel and probably Marco are on the loose."

"And there's not a darn thing you can do about it?"

"Right." He took a swallow of coffee and pushed away his plate. "I'm on edge about Candy and Crusher, about them getting what amounts to a SWAT team together."

"You want to be on the team," I said, the light dawning.

"Yeah, it's what I do. What I did, anyway. I hate waiting on the sidelines."

"Well, call her right now. Tell her you're on the way. You can drop me at home and go kick Vlad butt."

He smiled but shook his head. "I don't want to leave you unprotected. I may not understand what's going on with Triton or that vampire madness thing Ray mentioned, but the darkness smacks of the image Kevin got on video."

The creepies marched up my spine. "I thought the same thing, but the madness is attacking nest leaders, not lone vampires. Besides, if the object is still to take control of the nest, Laurel and Marco will be after Ray, not me."

"You're probably right, but I'm not leaving you alone."

"Stubborn man. Are you sure Candy hasn't left a message on your cell?"

"Checked while we were with Jackson."

"Then check your e-mail when we go back to your place. I'm sure she'll give you a heads-up."

"Not if there's a chance the mission would be compromised."

I heaved a frustrated breath. "Then I guess I'll just have to find a way to keep you occupied."

A wicked grin spread over his face. "How do you propose to do that?"

I pretended to think. "We could shop for those accessories your Realtor wants in your condo."

He growled.

"Or I could give that magnificent super bod of yours a good workout, starting with—"

He grabbed my hand and jerked me from the booth. The twenty-dollar bill he threw was still floating to the table when we were out the door.

I half expected to see Pandora waiting for us at Saber's place. She wasn't, and I was starting to worry about her. Then Saber kissed me in the elevator, and she slipped my mind. She was an ancient shape-shifter. She could take care of herself.

We'd just turned the lights on in the living room when Saber's cell phone rang. He snatched it off his belt, checked caller ID, and immediately put it on speaker.

"Jo-Jo, what's up?"

"The price of gas, again. Is Highness with you?"

"She is."

"Good. I'm calling about the stuff you e-mailed to me. First, this isn't the knife Marco had in Atlanta. Not that I saw all the knives he might have, but this isn't the one he cut me with. Second, Marco didn't smell like oranges. He smelled kind of funky, but not like citrus."

I met Saber's gaze and shrugged.

"You were right about the tracker bugs, though. There was one in the computer casing and in my cell. I had the guy save the bugs in a baggie if you need them for evidence."

"We probably won't need them, but keep them handy."

"Will do. I can't believe Ike was killed, and that poor Donita found him. How is she?"

"Looking to get a new job far away from Daytona," I said.

"I would be, too. Highness, consort of Highness, I feel awful that I put you in any danger."

"No problem," I said. "Laurel was scheming long before you came to town. So how is the life of a big-time comic?"

"Weird, busy, and good. Vince has me booked on Leno August thirteenth. Can you believe it? Vince pulled it off!"

"That's great, Jo-Jo. We'll be sure to watch the show. What about your other gigs? Are you still in Vegas?"

"Yeah, for tonight. Tomorrow I go to L.A., then I'm booked in Reno in a few weeks in September, but something else came up, and I could use your help at that end, if you're willing."

"Help with what?"

"The manager from the Riot, you know, where I did open mike night? Well, he called to ask if I could do a benefit this coming Saturday."

"In five days?"

"One of the acts they booked had to cancel, and I feel like I owe the guy, you know?"

"I know, but how can I help?"

"Would you book a hotel room for me? Something on the island or right downtown? I'll need the room for two nights, Friday and Saturday, but with a check-in time of about five o'clock on Saturday morning."

"That's it? You just want me to book a room?"

"Well, and if you could, pick me up at the St. Augustine airport. Vince is letting me take the private jet back, and we land about four. I hate to ask you, really, but Vince has me so busy, I'm writing new material all the time. Vince's wife told me to hire a personal assistant, but how am I supposed to find someone fast who wants to work for a vampire? Never mind one who understands my sleep schedule."

Bells went off in my head: Donita.

"Princess Ci? You there?"

Okay, so now was not the time to bring up my scathingly

brilliant idea, but I'd tell him soon. After I talked to Donita, if Jo-Jo didn't tumble to the idea himself.

"I'm here, and I'll make the reservation. And, Jo-Jo, break a leg on Leno."

Saber snapped the phone shut, crossed his arms, and gave me his stern look.

"Don't you think it's a lot too soon to mention Donita to Jo-Jo?"

"You read my mind?"

"Your expression, and I don't want you to call Jo-Jo back."

"Come on, it's a perfect solution. He needs help, she wants a big change, and she can do the job. Win-win."

"Humph. Isn't August thirteenth your anniversary?"

He was right. It would be a whole year since Maggie unearthed me and set me free.

"It is, and the thirteenth is in two days."

"Did you have plans to celebrate?"

"Not unless I celebrate with you."

"Hell, yeah, we're gonna celebrate. We'll TiVo Jo-Jo." He cupped the back of my head with his right hand and brushed his lips over mine.

"Now what were you going to do with my bod?"

NINETEEN

Triton came to me in a dream.

I stood at his mind door, deciding whether to knock. The door cracked to show a thin, glowing line, then blew wide open. I was sucked into a blinding light, falling through space and splashing into an azure sea awash in foam.

Triton flashed the wide smile I knew from his boyhood. "Remember this?"

I wiped water from my eyes and found us bobbing in the water beyond the breakers as if we were body surfing, waiting for a wave. Then he took my hand and dragged me to the ocean floor where a treasure chest was wedged into a coral bed.

"Open it," he mouthed.

I did, but it was empty.

"Look deeper."

I caught the top and side of the rough box and leaned inside. A tiny golden dot suddenly appeared where there had been only a void. As if in slow motion, the dot floated higher.

"Catch it," he commanded, but when I reached in, my hand plunged into a cold, oily mass that crawled over my skin.

When I opened my mouth to cry out to Triton, the black ooze dove into my mouth and down my throat, thickening until I couldn't breathe.

I jerked awake to find my face buried in the pillow. Duh. No wonder I was smothering. It was a dream, just a dream.

Still, it was almost dawn before my heartbeat slowed to its normal rate, and I dared to shut my eyes.

Tuesday afternoon, I awoke almost an hour earlier than usual, and with a bad-dream hangover. Or maybe it was a slept-before-daylight, broke-my-routine hangover, but I'd been exhausted. From Ike's murder to learning of Saber's past, the emotions of the last day and a half had me feeling like I'd Hoover-sucked my own aura.

The sound of keyboard keys periodically clacking got me moving. Poor Saber, typing one-handed. I brushed my teeth, wondering how good his healing powers were and if the cast was already for show more than stabilizing the broken wrist. But since only a handful of people must have known about his rapid healing, he had to leave the cast on for now.

By the time I'd washed my face and scraped my hair into a ponytail with the stretched out scrunchie I'd been using for two days, I felt better. And worse. I needed a new scrunchie, not to mention a change of clothes. The jeans and top I'd worn for two days were ripe, and I don't even sweat. And, damn. I was supposed to be watching Maggie's doorstep for cabinet hardware on back order, and watering her plants.

I stopped in the office doorway, intending to tell Saber I needed to make a run home. He looked up and grinned.

"Hey, good news. I got a coded e-mail from Candy, and she's got a team together."

"That's great. When are they hitting Vlad?"

"Maybe tonight, but probably not until Thursday. They're planning strategy while they unravel some red tape."

"Are you still bummed about not being there?"

He shrugged. "Not much. I got a call from Jackie, my Realtor. She wants to show the condo tonight and several times every day this week. Think you can help me speed shop for all that stuff she wants me to get?"

The Triton-dream hangover vanished. I had a mission, and I could pick up a change of clothes while we were shopping.

In the next two hours we hit Tuesday Morning in Ormond Beach, a Target, and a Wal-Mart. I'd decided against buying clothes since we were on a tight deadline, but I did check off all the items on the staging list.

"What do you say to going back to St. Augustine tonight?"

"Fine by me, but don't you want to be around in case Laurel and Marco cause problems?"

"If they do, the damage will be done before I can get there. Wherever there may be. With Jackie showing the condo this week, it'd be easier to be gone."

"Good point." Yippee. Fresh clothing and my own shampoo.

"If you want, I can stay at Neil's place. I've got the key, and he won't mind."

"He might not, but I would. Bring your laptop, and set up Operation Vlad at my place."

"Done."

"Purely out of curiosity, why did you decide to buy a condo instead of a house?"

"You mean somewhere more remote in case vamps—or back then, weres—came after me?"

I nodded.

"I thought about it, but I didn't want to fool with maintaining a house and yard." He looked over and grinned. "Plus, I knew the resale value on the condo would be damn good."

"Now you're ready to take on the upkeep of a house?"

He reached over the console to take my hand. "I'm ready."

By five that afternoon, we had accessorized Saber's place to HGTV perfection. Aside from adding colorful vases, throw pillows, and art, we'd assembled a bistro set. We also packed Saber's sensitive files and books with titles like *The Vampire Slayer Handbook*. Okay, so that wasn't a real title, but those books came off the shelf, and the Starbloods came out of the fridge. Wouldn't do for a potential buyer to see *that*.

Once we'd finished staging, we spit-shined the condo to a show-ready gloss. Saber threw a week's worth of clothes and toiletries together, and we headed out.

Saber had just shut the tail door on the SUV when I heard a plaintive mewling echo in the concrete parking garage.

"You hear that?" I asked Saber.

"Yes, but it doesn't sound like Pandora, if that's what you're thinking."

"But what if it is? Help me look, would you? She's been gone over twenty-four hours now. She might be hurt."

"Cesca, I'm telling you, Pandora can take care of herself. If there's another cat down here, it probably belongs to one of the owners."

"I know, and I won't take it home. Promise. I just need to be sure."

I heard him mutter, "Famous last words," before I began calling. Two *Here, kitty kitties* later, a little ball of pure white fur edged from behind the rear tire of a Jaguar and tottered toward me.

"Awww, hello, little one."

I ignored Saber's "Here we go," and scooped up the kitten. She fit in one hand, and when huge crystal blue eyes blinked at me, my heart turned over.

"Oh, Saber, she's so tiny and skinny." I gently petted the top of her head.

"We need to leave her here so the owner can find her."

"But what if the owner doesn't find her in time? Or is out of town? Or what if she's a stray?"

"What if Pandora thinks she's dinner?"

"Oh. Hadn't thought of that. You're right."

I carried the kitten, now purring in my cupped hands, to the alcove by the staircase, rubbed my cheek against her downy fur, and set her down on the cement.

"Okay," I said, "let's roll."

Saber did. He rolled those sexy cobalt eyes at me, and then stomped toward a door marked Storage. He fumbled with a key and disappeared inside. A couple of thuds later, he came out with a medium-sized cardboard box, and relocked the door.

"Here." He thrust the box at me, opened the rear door of the SUV, and handed me a towel. "Get her settled while I leave a note for the office."

I snagged the back strap of his sling. "Saber, if you're allergic, or you really don't want me to take her, I won't."

He gave me a rueful grin. "You think I can leave her now that I found her?"

In a flash of warmth, I knew he wasn't talking about just the kitten.

"Uh, no?"

"Uh, no is right." He pulled me in for a quick kiss. "Go take care of Snowball, so we can hit the road."

Snowball?

I didn't say it. I never brought it up, not in the hour it took to get back to St. Augustine. Not when we stopped to get Saber a fast-food burger. Not even when Saber stopped at Wal-Mart to buy kitten food, a litter box, and toys. Nope, I never one single time mentioned that he had named the kitten before we ever had her in the car.

Must've been our night for felines, because Pandora, in her house cat form, perched on the tiki bar on my patio.

"Pandora, geez, where have you been? I've been worried."

Saber stood next to me, and Pandora stretched to look into the box at Snowball.

"She's not a snack," Saber said, shifting the box away.

Pandora huffed, than turned her amber eyes to me.

Your home is secure.

"Thanks, but what about picking up the vampire trail?"

They flew west and south. I lost the scent in a few hours.

Saber cocked a brow.

"She said," I translated as I unlocked the door, "that they went west and south, and she lost them after a few hours."

"Could be anywhere by now. Here." He shifted Snowball's box to me. "I'll get the other things from the car while you talk to Pandora."

I nodded, pushed the door open, and put Snowball's box on the coffee table before I hit the code to turn off the alarm. Pandora padded in behind me, pausing to sniff each room in general, then stretching up to sniff Snowball again.

"Uh, Pandora, it's just a plain kitten."

She will sense spirits for you.

"Okay, good to know. Do you have anything else to report about the vamps? Did you tell Triton about the trouble? Is that where you've been all this time?"

She swung her head around. *Triton will speak to you. Listen. I will keep watch.*

With that, she trotted out my open door.

Triton would speak to me, huh? He'd better, and he'd darn well better speak to me clearly, not through another dream. I was so over these veiled messages.

Saber and I settled Snowball and organized Saber's command central space in the kitchen. Laptop on the table, VPA files in their storage box stowed underneath.

I checked Maggie's Victorian wraparound porch for the cabinet hardware. No delivery yet, so I watered her plants which, thankfully, were still thriving. On the way back to my cottage, I turned on my vamp hearing to see if the Listers were home yet. Silence. Good.

Saber got to work on entering digitized log information of Laurel's movements into a GPS charting software program. The printouts would not only time stamp everywhere Laurel had been but would also plot the times her tracker had been working and when it hadn't.

I remembered to make the hotel reservation for Jo-Jo, and since I'd sadly neglected my art institute classes, I booted up my own computer.

When Saber went to bed, I played with Snowball until I wore her out again. Then it was time to knock on Triton's mind door. If nothing else, I'd tell him to stay out of my dreams.

I'd missed the cushy embrace of my leather couch and took a moment to get comfy. With the charm in my left hand, the static quickly morphed into the sound of waves breaking on a shore. Triton's mind door appeared in my third eye, already cracked as if he knew I was coming.

"Do you know what's been happening?"

I know.

"A vampire named Ray mentioned a madness in the senior vampires. And a darkness. Is that what you're hiding from?"

The darkness is the Void. It consumes powers, and its victims descend into madness.

I blinked. I was finally getting real answers instead of double talk?

"Why does this void thing eat vamp powers?"

It devours the power of all who are Other. Vampires, faeries, the elves.

"Wait. Faeries and elves are real?"

Francesca.

"Don't take that long-suffering tone with me. I get it. Void thing is hungry and shape-shifters are on the menu, too."

Yes. We must destroy it.

"Well, of course we must. You get me the destroyer hand-book, and I'll jump right on it."

In my mind's eye, Triton shook his head. *The Void is not a joke.*

"I'm not laughing. I'm trying to understand. Don't you give this thing more power by fearing it?"

It feeds regardless. You must help me.

"How? From behind the scenes, like the way you held land in trust for me? Wanna talk about that?"

You know, then.

"I know. How much do I owe you for back taxes? You might as well tell me, because you know I won't be in debt."

What you owe can be paid when we meet.

"There you go with nonanswers again."

I must go, but be ready to act when it's time.

The door slammed shut. Damn it.

August thirteenth. I woke slowly from a dreamless sleep, savor-ing memories of this time last year. The lucky day for me when Maggie's hefty construction foreman had stepped just so on a rotten part of the kitchen floor and fallen into the tiny base-ment where I had been trapped for over two hundred years.

The man had landed on the lid of my coffin and might've broken through that, too, except that the wood had been darn near petrified when King Normand had put me there. After another couple of hundred years of curing, it didn't give an inch.

His plunge had jarred me, though, and if I screeched a little, who could blame me? Maggie didn't, even if it did cost her the man's construction expertise. He scrambled out of the hole he'd made yelling about the dead talking, and dashed out of the house just short of vampire speed.

Maggie? She lowered herself into the hole and removed the worst of the debris from the coffin, talking to herself the whole time. When she tentatively knocked on the lid, I knocked back.

"Hello out there," I remembered saying. "Please don't be afraid. I'm not going to hurt you."

Okay, in retrospect, that sounded lame, but my friend Maggie is about as fearless as they come. When she said to hang on and she'd get me out, I stopped her.

"I'm, well, I'm a vampire, and I've been here a terribly long time, so before you release me, may I ask for three things? Please?"

"What do you need?" she'd asked.

"Blood, a new frock, and a hairbrush."

"Give me a few hours," she'd declared, and she was as good as her word.

She'd come back with Neil, who grumbled that Maggie was insane, but she'd prevailed. She put Neil to work cutting the silver-laced chains fastened to the coffin while she drilled a hole in the side of the coffin near my head. After centuries of using vampire hearing to eavesdrop on the distant, changing world, so much noise from power tools right outside my box was deafening.

When the hole was drilled clear through, a small beam of filtered light let me see with my physical eyes. Excited, elated, exuberant. Words couldn't touch the myriad emotions rioting in my heart in that moment. I would've cried if I'd been hydrated enough to make tears. Clever Maggie soon fixed that.

She stuck an extra long straw through the hole, explained how to use it, then put the other end of the straw in bottle after bottle of blood. I sucked them dry without feeling the least bit queasy from the smell, and then Maggie fed me water chasers through a clean straw.

When the chains lay on the basement floor, Maggie and Neil took tire tools to each end of the coffin and gently pried the lid loose. I pushed from inside, and, with a whoosh of fresh air, I was free.

Neil took one look at me and brandished the tire iron. Maggie? She asked me my name.

"Francesca Melisenda Alejandra Marinelli," I'd told the petite yellow-haired angel.

She'd stepped closer, put out her hand to take mine, and said, "I'm Maggie O'Halloran. Welcome to the world."

That sealed it. Maggie became my best friend forever.

The baggy blue nylon shorts, equally baggy T-shirt, and rubber flip-flops she brought for me to change into seemed indecent at first. Of course, that was before I saw my first bikini. I thought the bikini bra was a fabric sample. Now the hairbrush Maggie gave me? That was the Holy Grail.

What a long way I had come. Correction, we had all come. Thanks to Maggie, I had a new lease on afterlife. Thanks to Saber, I had a sex life. Above all, I had a family of my heart, friends, and a future.

And I'd better get moving if I wanted to enjoy what was left of the day.

I went to the kitchen to snag my Starbloods, expecting to see Saber hunched over his laptop, but he wasn't in the house. Neither was Snowball, and I wondered if Saber had taken her to PetSmart. If he came back with one of those huge scratching post hotels, I was arranging an intervention.

A long, leisurely shower and hair washing later, I was in a short, silky robe, flatironing my wild hair as straight as I could get it.

I was just about finished, when a huge bouquet of flowers appeared, reflected in the mirror with Saber peering through the foliage.

"Happy anniversary, Princesca."

My eyes swam with tears, and I dropped the flatiron on the counter as I turned.

"Oh, Saber."

I touched one of the red roses mixed with white calla lilies and ferns. Then I noticed the art deco–style vase he held with his good hand, and steadied with the hand in the sling.

"Is this the vase we saw at Tuesday Morning in Ormond Beach?"

He grinned. "I found it at the store here, and took it to the florist to fill. These are the flowers you like, right?"

Dear man. "They're perfect. Thank you."

I took the flowers from him and leaned in for a kiss, when a white, whiskered face peeked out of Saber's sling.

"Meow?" the kitten squeaked.

Saber pulled me the rest of the way into his body. "Never mind her. Kiss me."

I did until I felt little claws dig into my robe. Then I couldn't help but laugh.

"Mood spoiler," Saber said to Snowball, before swatting my butt. "Go get dressed. I have a full schedule planned."

When I finished my hair and makeup, I slipped into my favorite denim Capris, an icy blue bra top camisole, and sandals. The outfit was dressy enough for nearly anything Saber had planned, and with the mermaid charm tucked into my cleavage and a spray of the gardenia perfume Saber had given me for my birthday, I was ready.

My steps faltered when I entered the living room. On the coffee table were a bouquet of daises, a gallon of Publix sweet tea, a package of Fig Newtons, and three gift cards.

"The flowers," Saber said, "are from Millie and the Jag Queens. The bookstore gift card and tea are from your tour guide friends, Janie and Mick."

The Fig Newtons and Blockbuster gift card were from Maggie, I knew. That cookie was one of the first solid foods I'd nibbled on about a month after I'd come out of the coffin, and we'd spent so much time at Blockbuster in my crash course to get up to speed with the twenty-first century, the staff knew us by name. The surf shop gift card was from my hang-ten buddy, Neil. Not that I can hang ten, or even five, but Neil and I had bonded through surfing. A far cry from when he was ready to bash me with the tire iron.

Saber cupped my cheek, brushed a tear away with his thumb.

"They really like me."

"Yes, Sally Field, they do, but no crying on your very first anniversary. We have things to do."

The rest of Wednesday afternoon and evening, Saber and I made memories. First we strolled St. George Street, had a bite of free pizza (I took the smallest one), and then stopped to taste-test gelato. The whipped cream–looking treat coats the tongue like a lover's kiss, and I couldn't resist testing three flavors. Between the gelato and tiny bit of pizza, my stomach groaned. I can eat real food, and I eat a touch more now than I used to, but my stomach is too shrunken to tolerate much.

We headed to the bay front next. Specifically to the marina. Surprise! We were taking the sunset sail on the *Schooner Freedom*, the replica of a nineteenth-century blockade-runner. For two hours, Saber and I sat hip-to-hip near the bow and held hands. The nearly full moon rose early, and we watched dolphins riding the ship's wake as they escorted us past the city sights.

After dinner on the second-story veranda at A1A Ale overlooking the bay (Saber ate, I picked), he took me back to the bay front, this time to the horse-drawn carriages. One carriage with white bows and bunting on the sides displayed a sign on the back reading Happy Anniversary.

"Saber," was all I choked out before he kissed me.

Our driver was a man in his fifties with a careworn face, shaggy salt-and-pepper hair in a thin ponytail, and look-into-your-soul blue gray eyes. I knew that intense gaze from somewhere but couldn't call up the memory. Then again, duh, I likely saw him every time I guided a ghost tour. Saber had to have paid the man something extra, though, because the driver didn't start the tour spiel that was part of the whole tour-by-carriage gig.

Saber must've read my mind, because he held me close and whispered, "He's just driving us tonight so we can enjoy the evening and cuddle."

"Works for me," I murmured, pulling his head closer for a kiss.

We kissed again at the Love Tree. Actually got out of the carriage to stand under the palm tree that grows right out of an oak tree. The legend is that if you kiss your lover under the commingled trees, your love will last forever.

When the hour-long carriage ride ended back at the bay front, the driver turned his intense gaze on me. He winked, and in a rusty voice said, "Never underestimate the power of love."

Caught off guard, I could only smile, thank him, and take Saber's hand to step out of the rig.

As I glanced at the driver a last time, a shiver shimmied up my spine.

"You cold?" Saber asked. "Your blue hoodie is in the car."

"It is?"

He dropped a kiss on my nose. "Yep, because we have one more excursion before your anniversary night is over."

A walk on the beach in the almost full moonlight. What could be more romantic? A yellow comforter, a bottle of sweet tea for me, wine for Saber, and daringly making love on the beach with just the shadows of the dunes to give us the illusion of privacy.

We stayed on the beach for hours, talking, touching, just being together. My heart was so full, my body so sated, that I drifted to sleep in the cocoon of Saber's arms later, knowing what feeling cherished truly meant.

Thursday afternoon, we were back to business, but I didn't mind in the least.

Saber wrote a coded message to Candy while I first checked for Maggie's package (not there), then wrote thank-you notes for my anniversary gifts. Oh, I'd called, too, and left messages, because no one answered their phones. But good manners were important, and writing a note was an extra way to show how much I appreciated my friends.

Snowball wreaked havoc batting my cards and stamps around, but she was now snug in Saber's sling. The sling he didn't need anymore and hadn't been wearing for the past day, but Snowball had dragged the thing to Saber and meowed until he put it on.

"You work tonight?" he asked as I finished sealing and stamping my last note.

"Shoot, I knew I forgot something. I'll call, but I imagine I'm back on the schedule, since I've been off for three days. Will you stay here to wait for word from Candy?"

He rubbed the back of his neck. "I thought I'd go with you and run interference if that ghost hunter shows."

Elise Williams, owner of Old Coast Ghost Tours, confirmed that I worked the early shift tonight and Friday, but was off on the weekend. Then she told me what a riot my friend had been on Leno Wednesday night. My bad. I'd forgotten all about Jo-Jo's appearance.

"That spot increased our business," Elise said. "In fact, your tours are sold out for tonight and tomorrow."

"They are?"

"I've asked Janie and Mick to help you out. Keep the autograph hounds from bothering you."

Autograph hounds?

I must've looked queasy as I said good-bye, because Saber got up to steady me.

I gripped his shirt. "Did you happen to remember about Jo-Jo being on Leno?"

"I set the DVR. You want to see it?"

"Yeah, and I think it should be now."

We hit fast-forward until Jo-Jo appeared on the screen. Then Saber rewound a smidge and hit Play. With Leno's usual flair, he introduced Jo-Jo, and the curtains parted.

"Good evening, thank you. Yes, it's true I'm a vampire. Hard to tell me apart from anyone else in L.A., isn't it?"

The joke elicited chuckles, and Jo-Jo went on with some of the jokes he did during open mike night, and then juggled. Judging by the laughter, Leno's audience thought Jo-Jo was hilarious, but why did Elise think this had increased business?

When Jo-Jo sat with Leno, I knew.

Leno got Jo-Jo to talk about his court jester days, rubbing elbows with royals. That's when Jo-Jo said he had feared getting royally flushed when he came to St. Augustine, but that Princess Ci was one of the good ones. He mentioned my ghost tour job, then extolled the glories of living in a town where the local princess didn't want to rule over other vamps.

"Aw, geez." I dropped my head in my hands.

Saber was more succinct. "Shit. That's gonna piss off the Covenant from coast to coast."

"You think Gorman will show up at the tour tonight?"

"We'll find out real damn soon."

TWENTY

Gorman wasn't lying in wait at the tour substation. Instead, a crowd of thirty ghost tourists chattered loudly enough to wake the, um, dead.

Janie in a Victorian costume and Mick in his Spanish soldier suit hurried toward Saber and me, and someone in the crowd yelled, "There she is!"

Saber thrust me behind him just as Janie and Mick reached us. Mick stood shoulder to shoulder with Saber against the stampede, and Janie huddled next to me.

"Back off, folks. Now." Saber's voice cracked across the space, and everyone froze.

"Wow, are you the bodyguard?"

"No, the boyfriend."

The crowd laughed but fell back, and Mick spoke up.

"Ladies and gentlemen, this is a ghost tour, not a rock concert. We need some order here."

When the group energy downshifted from crazed to curious, I stepped from behind Saber and smoothed the skirt of my sapphire Regency gown.

"I'm delighted you all came out for the tour, but we do have a schedule to keep with the ghosts. So, please gather around me in an orderly fashion, and we'll begin."

I introduced Janie and Mick, and off we went without another incident. Okay, I did have writer's cramp at the end of the evening from signing autographs. I felt like a fraud, impersonating a celebrity, but it would have been rude to refuse. Vampire superpowers I may not have, but I have manners in spades.

When the last tourist walked jauntily off, I hugged Janie and Mick.

"Thanks for your help, and for your anniversary gifts."

"You thanked us in your phone message," Janie teased. "I bet you sent a note, too, didn't you?"

I nodded, and she rolled her eyes.

"You're terminally polite, you know that?"

"You want crowd control help tomorrow, Cesca?" Mick asked. "I heard another thirty people signed up for that one."

"You two don't have something better to do?"

"Lots, but we can do that later, can't we, Janie? It was kind of fun to be part of your entourage."

I groaned. "Please, stop. I want this hubbub to die down."

We chatted a few minutes more, but Saber was getting antsy about the raid on Vlad's place. After we'd parted, it dawned on me that Kevin Miller hadn't been on the tour. Maybe he'd given up waiting for me to come back to work and had gone home, but my little voice nagged that something was off.

*   *   *

Candy was supposed to call with her raiding-Vlad's-nest report, but hours dragged by while we waited.

I gave halfhearted attention to my homework while Saber fidgeted, watched ESPN, played with Snowball until he wore her out, then paced. He was jumping out of his skin by the time midnight rolled around, but five minutes later, his cell rang.

A quick check of caller ID, and he turned on the speaker.

"Candy, you guys good?" he asked.

A loud pop in the background, a little screech, and a curse crackled over the speaker. I shot out of my chair. One beat, two, and finally Candy spoke.

"Sorry, Saber. Crusher just opened some champagne all over me."

I exhaled on a whoosh of breath as Saber pulled me down beside him. "I take it the night went well?"

"Well is relative. We've got some answers, and we've got Vlad in custody. That's why I'm callin' so late."

"You made a capture, not a kill?"

"Got Vlad with a stun gun. I didn't think it would work, but one of the guys on the task force nailed him. Once he was down, we got the silver shackles and guards on him and swept the building."

"Candy, tell us what happened."

"Us? Is Cesca there?" Candy laughed. "Well, a course she is. Okay, here's the skinny.

"From what we got out of three different vamps, Marco is down your way. He put his tracker in some poor homeless guy who was probably more dead than alive to begin with. Vlad stuck him in a hole of a room where he died."

I glanced at Saber and grimaced.

"So you've got Vlad on felony murder. Did the vamps tell you why Marco is in Florida?"

"Oh, yeah. Most of 'em couldn't tell us enough, but Jemina is apparently a woman scorned, and she spilled that Marco's workin' with Laurel. She told us Vlad wanted Ike removed, and Marco went to do the job."

"That fits our theory. You find any payment records to Vlad from Ike?"

"We found reams of records, and it's fascinatin' stuff. We also found at least a partial list of vamps who are rakin' in tributes across the country, but this next part is weird."

"Hit me."

"The vamps in major nests are in turn makin' payments to someone else. Someone higher, I have to assume. The amount varies, but it goes to an offshore account."

"Shit."

"By the truckloads. I've already got the forensic accounting team on this, but I don't know how far they'll get before the owner of the account finds out we're tracing it.

"It'll be closed and another one opened."

"Yeah. The big question is, who or what could possibly have that much control over vampires?"

The madness, Ray's voice whispered in my head.

"The what?" Candy asked.

I blinked at Saber. "Did I say that out loud?"

Saber gave me a questioning look. "Yeah, you did. Are you getting something psychically?"

"I'm not sure how I got it," I said, rubbing the goose bumps that erupted on my skin, "but I think it ties to what Ray told us on Monday."

"Wait, people. Catch me up. Who is Ray?"

"Ray," I began, "is a vamp who was Ike's friend and attorney. Ike willed his worldly goods to Ray, so Ray takes over Ike's nest."

"Gotcha. Go on."

"We interviewed him and the rest of Ike's vamps on Monday night, and Ray told us privately that there was a madness affecting the major nest vampires. He didn't elaborate, but you could tell he's seriously alarmed."

"I don't suppose Laurel's tracker is workin'," Candy said.

"Negative, it appears to have been removed entirely. As of Monday, Ray had temporarily shut down the club, and he's keeping his vamps nestbound."

"No reports of activity that would point to Marco and Laurel bein' on a rampage?"

"Been as quiet as a tomb."

Candy was quiet a long minute.

"All right, here's what we'll do. I'll hurry the forensic accounting team along, and you two see if you can get more information out of Ray. Crusher and I will work on Vlad, maybe even give him a chance to cut a deal if he'll tell us what's goin' on. Meantime, I'm puttin' out an alert to headquarters and every VPA office in the country."

"You getting Homeland Security involved?" Saber asked.

"And the FBI and freakin' CIA if I have to. We've got to bring these suckers down. Every last one of them."

"Won't Mr. Big with the offshore account just come after the next heads of nests?" I asked.

"Not if we can get one of the honchos to roll on this guy." Candy sighed. "I'll admit the chances of that are slim and none, but Slim ain't left town yet. And, Saber, you need any backup, you call us. Crusher can be down there double time with half an army of his freelancers."

"Good to know. We'll talk to Ray tonight and check in if we learn anything new."

Saber snapped the phone shut and tapped it on his knee. I didn't like his speculative expression.

"Are we going to Daytona now?" I asked.

"No, I don't want to disturb the perimeter Ray has set up."

"What perimeter?"

"Except for last night during our date, I've been checking in with him." His lips twitched. "Remember how vampires like to have psychics or witches in their camps?"

"I was one, and what's funny about it?"

"It seems that Suzy is also a fairly powerful witch, and has set wards on the property."

"Her witchy powers didn't go haywire when she was turned?"

"Apparently not. That's why I don't want to go out in person, but if we call Ray to question him, you think you might be able to get in his head enough to read him?"

"I can try."

Saber jerked his chin toward the computer. "Turn that off so the mail alert doesn't ding."

I did, and also grabbed a pad and pen as he dialed Ray. I didn't know Saber had the number, but then I didn't know the residence had a phone line.

"Nest residence," Miranda said in her crisp British accent.

"Hello, Miranda, this is Saber. Is Ray available?"

"He has Tower engaged in a rousing game of chess, but let me call him, Mr. Saber."

Tower played chess? Suzy the vampire cheerleader was a witch? I was starting to feel like an underachiever.

"Saber, is there any news?"

"That's why I'm calling. Vlad is in custody, and the vamps in his nest are cooperating with the VPA."

"And they have confirmed what?"

"Vlad wanted Ike out. He sent the vamp we told you about, Marco, to work with Laurel and get the job done."

"Marco is the one who is immune to silver?"

"If the reports are true, yes."

"Are Laurel and this Marco still at large?"

"'Fraid so. The VPA in Florida is on alert. I notified the agency Monday that they were Rampants, but these two are flying off the radar."

"So it is advisable to keep the nest secure?"

"Yeah, though you might be able to help us get a break if you're willing to help."

Ray paused. "Help how?"

Saber gave me the high sign to turn on the mind probing, but I was already there. Not picking up anything yet, but tuning in as best I could. I doodled on the pad to clear my mind.

"You mentioned that the upper-level vampires, the ones running the bigger nests, were being afflicted in some way. You called it a madness, but can you be more specific?"

"*Un momento.*"

We heard footsteps, voices in the background, then a door closing before Ray spoke again.

"You understand I can only give you my observations, yes?"

"That's fine," Saber said. "Anything to go on will help."

"Rico—that is, Richardo, the head of the South Beach nest—could be somewhat fearsome, but was stable in temperament."

I closed my eyes and let Ray's voice wash over me.

"Months ago, perhaps in October, Rico became more erratic in his behavior. At first, he lashed out at his nestlings over small matters that he shrugged off in the past. Then he grew more easily enraged, meting out harsh punishment to those who would before have been given only a reprimand."

"Did he feel his authority was being challenged?"

"I do not think so, and yet he grew to be more and more paranoid, especially since March. I began to hear the same thing from vampires in other major nests. Their leaders were following a similar pattern."

"Besides Ike asking you to investigate Laurel, was there anything in particular that made you leave?"

"Rico was becoming insular. Seeing only his advisors."

Of which Ray was one. I slid into his memories and watched as he entered a large, dark chamber. A magnificent chandelier hung in the center of the room, yet only a few candles lit the room. Rico sat in a high-backed armchair crowded into a corner. No windows ran along those walls, though both the other walls were lined with windows. I had the impression of a fabulous mansion that had once bathed in the south Florida sun. Now shadows crept along the floors, an oozing, oily fog.

"What happened when you asked to leave?" Saber asked.

I flinched as the scene unfolded in Ray's memory. Rico rose from his armchair, and the candlelight caught his gaunt face. He gestured wildly and shouted in Spanish about Ramon's betrayal. Ramon—Ray—assured Rico he would return; Rico wouldn't hear him. He backhanded Ray, but the blow that should've launched Ray across the room barely snapped his head to the side.

Rico is starving. His energy is being drained.

I wrote the words on the pad without conscious thought, without even opening my eyes, but Saber must have seen it.

"Did you notice physical differences in Rico? Did his habits change? Did he seem to age?"

Ray sighed. "You remember when some of the independently living Miami vampires disappeared?"

"Yes."

I remembered, too, because Saber had gone to Miami to investigate right after we started dating.

"Rico—"

Ray broke off, but the scene in his mind kept playing. Vampires and a few humans who seemed to be spouses were dragged before Rico. If the vampires would join his nest, he would spare them. Those who resisted . . .

I snapped my eyes open and clutched at Saber's good arm, but it was too late to stop the images of blood spurting as Rico tore out their throats.

"Let me simply say Rico was feeding more often, and yet the feedings did not sustain his energy."

"Damn it to hell."

"So it would seem," Ray replied. "I have shared with you. What are you not sharing with me?"

"Before I tell you, let me ask you one more thing. Does Rico have an accountant?"

"One who is a vampire, yes. He was one of Rico's advisors. Or I suppose he still is, if he lives."

"Did this vampire mention Rico was paying another vamp?"

"He did not know who Rico paid, but money transfers were made."

"To an offshore account?" Saber pressed.

"Yes. What have you found?"

"The raid on Vlad's nest turned up records of payments from minor nests to him, and from him to an offshore account. The feds are tracing it, but would you speculate that whatever controls the account is responsible for this madness thing?"

"*Madre de—* It is *la oscuridad*, Saber. The darkness. I can say only two more things. Do not be surprised if the account disappears."

"Yeah, we're figuring that's a good possibility."

"I would call it a certainty. Tell the princess that I allowed her to see into my memories so she will recognize the black fog. The darkness. Do not let it consume her."

"Black fog?" Saber paused. "Ray?"

The line was dead.

I collapsed back on the couch as Saber shut the cell phone and then pulled me into his arms.

"What the hell did you see?"

"Rico killed at least ten vampires and their human mates, but he looks almost emaciated. Like something is draining his life force, not just his aura energy."

"The black fog?"

"I saw it in the room, sort of spread out over the floor."

"Is that why you're shaking?"

I took a deep breath. "No, I'm shaking because I forgot to tell you that I got info out of Triton. He called this darkness thing the Void. He said it preys on the power of vamps and magical beings."

"Humans, too?"

"He didn't say, but the black fog in Rico's house looked similar to the dark shadows Kevin caught on video last week."

I felt Saber's lips in my hair. "I noticed Kevin wasn't on the tour tonight."

"I know. When I realized he wasn't there, I figured he'd left town. He told me he had a limited time here. A few weeks, I think, but I don't remember more than that."

"And now you're afraid he's, what?"

"I don't know. He wore enough silver crosses to ward off most any vamp, but my little voice is screeching that something is wrong."

"Did he give you a card? Tell you where he was staying?"

I thought back to the first time I'd met Kevin, then sprinted to my closet. The pirate outfit. If I'd kept the card he'd shoved at me, it had to be in the pocket.

It was, and it listed Kevin's address, phone number, MySpace page, and a paranormal investigation website. Another number was handwritten on the card.

"Find it?"

"I did, but it's too late to call if he's gone home. I'll check his MySpace page first."

"How will that help?"

I activated my laptop screen. "He told one of the groups last week that he'd upload his videos to some Web page or MySpace. I can't remember which one, so I'm starting with this."

The page came up in pieces, and I gave a quick glance at his blog titles.

"There." From over my shoulder, Saber pointed at Kevin's last blog entry. "St. Augustine Shadow Man?"

I clicked, brought up the blog dated Thursday morning, and scanned it. Basically, he wrote about the amorphous shadow he'd caught on video and mentioned the differences between it and a typical shadow man. He gave a link to his video, and, when I clicked it, the two videos of the shadow and the light entities played across the screen.

"Is this the shadow you saw when you were reading Ray?"

"It's similar, but the one in the vision stayed low to the floor. It didn't loom up behind Rico or Ray. Or if it did, I didn't see it."

I tapped a nail on Kevin's card where it lay next to my laptop and stared at the scrawled phone number. I recognized the exchange as a local one. His hotel? It went against every mannerly instinct I had to call so late, but what was the worst that could happen if I called? I'd wake him up? I'd disturb a tryst between Kevin and Leah, or Kevin and Caro? Heck, the hotel operator might tell me Kevin had checked out, and I could shut my little voice up entirely.

"I'm calling," I said, and scooched away from my desk to go grab the cordless in the kitchen.

I stood in the kitchen doorway, biting my lip as I punched in the number.

"Is Kevin Miller still checked in?" I asked when an operator answered.

The woman who was either sleepy or bored out of her skull asked me to hold, and then the line rang.

Once, twice. I let it ring five times before I hit the Off key and put the unit back on the charger.

"Not there, huh?"

"No, but he's apparently still checked in."

"Maybe he's out with those girls he hooked up with."

"Maybe. I wish my little voice believed that."

Saber sighed and scooped his keys off the coffee table. "Come on."

"Where are we going?"

"To Kevin's hotel."

Night clerk Beth Gravis wasn't happy when Saber introduced himself, showed her his badge, and asked her to let us into Kevin's room. Nope, not happy even when Saber flashed his sexy smile.

"Is he a scam artist? I just upgraded him to a patio room two days ago, and I'll be in trouble if he's skipped on the bill."

"It's nothing like that," Saber said. "We're concerned he's had an accident."

Alarm flared in her hazel eyes. "Should I call an ambulance?"

"Let's see if he needs one first."

Beth didn't grumble as she led us to Kevin's first-floor room, not with her lips pursed in a thin white line. She jammed the card key in the slot and pushed hard on the lever handle.

As the door swung open, I saw a flash of movement in the dimly lit room.

And smelled jalapeño, garlic, and cheap cigar.

"Saber, it's Gorman."

But Saber already had his Glock in his hand when he lurched inside. Beth and I crowded in on his heels.

"Gorman, stop right there, or I swear I'll shoot you and enjoy it."

Frozen in the threshold of the sliding glass door I assumed led to the patio and pool, Gorman sneered. "You wouldn't shoot an unarmed man."

"You want to test me? Lace your hands behind your head. Do it now."

As Gorman complied, Beth said, "Vic?"

I peered at her slack-with-confusion expression. "You know Victor Gorman?"

Beth swallowed. "He works here. He's one of our maintenance engineers. He told me this Mr. Miller was writing a hotel review and talked me into the upgrade."

"To this specific room?" Saber asked.

"Yes. Should I call the police?"

Saber nodded, and Beth scurried off, leaving the heavy door to clunk closed behind her.

"Keep your hands laced and sit in the chair."

I held my breath while Gorman complied, and I scanned the room for signs of, what? The Covenant didn't take kindly to vamp-friendly humans, but would Gorman harm Kevin?

The bed was made, clothes hung in the open closet, and from peeking in the bathroom, I could see toiletries strewn on the counter. Kevin's cameras and other equipment appeared to be missing, but maybe he was ghostbusting on his own tonight. Wait, Kevin's laptop lid was half-closed. That didn't fit.

"Saber, I think he's been on Kevin's computer."

Saber hardened his cop face. "Is that right, Gorman? What were you looking for?"

"I got the right to remain silent."

"Cesca, see if Kevin's stuffed in the bathtub."

Gorman snorted. "He ain't in there. He left with two gals afore dark."

"Where'd they go?"

"How the hell should I know? Can I put my hands down now?"

"No. What's the deal with having Kevin moved to this room?"

"I ain't sayin'."

"Fine by me. I'm happy to see you stay in jail. You should be there for attempted murder, but Cesca won't press charges."

Gorman's eyes shifted to me then away. "I was just fixin' the slidin' glass door catch."

"Right. At one thirty in the morning."

I saw police car lights strobe through the window, then heard the hotel room door lock tumble and open.

Saber didn't move, but I whirled to face an astonished Kevin. Before he could speak, the EMF meter he held suddenly screeched, and then St. Augustine's finest burst through the sliding glass door.

An hour later, the cops had sorted out the story. While Kevin, Leah, and Caro had gone on a lighthouse ghost tour, Gorman had entered Kevin's room by simply jiggling the sliding glass door lock until it failed. Something he knew the lock would do because he purposely hadn't fixed it. At which point Beth had muttered, "He is so fired."

When pressed as to why he'd broken in, Gorman admitted he'd been on Kevin's computer looking for the list of vampires who were moving to St. Augustine. Why he thought such a list existed, never mind why Kevin would have it, boggled the intellect. Then again, that was Gorman. And, though he was cuffed and led away, I was betting he wouldn't stay in jail long. He must have a bail bondsman on speed dial.

Kevin said that, after the tour, he and the girls had trolled the lighthouse neighborhood, and made contact with a spirit who called himself the Mariner. Or that's what he thought the voice said when he'd listened to it in a near-empty all-night restaurant. Saber and I declined his invitation to hear the recording for ourselves and left the hotel with a word of thanks to Beth.

Relieved as I was that Kevin was safe, my body didn't seem to have the memo yet. My shoulders had more knots than the berry farm, so much so that Saber noticed.

"Why don't you go surfing this morning?" he said as we got into his car. "You haven't been out in a week, and it might relax you."

He was right. I'd missed the exercise and the Zen-ness of simply feeling the ocean roll under my board.

"And tomorrow afternoon when you get up, I'll have the information you need to claim your land. You can start ripping out vines to your fang's content."

"Are you trying to keep me busy?"

"I'm trying to take your mind off things neither of us can do a damned thing about right now."

"What about taking your mind off things?"

"You've got a king-size bed that can help me out there, so long as you're in it with me."

I took his hand and squeezed. "Home, Saber."

*　*　*

The waves on Friday morning weren't the stuff of surfer dreams, but my spirits rose the moment I hit the water.

I joined some other surfers I knew by face more than name, and hung with them awhile. Later, I paddled out farther than the others, just to sit and be, but about levitated off the board when something hit my right foot.

Last time that happened, a dead body had surfaced. This time a dorsal fin broke the water in an arc. Not a shark, a dolphin. Whew! I watched as it swam nearer, and wondered for a moment if it could be Triton in his shape-shifted form. But no, the moon would be full tomorrow. Triton changed only at the dark of the moon. Well, he did unless his inner shifting clock had changed over the centuries.

"Triton?" I said as the dolphin approached.

It dove under my board, then did a Marineland-worthy leap out of the water on the other side.

"Triton, damn it, if that's you, you'd better get your flipper over here now."

The dolphin bobbed up near my left leg, clicked and whistled, but a fast mind probe told me this wasn't Triton. This was a dolphin out to play, willing to connect with me. I reached to touch, and it lifted its beak to my hand. For a moment suspended in simple, profound accordance, we met gazes. Then the dolphin slowly rolled away from me. It circled back once more before arching away toward the shore.

I paddled hard to follow, and in an exhilarating minute, we had both caught a wave, the dolphin and me.

We were nearing the shallower water when the dolphin peeled off. I rode the wave until it fizzled into froth, and packed it in for the day.

How can you top surfing with a dolphin for a natural high?

Something in me must've healed that morning, because I felt better than I had in a week when I woke up Friday afternoon.

It helped that Saber had news. First, Kevin had called to thank us for catching Gorman. I knew Kevin would be on my tour tonight, even if he had to crash it, and I didn't care.

The second bit of good news was that Saber had sweet-talked his former Realtor, Amanda, into giving him the information I needed to claim my property. I'd wait to file on Monday, but I could hardly wait to talk with Maggie about fixing up the place.

Even Candy had checked in with cautiously optimistic news. Vlad stonewalled them in the interrogation, but the offshore account hadn't been closed yet.

The one surprise was having visitors ring my doorbell at six fifteen that evening. I didn't recognize the two men in their sixties dressed in green polo shirts and gray Sansabelt slacks that I spied through the peephole, but they weren't selling Amway.

Saber stood at my back, hand on his holster as I opened the door.

"Ms. Marinelli?" the slightly taller and thinner man said.

"Yes?"

"I'm Reggie Princeton, president of the local Covenant organization, and this"—he indicated Polo II—"is our vice president, Phil Jameson."

"Gentlemen," I said, being pleasant as you please, though my muscles tensed for trouble.

"I'm Deke Saber. What do you men want?"

"To apologize for the actions of Victor Gorman," Reggie said without hesitation.

"Which actions, exactly?" Saber pushed.

"All of them. The stalking, the threats, the arrow incident. None of his actions have been or will be sanctioned by our branch of the Covenant."

"Why not?" Saber asked. "That's part of what you do. Provoke vamps until they defend themselves, then call for an execution."

"Some branches do those things," Phil piped up. "We don't. Not anymore."

"Ms. Marinelli has proven herself harmless," Reggie said.

"And?" Saber pressed.

"And our activities are under law enforcement scrutiny. From now on, we'll merely keep an eye out and report problem vampires to the VPA for them to deal with. Gorman has been a—"

"Rambo wannabe?" I supplied.

Reggie smiled. "I was going to say he's been a challenge to deal with since he joined, but your description is on target."

"We appreciate knowing your new policy," Saber said, "but what are you going to do about Gorman?"

"We're tossing him out at the meeting tonight," Phil stated. "That's the worst we can do to him."

"Um, can't you do something less than your worst?" I asked. "Like fine him, or give him some very specific job?"

Phil's eyes bulged. "You want us to keep him?"

I shrugged. "It's better for someone to have an eye on him than for him to go completely renegade."

Reggie and Phil exchanged a look. "You have a point, but Gorman is stuck on half-cocked. We don't want to be blamed if he attacks you again."

"What if," Saber said, "you demand that he surrender his weapons, and tell him he's not allowed to restock until you tell him to?"

"Knowing Gorman, he'll start screaming about his Second Amendment rights."

Saber shrugged. "Tell him it's that, or he's out of the club, and that you'll inform me that he is conspiring to commit murder."

Reggie gulped. "You'd trump up charges against him?"

"I'll do what I have to do to keep Cesca safe."

Reggie jerked a nod. "All right, but let me ask you something. Gorman is riled up about this Jo-Jo fellow coming back to town, and about rumors that a whole lot of vampires are moving here. How much of that is true?"

I couldn't help rolling my eyes. "Jo-Jo," I said firmly, "is doing a benefit here Saturday night and leaving again on Sunday. As for the other, there are no masses of vampires moving to St. Augustine that I know of."

"And if more vamps were to move here," Saber said, "they have the right to live where they want so long as they comply with VPA regulations and obey the same laws all of us do."

Reggie and Phil reluctantly agreed, then turned their attention back to me.

"You really have no intention of setting up a nest?" Reggie asked.

"Mr. Princeton, even if I wanted to, which I don't, my cottage isn't big enough to house a vampire nest."

Phil hooked a thumb over his shoulder. "What about the big house?"

"That's Maggie's home, not mine."

"It seems Gorman has misinformed us about a lot of things, Ms. Marinelli."

"Will you keep him in the fold?"

Reggie cracked a wry smile. "As long as you remember this was your idea."

"Or until we get fed up enough to knock him off ourselves," Phil added.

Reggie and Phil said cordial farewells and had just closed the gate when Hugh Lister stormed through the jasmine hedge. I braced myself for his onslaught.

"What did those two Covenant men want?" Hugh demanded.

I blinked. "You know them?"

"Know of them. Did they threaten you?"

"Uh, no."

"Good."

"Good? I thought you hated us."

"I hate your loud parties and your late night shenanigans, and I don't trust you one little bit, missy."

"But?" Saber asked.

"I'll be goddamned if some two-bit hate group gets away with scaring you off."

Mouth open, I watched Hugh slam back into his house before I looked at Saber.

"Bless his holy name."

TWENTY-ONE

~

Friday night's tour went off without a hitch, other than that I again spent as much time signing autographs as I did telling ghost stories.

Kevin, Caro, and Leah showed up and made three more than we were supposed to have, but I didn't complain. I introduced them to Mick and Janie, and Kevin showed off some of the video he'd shot during the tour. This time, he'd caught a few white shadows hovering around me and other members of the group, but nary a hint of a black shadow.

Saber teased me about Kevin as we walked home hand in hand.

"I think you're starting to take the wounded under your wing like Neil says Maggie does."

"Kevin's a little weird, but he's not wounded."

"And Jo-Jo was wounded and a lot weird, but he grew on you." Saber grinned. "And then there's Snowball."

"Oh, no, bud. I'm not taking the fall for Snowball. I felt sorry for her, but you're the one who named her."

"Okay, you've got me there."

I grinned. "I've had you a lot of places."

"Yeah, you have," he said, drawling out his words. "Want to go for a new one?"

Saber *said* he had to check on Neil's place, but what he *did* was seduce me into Neil's solar hot tub for a romp. Even with his arm still in the cast, the hot tub was another reason to love Saber's soon to be new house.

Later, while Saber slept back at my place, I killed time before picking Jo-Jo up at the regional airport by first working on my design classes, then playing with Snowball. She spooked me a few times when she stopped batting a toy to stare at the door, arch her back, and hiss, but I sent out feelers and didn't sense anyone there.

Except for the third time when I heard Pandora chuff on the patio. If Snowball had been a dog, she'd have gone on point. I scooped her in my arms and cracked the door. Pandora in her full panther size sat smack on the threshold.

"Where have you been?" I spoke softly enough not to disturb Saber. "I thought you were supposed to stay nearby."

Old Wizard had need of me, but you have been safe.

"Old Wizard?" Then I remembered. "Oh, the guy who's at the big meeting. The guy you, um, live with. Right."

The time of the first resolution is near. Be prepared to claim your power, Princess Vampire.

Pandora rose and turned.

"Come on, Pandora, give me a straight answer. What the hell is the first resolution?"

I will be there when you need me.

She padded toward the gate.

"When I need you for what?"

Silence.

"Pandora, it really ticks me off when you do this."

More silence. Snowball relaxed and batted the feather toy I forgot I held.

At three forty-five by the light of the full moon, I drove to the airport. Jo-Jo bounded into the all but deserted terminal toting a fancy piece of carry-on luggage.

"Highness! Good to see you!" he gushed, then gave me air kisses.

Air kisses? This from the vamp who'd been prostrate at my feet two weeks ago?

Jo-Jo dropped more surprises on me en route to his hotel.

"Vince is negotiating a deal to star me in a remake of *The Court Jester*. You know, that movie? The original starred Danny Kaye. Anyway, the shooting schedule could be tricky, what with me only up at night, but Vince says if this company wants to do it bad enough, they'll work it out with the unions. They might even shoot part of it here."

"The tourism bureau will love it." And they would, but Gorman wouldn't. Might have to call my new Covenant contacts with a heads up.

"I hope I don't have to sing," Jo-Jo went on. "That could be trickier than night shooting. Now, guess who I looked up?"

"In Vegas or L.A.?"

"Daytona. I called Donita and offered her a job as my per-sonal assistant. She took it, and she's coming up to meet me tomorrow night before the gig. Isn't that a stroke of genius?"

"It's perfect for both of you," I said, grinning to myself, "but I didn't think she had her car back."

"She doesn't. She's catching a ride with someone who's coming up for the show at the Riot."

"You said there were other acts, Jo-Jo. What time does the whole show start?"

"At eight, but I go on at nine and ten thirty. You will be there, right, Highness? For at least one show?"

For all the air kissing, that little bit of insecurity reassured me Jo-Jo hadn't gone completely Hollywood.

"We'll be there."

I felt jumpy all afternoon on Saturday but figured the cause was either the full moon or simply anticipating Jo-Jo's per-formance. When it was time to get ready, I paired black jeans with a lime green top and sandals, and put my hair in a pony-tail. Saber wore black jeans, too, but with a blue shirt that made his cobalt eyes look like a stormy ocean.

We were headed out the door at eight fifteen when Candy called. Saber took the call with the speaker feature on as we hustled to the car.

"Vlad's dead," she said tersely. "He was startin' to look ill, so we decided to move him while he slept. Son of a bitch woke up, broke out of the building, and ran into the sun. He fried before we could put out the fire."

I shuddered and blocked the scene my imagination conjured.

"So much for getting his cooperation."

"We lost the offshore account, too. It was closed at the last minute yesterday."

"Did the investigators get enough to trace it?"

"I'm not sure yet, but the whole thing with Vlad is buggin' me. He seemed to weaken and age while we had him in custody."

I immediately thought of Rico, the black fog Void sucking his life force.

"You two have any idea why that would happen?"

"He was being energy drained," I told her as we reached Saber's car.

"How is that possible? We didn't let anyone near him."

"You didn't have to," I said. "Something is getting to vamps wherever they are."

"What?"

I looked at Saber, waited for him to tell her, but he shook his head.

"Candy, our intel on this isn't confirmed. We'll do some checking and call you later."

"All right, but keep me in the loop."

Saber disconnected and faced me. "You okay about Vlad going up in flames?"

"It's gross, but the real question is how he awoke in the first place."

"The Void gave him a super shot of energy?"

"I don't want to think about it."

But I couldn't help it, and my jumpy feelings shifted into overdrive as we sped through traffic to the island.

My nerves frayed to shreds when we found the parking lot near full but strangely quiet. No smokers stood outside as they had last time. And then we spotted Pandora in her house-cat form waiting at the club door.

The vampires you seek are inside. Go quickly. Help is waiting.

Stark fear ripped though me, and Pandora sprinted around the building before I finished relaying her message to Saber.

"Do you think Laurel and Marco have killed everyone?" I whispered.

"No, but they're holding a hundred or more hostages we have to keep alive."

"Please let them be in thrall."

"Amen." He drew his Glock, held it by his thigh, and reached for the huge half-moon door handle.

I gripped his cast to stop him. "Wait. Do we have a plan?"

"We take whatever help is waiting, and we end it."

"That's the whole plan?"

"Honey, vamps don't do hostage negotiation. We know the basic layout of the building. I'll take the first clear shots I have, and you wing it for all you're worth."

Wing it, right.

He pulled the heavy door open, and we stepped from the lights of the street into the dim club foyer. The smell hit me first. Not death. A sweet orange tang that clogged my throat.

I glanced at Saber. Mouth clamped tight, he jerked his chin. *Move*, I heard him say in my head.

I stutter-stepped, then stopped, eyes on Saber's face. I hadn't really heard him, had I? I'd read him. Had to. I didn't have time for another shock now.

I eased into the club proper, Saber at my back, dread fisting tighter in my chest with each shallow breath. I scanned the humans frozen in place, figures in a wax museum. Grateful the thrall left them senseless, I edged deeper into the bodies suspended in time.

Sudden movement on the stage drew my attention, and a man stepped into the glare of two spotlights.

No, not a man.

The monster from my past. The vampire I'd convinced myself was dead.

Marco Sánchez.

Everything stilled in me. Blood. Breath. Life.

However he had disguised himself in Atlanta, tonight he'd stripped his mask. Midnight black hair the color of his soul. Dark, cruel eyes with the same glint of evil glee I remembered.

He stood on the stage dressed entirely in black, brandishing a short sword that flashed silver in the spotlights. As I watched, he paused, shielded his eyes, and made a pretense of seeing me.

"Ah, Francesca, Princess of the House of Normand," he said with a mocking bow. "Welcome to my little reunion soiree."

His voice made every drop of blood in my body go icy, but I controlled a shudder and looked at the others on the stage. Just out of the glare of the spotlights. Jo-Jo slumped in a chair, his hands bound behind him, Donita kneeling at his feet. She didn't seem to be harmed, but neither did she seem completely in thrall. Shock waves of terror quivered from her.

Another female hunched across the stage floor from Donita. Laurel. Half-clothed, a grotesque tattoo of burn marks on her bare arms, and an oozing slash on her upper chest. She still wore Saber's silver handcuffs and cowered beside Marco, yet her eyes flashed with rage.

"Now, now, Francesca," Marco chided. "Is this any way to greet an old friend? Come closer."

I turned to Saber, but he was frozen, too. My heart seized.

"Do not look to your tame mortal for help, Francesca," Marco said silkily. "He will do as I tell him. Shall I demonstrate? You, throw down your weapon."

Saber complied, but I saw the spark in his eyes and remembered. He was immune to enthrallment. Playing along.

"Wing it. I'll move in when you distract him."

A rush of relief made tears prickle my eyes. Then Marco ruined the moment.

"Francesca, my love. I will let them all live if you will come to me."

Manipulative hell spawn. He gave me no choice.

Raw nerves scraped against each other as I moved toward the stage, picking my way through standing waiters and seated patrons, all in suspended animation. Thankfully, the thrall over everyone in the club save Donita and Saber seemed total.

"Don't pull anything funny," Laurel warned.

Marco laughed. "What can she do, you stupid bitch? My Francesca was ever a pathetic excuse for a vampire. She missed being human, but was too much the good girl to end her life."

I winced at the truth.

"See how she cringes at my barb? She is still the same, oblivious to her powers, or she would have known I had a spy watching her."

I cut my gaze to Jo-Jo, and Marco laughed again.

"Laurel was the spy, not Jo-Jo."

"Focus, honey," Saber said in my head. *"Play him."*

I fought to wet my dry mouth and scrambled for something to say as I neared the base of the stage.

"If Laurel is your little fanged friend, why have you tortured her? And *what* is with that orange smell?"

He gave me a venomous grin. "You insulted me in the old days when you said my scent offended you."

Everything about Marco offended me, but I flashed to the last time I'd seen him. He'd been a vampire for more than three years, yet his body held the odor of cumin and datil peppers, the spices his mother had used to cook, the smell that permeated his home. Marco sweated the smell before he was turned, and it lingered after.

"Ah, I see you recall. Sadly, I am still afflicted with my own signature scent. I had to disguise that from you, Francesca, or ruin my surprise. You are surprised to see me, are you not?"

"Brutally so," I snapped. "Did you wear contacts as part of your disguise, Marco? To change the color of your eyes?"

"Ah, then Jo-Jo did describe me to you. Indeed, I went to much trouble to hide my identity until the time was right."

"What's the deal with Laurel?" I pressed as I neared the foot of the stage and a yawning hole beneath it.

Marco waved a dismissive hand. "Possessive ingrate, she tried to shoot you. Against my direct orders."

Anger burned into my fear. "Laurel was the sniper?"

"With deplorable aim. I killed Ike for her and for Vlad, and even left my favorite short sword behind. Yet this cow whines that I have not killed Ray." Marco spat on the floor. "Laurel is an encumbrance who would get in the way of my plans for you."

"Plans?" I strove to keep my voice steady, to keep him talking, to stay calm.

But I nearly flew to the catwalk when a shadow startled me from the space under the stage. Triton, in-the-flesh Triton, rose from the shadows just enough to tug at my jeans pocket. He slipped something heavy inside the pocket, patted my butt, and melted into the darkness again.

"Who is there, Francesca?" Marco demanded, taking two swift steps toward me.

"A cat under the stage," I blurted, winging it. "The thing startled me. That's all."

"You lie," Marco snarled, sword raised.

Pandora meowed, loud and long. I smiled.

"Actually, I don't."

Pandora brushed past me and trotted up the stage steps.

With my heart slamming in my chest, I don't know where I got a spurt of courage at that point, but whatever Triton had put in my back pocket pulsed and grew warmer. I followed Pandora up the five steps, intent on my mission to distract Marco. Did he know I could suck energy? Not unless Laurel had told him. She'd warned me not to try anything, but maybe that had been a hint, not a warning.

"You mentioned plans, Marco?" I stopped on the stage, subtly began drawing his energy, and prayed he didn't notice. "If you had such big plans for me, why didn't you come for me right after the villager uprising? I at least expected you to come after Normand's treasure."

"Ah, yes, you know me well," he said, strutting to where Laurel cringed from him. "Come closer, or I will behead Laurel as I did Ike. Or shall it be Jo-Jo and his little friend?"

I gritted my teeth and took the smallest baby steps I could, still sipping his energy, the thing in my butt pocket pulsing with even more heat.

"Your story, Marco?"

"Sadly, the villagers turned on me, as you must have known they would. I was gravely injured by the fire, but my father— you remember my father, Francesca?"

"I remember." I inched nearer, steadily sucking from Marco, even though each orange-flavored sip made my stomach churn. "Your dad was a Spanish soldier rumored to be a silversmith."

"The rumor was true. He was a silversmith, and a very fine one in spite of the scandal in *España*." Marco had drawn himself up straight, ready to take umbrage for any insult, but suddenly laughed. "Ah, yes, *mi padre*. A tender but stupid man. He took pity on me, hid me in his workshop. I begged him not to leave me where the silver would harm me. Do you know what he said, Francesca?"

I shook my head. I was less than ten feet from Marco, and the right side of my butt felt like a vibrating live coal, sending shock waves into bones, my skull. Hell, into my DNA.

"He said perhaps the silver would purify my soul and bring me back to him. Instead, the exposure made me immune. Or perhaps it was the exposure of being in his shop all those years before I was turned, but no matter. My flesh did not heal properly after the fire, but I gained strength enough to kill *mi padre* and feast on his blood."

I gagged and snapped my psychic shield in place to keep from seeing more of the scene in Marco's vivid memory.

"So you really are immune to silver?"

Marco shrugged almost humbly. "I did, of course, continue

exposing myself to the metal over the centuries to ensure and build my immunity."

I pulled a little more of his energy, my body throbbing now, a tuning fork on speed.

"Why have you shown up after all this time, Marco? You still haven't told me your big plan."

"It is the same as it ever was. I take you, Princess of the House of Normand, and together we rule. It is just as well that the magic symbols stopped me from reaching you before. We will have more influence now."

"What magic symbols?"

He stared, his eyes unfocused, as if he'd lost his train of thought, then shook himself.

"You might be a pathetic excuse for a vampire now, but day-walkers are rare and have legendary powers. I have been chosen to teach you"—he paused—"to fulfill your destiny as King Normand's daughter."

Gads, Marco was slurring his words. Had he noticed? Whether it was me energy-sucking him or the thing in my pocket affecting him, I had to keep him talking.

"Marco," I scoffed, "Normand wasn't real royalty."

"Normand," Marco said slowly, "was a bastard son of the French royal house." A pause. He was weakening. "It is the reason I gave myself to the vampires." Another pause. "I could achieve power I would never have as the son of a soldier."

Marco weaved on his feet. I took two steps closer to his side, almost within touching distance but out of Saber's line of fire. I thought we had him, thought Saber would open fire. Instead, Marco whipped the short sword to my throat. His hand trembled, and I felt the blade slice into the side of my neck.

Rage flooded my vision, my being.

I jumped, pulling hard and fast on his energy. At some point I realized I was hovering eight feet in the air, but I held my focus. I drained Marco.

He dropped his sword and fell to his knees, but I didn't stop sucking his aura. I couldn't. Not even when the air between us turned black. My soul seemed to quake with the force of whatever Triton had put in my pocket. I had to hang on until Saber came.

Then Marco began to wither like a raisin, and I faltered.

Laurel crawled toward Marco's sword, and Saber shouted, "Stop her."

I swooped to the stage and kicked the sword away.

"Kill him. Behead the bastard," Laurel screamed.

"No," Triton said, suddenly on my right.

Saber was there, too, on my left. He took my shoulders and shook me.

"Cesca, stop now. Stop pulling Marco's energy before you kill him."

"But he must die," Laurel screeched.

"He'll be executed legally. Cesca, listen to me. His energy is black. It's infecting you. Stop."

"No," Triton snapped, jerking me from Saber's arms. "Marco must die now, or he'll escape execution. The blackness is the sign of the Void. Marco must die and by your hand, Cesca. It's the only way."

"Let go!"

I sobbed and wrenched free of Triton, stumbled back. My right butt cheek burned, my throat felt like I'd swallowed oil, and I couldn't think for the shrieking pain in my skull.

"Triton, I can't kill him. I can't."

"Then give me the disk in your pocket. Now, Cesca. I need the medallion now."

I expected the disk to burn me. It didn't, and some instinct made me look at the medallion more closely. Hexagon-shaped, the size and thickness of a jelly jar lid, the clear crystal was shot through with silver and gold lines and framed in copper. A smattering of ancient-looking symbols were etched into the copper rim. I made out part of a musical note, and the Greek letter for *Mu* as the medallion beat its pulse into me, strong, slow, comforting. My heartbeat fell into synch.

Just as it did, Triton cupped my hand and jerked me down to where Marco lay on his back. He flipped my hand palm down and pressed the medallion to Marco's chest, over his heart. With Triton's hand pushing on mine, he muttered a string of words in a language I didn't recognize.

Brilliant, blinding rays of white light burst from every surface of the medallion, and beamed into Marco. One moment he was there on the floor, the next he had vanished. I gaped, started to ask what happened to him, but Laurel lurched forward.

"Mine," she screeched, clawing at the medallion.

At her touch, the light arched into her. She writhed on the stage as if snakes infected her body. Then she, too, dissolved into nothing, and the light collapsed into the disk.

My fingers curled around the medallion as I stared into Triton's deep brown eyes.

"You killed them," I whispered. "You made me help you murder them."

Triton shook his head, and a stray lock of his tobacco brown hair fell across his forehead.

"We didn't kill Marco, Cesca. We released his soul, and his body left with it. The female released herself."

I glanced at the stage floor where Saber's handcuffs lay empty, then at the medallion in my hand.

"What the hell is this thing?"

"I don't have time to explain." He snatched the disk and dropped it in his shirt pocket. "Trust me now as you trusted me before. The dark forces have lost two minions."

He kissed my cheek, murmured in Greek, "Until later, dear friend," and bolted off the stage before I could react.

I don't know how long I knelt, stunned and alone, before Saber's arms closed around me and drew me off the floor. I sobbed and buried my face in his shoulder.

"Cesca, honey," he crooned as he stroked my hair. "Stay with me. I need you. Come on, now. The bad guys are gone, but we have a stage to clean up and people who are still enthralled."

I blinked at him. "They are?"

"Every damn one of them. I don't know why they're still bound, but you have to release them. You can break down later."

I hiccupped. "I suppose this is a bad time to tell you, but I don't know how to release them."

A footstep thudded on the stage.

"I do."

TWENTY-TWO

⌒

We whirled toward the baritone voice—Saber tensed to fire his weapon, me darn near fainting when I saw the carriage driver from Wednesday night.

Except tonight he looked completely different.

He wore baggy black pants, a loose white tunic, and a midnight blue, honest-to-gosh full-length cape. His gray hair had seemed thin and dirty on Wednesday, but now it flowed to his shoulders like a white water wave.

He stood with his hands resting lightly on Jo-Jo's shoulders. Pandora in full panther size sat on her haunches beside him.

I looked into Pandora's eyes. "Your wizard, I presume?"

Pandora chuffed, but the man laughed.

"I am Cosmil, at your service. I promise, I offer no harm, only help."

"If you know how to break a vampire enthrallment, you're on," Saber said and holstered his Glock.

"I even know why the spell did not break when Marco vanished. It is because, Princess, in taking his energy, you assumed responsibility for what he left behind."

A flare of panic burned my gut. "Am I infected with Marco's dark energy?"

"No, though I will teach you how to release unwanted energy as well."

"Can we get back on track?" Saber said. "It's ten o'clock, and a few hundred people are missing over an hour of time."

"It's really ten?"

"Time flies when you're killing bad guys. Did Jo-Jo say when the show was supposed to end?"

"Eleven, I think. Is there a program on the tables?"

As soon as I turned to look, a folded sheet of paper lifted off the nearest table and floated to me. Bemused, I plucked it out of the air.

"Eleven is right. Jo-Jo was supposed to be on at nine and again at ten thirty. But what are we going to do about the clocks and everyone's watches?"

Saber eyed Cosmil. "How long will it take to teach Cesca to undo the enthrallment and get everyone functioning?"

"Fifteen minutes, perhaps twenty. I will change timepieces, if you like."

"That'll do. Let's move. Cosmil, help me get Jo-Jo and Donita backstage. Cesca, grab the cuffs and sword, would you?"

"Nuh-uh. Allergic to silver, remember?"

Cosmil coughed. "I believe you will find your allergy is less severe if not entirely gone."

"Is this a sucking Marco's energy thing, too?"

Cosmil spread his hands and smiled. "You have assumed a new power, Princess."

"I don't want anything of Marco's."

"Cesca, if you can touch silver now, you can wear it. Think new options in jewelry, and deal. Cosmil, your help, please?"

New options in jewelry? Okay, that was a plus. Gold *was* outrageously expensive.

Still, I handled the sword and handcuffs gingerly. They gave my fingers only the slightest sting. Not so much a burn as a vibration. Not like the mermaid charm. Softer.

Pandora and I followed Saber and Cosmil as they led the apparently sleepwalking Donita and Jo-Jo into a dressing room. When they were seated, I frowned at Jo-Jo.

"Is Jo-Jo hurt or enthralled?"

"Neither. He was struggling to protect the woman, so I cast a sleep spell to calm him."

"Marco didn't notice?" Saber asked.

"Marco saw what he chose to see."

Saber made a hurry-up gesture. "Time's ticking. Now what?"

"First I'll instruct the princess in waking Donita. She had some immunity to enthrallment, and is more terrorized."

I brushed my fingers over Donita's shoulder.

"Good. Your instincts are good. Now send your will that she awakens with no unpleasant memories of this night."

"And no missing time?"

"Yes. I will awaken Jo-Jo as you release the woman, but I will not be here when they are conscious again. Meet me in the hall so we may unenthrall the others."

Between Marco and the medallion incident, I should have been a wreck. Instead, I felt strong and secure. I could do this.

Hell, I'd finally flown when it counted. This should be a relative snap.

Course, I could be back in denial land, too.

Cosmil nodded when he was ready, and I put all my focus into willing my intent into Donita. Maybe a half second ticked by, then both she and Jo-Jo awoke.

I expected Jo-Jo to remember Marco, but Pandora in her house cat form landed in his lap just as he came to.

"Ooof," Jo-Jo said, then stiffened. "Who let this cat in?"

"We did." I grinned at his horrified expression. Bless her, Pandora did know how to make an entrance.

"What a gorgeous feline you are," Donita crooned, and Pandora abandoned Jo-Jo for her.

Saber cleared his throat. "We just wanted to say hello before you go on again."

Jo-Jo frowned, confusion evident in his eyes. Was he remembering?

When he shrugged, I released a breath I hadn't known I held.

"I wish you'd stay for the second show. I'd like to buy you a drink afterward. You know, for all your help."

Saber clapped a hand on Jo-Jo's shoulder. "Sorry, we have a long day tomorrow. But it's been a hell of a memorable night."

I snorted and left to find Cosmil.

Releasing a whole building of enthralled humans was a huge challenge, even with a wizard on the team. We had to include those people in the bathrooms, the storerooms, the office, even in the crannies where the techies were running the lights and sound show. Nerves fluttering like bat wings, I secluded myself in a shadowed corner. Cosmil stood behind me to provide an energy boost.

I raised my hands, palms toward the crowd, and broadcast my will with a vengeance. With a pop of electricity, activity in the room instantly resumed, and the noise level swelled. If Marco had hit the Pause button, I had pushed Play.

Pandora had stayed in the dressing room to distract Jo-Jo and Donita, so Saber and I walked into the humid night with Cosmil. A thousand questions pricked the tip of my tongue, but I didn't know if I should ask even one.

"We will meet again," Cosmil assured me as if he'd read my mind. Which he likely had. "I will send Pandora when I know you are ready."

Ready for what? hovered on my tongue, but I knew. Ready to unite my powers with Triton's. Humph. That'd be a cold day in every level of hell.

Cosmil chuckled. "No, it won't."

He turned south, away from downtown, and just as Pandora loped up to him, they both disappeared.

"Damn," I breathed. "And I thought flying saved gas."

The next two weeks passed at vampire speed.

Saber contacted Candy and Ray to relay that Marco and Laurel were exterminated. Ray heard a more edited version of events, I was sure. And, while I wasn't present for either conference, I knew the VPA was closing down nests nationwide. The good news was that many vamps had the money and credit ratings to buy their own homes. The housing market boomed in some locations, and Ray reopened Hot Blooded.

When Maggie got home from Savannah, I caught her up on

bits and pieces, but mostly we talked wedding plans. Oh, and I took her to see her dress. She cried happy tears for days.

I asked Saber about the apparent telepathy I'd experienced with him at the comedy club, but he acted like I'd taken another conk in the head with my surfboard. Since I didn't hear his thoughts again, I chalked it up to an aberration brought on by stress. Yep, Dr. Phil has nothing on me.

Saber sold his condo and bought Neil's house, closing on both the same day. Property deals must have been in the stars, because I filed the papers to claim my land from Triton's trust and had the deed before the end of the month. I thought for sure Triton would contact me about the transfer, but he didn't. I didn't know whether to be ticked or hurt, but I was glad I'd buried the mermaid charm in my jewelry box drawer.

Jo-Jo called with news that *The Court Jester* was a go, and that pieces of the film would be shot in St. Augustine in October. He wanted me to be an extra, and I told him I'd think about it. Sure, it could be interesting, but my ghosts were more fun.

One disturbing event occurred ten days after the showdown at the Riot. I received a DVD in the mail with Kevin Miller's return address on the package. The note inside read:

"Don't need this footage for my project, and have destroyed the original. This is the sole copy to do with what you want."

Good thing Saber was with me when I played the disk. Though I hadn't seen them, Kevin, Leah, and Caro had been in the club the night of Jo-Jo's show, and Kevin had set up a digital video recorder to run before he was enthralled. The camera had been aimed at the stage, and, though the picture was fuzzy, Kevin had inadvertently caught most of the confrontation between Marco and me. The DVR battery had died before the final scene played out, but seeing the video left me shivering for hours. Saber held me through the night to keep dreams at bay.

On the last Sunday of August, I decided to rip out the bushes and vines around the beach house. Saber was with Neil, watching the preseason football game he'd recorded on TiVo, but promised he'd join me later.

I took my surfboard with the idea that I'd reward myself for working, and after an hour, I'd cleared three sides of the bungalow. I also found a partial boardwalk to the beach, one with steps all but obliterated by sand. Since tramping over the dunes is a no-no, the hidden access meant the stretch of beach in front of my little shack was deserted. I had the ocean pretty much to myself, too.

I didn't need more invitation than that. I unloaded my board from the car, changed into my new coral flowered bathing suit, and hit the surf.

After one bitchin' ride after another, I paddled out farther to rest a few minutes before I caught the last wave of the day.

A splash on my left, and a dolphin leaped in a graceful arc, submerged, then swam directly at me. I tensed in case it bumped my board, but the dolphin dove under me and surfaced far on the other side. Then it swam lazily back, making clicks and whistles, and gently nudged my thigh with its beak.

Don't recognize me anymore?

I jerked sideways so hard, I nearly fell off my board.

"Triton?"

No, Flipper.

I gave him the evil eye as he bobbed beside me. "Do not

crack jokes with me. Not after what you pulled with that medallion thingie."

It's an amulet to be precise, and it had to be done. Marco was on the edge of being consumed by the Void.

"Then why didn't you hit Marco with the amulet yourself? Why make me a party to killing—"

Banishing.

"Banishing then. You could've done it on your own."

Triton shook his massive dolphin head. *Remember what Pandora told you about uniting our powers?*

"Yes, and I'm sick of hearing it."

Francesca, whether you admit it or not, whether we like it or not, whether you want to or not, uniting our powers is part of our destiny.

"Yeah? Well, destiny can take a hike if you keep being stealthy and secretive. Straight answers, Triton. Straight answers, or you'll be power tripping all over your flukes to get back in my good graces."

Come see me.

"You mean like this? Vampire to dolphin, or should we stay dry and hook up telepathically?"

Check your Sunday paper. Then come see me.

With that, Triton arched and dove under the water. I waited for him to surface again, but when he did, he was twenty feet away. Damn it.

Double damn when I realized I'd drifted toward the shore, and that Saber stood on the dune waiting for me.

I threw myself flat on the board and paddled, catching one more wave on the way in, then carried my board up the beach to meet Saber.

At the top of the steps, he clasped my free hand.

"Was that Triton?" he asked as we walked toward the shack.

"Yeah, and he about scared me half to death. How did you know it was him?"

"Aside from the fact you don't usually argue with dolphins, it's the dark of the moon. You told me he only shifts then. Plus, I saw this in the paper today."

He unfolded the business section and pointed.

I saw the headline "New in Town," then read the few column inches aloud.

"'Ocean Enchantments will specialize in shipwreck treasurers and kitschy maps purportedly drawn by mermaids. Owner Trey Delphinus.'" I met Saber's gaze. "The mermaid on the treasure map charm."

"Yeah." Saber paused a beat. "You're going to see him."

It wasn't a question.

"I have to if I want answers to my long list of questions about the Void and why he's recruited me to fight the damn thing. I was hoping you'd go with me."

"You think there will be sparks?"

I sighed and leaned my board against the shack.

"If you mean will I blow up at him, I just did, and, yeah, there's a darn good chance I will again. If you mean romantic sparks, I can only tell you this: When I faced Marco, I wasn't thinking about Triton rushing to help me. I was thinking about you."

Saber cracked a grin. "Sure you don't love me just for my big gun?"

"I love you," I said as I went on tiptoe to steal a kiss, "because you love me. Fangs and all."